After Dark

ALSO BY M. PIERCE

Night Owl
Last Light

After Dark

M. Pierce

St. Martin's Griffin New York

AFTER DARK. Copyright © 2015 by M. Pierce. All rights reserved. Printed in the United States of America. For information, address St. Martin's Press, 175 Fifth Avenue, New York, N.Y. 10010.

www.stmartins.com

Library of Congress Cataloging-in-Publication Data

Pierce, M.
    After dark / M. Pierce.—First edition.
        pages cm.—(The Night Owl trilogy ; 3)
    ISBN 978-1-250-05837-9 (trade paperback)
    ISBN 978-1-4668-6254-8 (e-book)
    1. Authors—Fiction.   2. Literary agents—Fiction.
    3. Man-woman relationships—Fiction.   I. Title.
    PS3616.I355A69 2015
    813'.6—dc23

                                    2015001985

St. Martin's Griffin books may be purchased for educational, business, or promotional use. For information on bulk purchases, please contact the Macmillan Corporate and Premium Sales Department at 1-800-221-7945, extension 5442, or write to specialmarkets@macmillan.com.

First Edition: March 2015

10 9 8 7 6 5 4 3 2 1

For Anna, always

Spend all you have for loveliness,
Buy it and never count the cost.

SARA TEASDALE, *"Barter"*

After Dark

Chapter 1

HANNAH

This is my favorite part. The beginning.

The crowd continues to clap and Gail Weider beams at us.

I pull Matt several feet onto the stage and he stops. He stands there woodenly, his expression blank, and then darts a look backstage. "I was contemplating running," he told me later.

Gail's smile falters.

My boyfriend and I are live on *Denver Buzz*, the biggest morning talk show in the city, and this is our chance to spin his fake death in our favor. A reclusive artist driven into hiding. A sensitive personality reacting to harmful circumstances. Stuff like that.

"Welcome," says Gail. She gestures to the couch. I know where we are supposed to sit, and I have been coached on good posture, eye contact, and affirmative answers. So has Matt.

But Matt is gone. The camera focuses on his stunned face. The applause dwindles.

"Come on," I whisper, coaxing him forward.

Abruptly, Gail crosses the stage and we flank Matt. The scene becomes comical. She grips his shoulder, I hold his hand, and we maneuver him toward the couch.

"Don't be shy, Mr. Sky. We're so excited to have you." Gail

plows off-script like a pro, her confidence undiminished. She exudes authority, and Matt and I look like children on her stage. At last, we get Matt seated. His hand is glued to mine.

This awkwardness is all my fault.

"Marry me," I'd whispered to Matt just moments before we stepped onstage. Had I sabotaged our TV appearance? The possibility never crossed my mind. In fact, the proposal didn't cross my mind until it rolled off my tongue. Oops . . .

"Matthew, Hannah." Gail nods at us.

"We're so happy to be here," I say. I pat Matt's knee. He remains comatose, and Gail launches into a spiel about how glad she is to see Matt safe, and yet how stunned she and the nation felt after the news of his death in December. She recounts the story. Her eyes sweep from the teleprompters to the crowd and back to us.

A silence follows, during which Matt is supposed to speak.

Even I know his lines.

I'm glad you brought this up, Gail. I've been looking forward to this opportunity to explain what happened, and why. First, I need to say that . . .

Matt glowers at the camera.

"We're getting married," he announces.

Dear God, he looks adorable. His bewilderment turns to anger. He glares a challenge at everyone, as if we are already at the altar and someone might object to our union.

The audience gives a collective gasp.

"Wow!" says Gail. A blissful smile breaks out on my face and Matt and I hug. Everyone claps. People get on their feet.

It's soap opera season finale meets touchdown in the studio. And the crowd goes wild . . .

I paused the video—*Denver Buzz, May 14, 2014*—and closed my laptop. The bedroom was dark. I padded to the window and watched a thick white cord of lightning reach down from the sky. Thunder followed in a long bass rumble.

I opened the window and tropically warm wind rushed over me. Our curtains streamed through the room. Finally—a storm to break the dry heat of June.

As I waited for the rain, my mind traveled back to that day, almost a month ago, when Matt and I appeared on TV and he announced to the nation that we were getting married.

The remainder of the show had focused on our whirlwind romance, our tumultuous relationship, and *Night Owl*, Matt's tell-all novel about us. Somehow, the news of our engagement eclipsed even Matt's phony death. We excused everything with love. Women in the audience dabbed their eyes—and the cameras ate it up—as Matt described his loneliness at the cabin. He was animated, gorgeous, and powerfully persuasive. "I realized that no amount of freedom was worth a life without Hannah," he told Gail, and a sigh rippled through the studio.

As Matt wove a tale for our rapt spectators, even I envisioned him storming off the mountain and back into my arms—all for love! We laughed and shared longing glances. I lowered my head when the story darkened. My hand played on his thigh.

After the last segment, Matt had dragged me off the set. My heart kicked into doubletime as we navigated the corridors backstage, stepping over wires and around video equipment. He hauled me into a dressing room. My phone began to ring.

I remembered thinking it was probably my boss and Matt's agent, Pamela Wing, and she was probably having an aneurysm. Or maybe she was cracking open a bottle of champagne. Impossible to say. Pam had arranged the talk show appearance and prepped Matt and me exhaustively, and we had proceeded to stray from every line in the script.

Matt's phone had started ringing, too. He ignored it. He slammed the dressing room door shut and pressed me against it. In the dark, I couldn't make out his expression.

"Hannah, what the hell was that?" His chest touched mine and I felt his wild pulse. "God, you're going to drive me to an early grave."

"I'm sorry. Are you angry? I—"

"Angry?" His breath fanned through my hair. His hands roamed down my body.

The scene is engraved on my memory: the way our cell phones rang relentlessly, the ringtone for my sister and then my mom sounding loudly, the way Matt kissed me and started to laugh, and the high fluttering happiness I felt because we had just announced our spontaneous engagement to the entire nation.

And then the way Matt had said, "You're a genius, Hannah. You're brilliant."

In the days following our TV appearance, Matt managed to put off everyone who asked about the engagement. He said it wasn't "a sure thing." He said that we planned to "continue living together" and were "keeping our options open." To Pam, he passed off the stunt as "Hannah's last-minute stroke of genius."

And with one another . . . we maintained a stilted silence on the matter.

I moved back into the condo with Matt. We returned to our routines. Three weeks passed, and I began to wonder if I had even asked. *Marry me.* Did I say those words? *We're getting married.* Did he believe those words?

The sweet smell of rain brought me back to the present moment. I perched on the windowsill and listened as Denver's dry pavement sighed beneath the downpour. The wind carried a spray of moisture that misted my face and legs.

You're a genius, Hannah.

I shut the window and walked to the office.

The door stood open, which meant Matt wasn't writing. I leaned against the frame and watched him. Something on the computer screen captivated him. He sat hunched forward, frowning and rubbing his jaw.

I giggled and his eyes shot up.

God . . . I loved to watch that smile dawning on his face.

"Little bird," he said. He pushed away from the keyboard and patted his thigh.

"I'm invited into the inner sanctum?" I moved around the desk and sat on his lap, and his arms tightened about me. He grinned at me. His hair was growing in blond, light roots clashing with black dye on the fringes. I ran my fingers through it and he nuzzled my chest. "Baby, we gotta do something about your hair."

"Mm." With his face between my boobs, Matt might agree to anything.

I rubbed his shoulders and he planted idle kisses along the neckline of my nightie. I stole a glance at the computer.

"Are you . . . on Twitter?"

"Mm." He got a handful of my rump and squeezed. "Interacting."

"Interacting?" I smiled. "That's kind of cute."

"With my readers. I'm on Facebook, too." His mouth drifted across my chest. "It was my editor's idea."

My eyes flickered to the Firefox browser. I rarely got a look at Matt's computer. The browser tabs read *Gmail, Twitter,* and . . . *Colo Real Estate*?

"Hey . . . Matt." Something in my voice stopped his wandering hands and lips. "Are you looking at houses?"

"What?" His head came up. "No."

"Uh, yes." I reached for the mouse and clicked on the *Colo Real Estate* tab. A page of Colorado homes loaded.

He glared at the screen.

"Whatever. Just looking."

At least he didn't lie and call it research.

A smile quirked my mouth—until I started to study the houses.

"You can't be serious," I said.

Matt eased out from under me and plopped me onto the office chair. He stalked to the wall, where he pretended a frame needed straightening.

"I *am* serious." He spoke to the painting. "Why can't I be serious? This place is tiny. You have no real room of your own. It's like a—"

"'Six built-in fireplaces,'" I read from the Web page. "'Experience the grandeur of two-story ceilings, the wine room, wet bar, and—'"

"What's wrong with—"

"Eight baths!" I shouted over him.

"Better than one."

"Oh my God. Six bedrooms? Oh here, look at this. There's a fountain in the driveway. That's perfectly normal."

"Looks nice." His voice tightened.

"Marble floors, gourmet kitchen—ha! A Romeo and Juliet balcony? Is that a thing?"

"What's wrong with a balcony?"

"These homes are in the millions."

"The rock and stucco—"

"Right, that one is just a million and a half." I swiveled to face him. "Look at me."

He continued adjusting the painting, right a little, left a little. Ignoring me. Like a child. At last, he turned and folded his arms, and he stared at a spot in my vicinity.

"You like Nate's house," he said.

"Still? Seriously?"

"Still what?"

"You are *still* jealous of the way I looked at Nate's home?"

"His home is nice. These homes are nice." He jabbed a finger toward the computer. "I don't see why we can't even consider living somewhere nice and spacious."

Weeks' worth of frustration and confusion boiled over. I hurtled out of the chair and headed for the door. "And I'm not even sure I want to buy a home with someone who practically proposed to me on national television and hasn't breathed a word about it since!"

I stormed to the bedroom and threw myself on the quilt. Like a child.

I lay in the dark, listening for Matt.

Rain spattered against the window. I heard the low *thump-thump* of his feet pacing the floor. Lightning shimmered on the wall and thunder reverberated over the Denver skyline.

At last, I heard him coming down the hall.

The mattress shifted.

"Are you awake?" he whispered.

"Yeah."

"I didn't propose," he said. "You did."

I rolled over. Matt sat on the edge of the bed, hands on knees, elbows locked. I crawled to him and slipped my arms around his shoulders. He relaxed in my hold.

"I guess . . . I did, yeah." I laid my ear against his back. Relief relaxed me, too. It felt good, and right, finally to be talking about this. "But you went along with it."

"Of course I did." He chuckled. "Why would I pass up such a perfect play?"

"Huh?"

"Love, I knew you weren't serious. Not completely." He twisted around and cupped my face. His eyes glimmered with amusement. "I knew it was for the show. I mean, we've known each other for a year. Not even. And think about that year . . ."

Matt trailed off and I thought about *that year.*

It was a year next month, in fact, if we counted our meeting online. Less than a year if we didn't count the Internet. Much less than a year if we didn't count Matt's meltdown in New York and our separation after his faked death.

So . . . we'd known one another for much less than a year.

A tight, painful feeling expanded in my chest.

"So w-why were you"—I cleared my throat—"looking at houses?"

"Because we need a bigger place."

I shook my head out of his grasp. "Do we? I don't see why we need a house if we're not—" My voice cracked. *If we're not getting married.* No, I wouldn't be the idiot who said that. The idiot who'd spent the past month hoping and dreaming.

"What is this?" A flash of lightning whitened Matt's eyes, which were somber now. "Hey, look at me." Again, he took my face between his hands. "Little bird, you barely know me. We barely know one another, if you think about it."

His words put a hairline crack in my heart. We did know one another. We'd been through so much. What was he saying?

"And marriage is about more than me," he continued. "More

than us. It's about family. There's a lot to consider, starting all that."

I pinched my tongue between my teeth. *Holy shit.* Matt wanted kids? We'd never had this discussion, and my desire to carry a child could be described as less than zero.

His voice gained confidence as he spoke.

"Of course we'll talk about marriage . . . someday. When we're ready, you know? When we're sure this is what we want. Marriage is very finalizing, or it ought to be." He released my face and stripped off his T-shirt, and for a second his gorgeous body distracted me. Those toned arms, that golden trail below his navel . . .

"I know," I snapped. "I know marriage is finalizing. I'm not an idiot."

"Come here. Don't be upset; we're talking." He tried to kiss my neck. I ducked.

"It was real for me," I said. "I was ready."

"What? Hannah . . ."

Matt wanted closeness—probably to confirm that we weren't having a serious fight. I knew how he worked. He drew comfort from intimacy. *See, Matt? I do know you.* He pulled on my shoulder. I stiffened and fought my instinct to melt against him.

"Stop." I pressed both hands to his chest. This wasn't play and he knew it. He frowned and stilled.

"What's the matter?" His voice grated with frustration.

"I *was* ready," I repeated. Tears rimmed my eyelids. "I was fucking ready, Matt. I was serious when I said, "marry me." The perfect play? Is everything a game for you?" I scrambled back on the sheets. "I can't believe you just said, 'when we're sure this is what we want.'" I sniffled and a tear fell. My cheeks burned. "I am . . . was sure. I'd been sure."

Matt watched me impassively. Oh, he could go so cold, even in the face of my emotion.

"What are you talking about?" he said. "Of course it was a game. It was a *story*, a simple narrative for simple people. Something they'd understand. Do you think I would seriously parade my engagement out for the public like that? God, it's like I said. You don't know me at all."

"No, I do know you." My fingers dug into the sheets. Nothing makes me indignant like humiliation. "You're manipulative, just like Seth said. Your own fucking brother said you're a master manipulator, and that's what you are, letting me and all those people think we were seriously getting married. I feel like such an idiot."

"Don't." Matt leaned in swiftly. He didn't touch me, but his breath touched my face and I froze. "Don't bring him into this. Do you think I'm lying when I say I love you?" He sneered. "Do you think I'm lying when I say you don't really know me? Hannah, I want things that . . ." He lowered his head so that he could look directly at me. I shrank beneath his frigid stare.

He wanted things that . . . *what?*

As suddenly as he'd leaned in, he withdrew. He stalked out of the room and left me shivering on our bed.

Chapter 2

MATT

Mike kept a framed picture of his family on his desk. Blonde, wife, two cherubic-looking children, and a goddamn golden retriever.

I pointed at the picture with my unlit cigarette.

No smoking allowed in my psychiatrist's office, of course.

"The dog," I said. "The dog is what makes this too much."

I sat in an overstuffed armchair and Mike sat on a couch beside me, his body angled toward mine. Everything about his posture said: *I am attentive to you.*

Mike's golden retriever grinned at me.

"It's like you're mocking me," I said. "Mocking the poor messed-up people who must sit in this chair. With your dog. With your golden family. Do you get that?"

"You're avoiding," Mike said.

"Right." I chewed my cigarette's filter. "God, I gotta quit smoking again."

"I could prescribe something to help with that."

"Thanks, but no thanks. I'm down to one or two a day anyway." I rose and walked to the broad window of Mike's high-rise office and I looked out at a sunny Denver morning. It was Monday. Hannah was at work and I was meeting with my psychiatrist for the first time in months because Hannah demanded it.

If I didn't get regular therapy, she wouldn't live with me.

That stipulation seemed fair enough, considering the last year.

"Let's talk about your relationship," Mike said. "Are congratulations in order?"

"God, not you, too," I muttered.

My mind tracked back to Friday night, when Hannah and I had finally discussed "the proposal." Yes, "the proposal," which I viewed as a ploy to manipulate public opinion. It had worked, too. Thousands of previously angry readers (*how dare that author fake his death and make us grieve?*) took to social media in support (*oh, their story is so romantic!*).

"No, no fucking congratulations. It wasn't real. That should be obvious."

"Another hoax?" said Mike. "People will get tired of your games."

"And I am tired of people!" I flung myself back into the armchair and resumed glaring at Mike's perfect family. "I am *tired* of explaining myself, *tired* of having to be one thing or another, *tired* of making up stories to justify my life." My head sank. I drove my fingers through my hair, short nails raking over my scalp. "Of course, Hannah thought it was real. She says she was ready. She says she believed it, that we were getting engaged."

"Ah. So she's tiring of your games, too."

"I love her," I snarled, "and that's no fucking game."

"But you aren't ready to put a ring on her finger?"

"I would do it in a heartbeat, if I thought she really knew me."

"What doesn't she know? As far as I can tell, she's seen you at your worst."

"Ha! My worst . . ." I rolled my eyes elaborately. What did Hannah know about my worst? What did I even know? I only understood, vaguely, that my desires ran deeper than blindfolds and handcuffs, rougher than role play and spankings, stranger—

"Matthew?"

I glanced at the clock. "Hour's up."

"Ever vigilant. In that case"—Mike withdrew a spiral notebook from his desk drawer—"I'm giving you some homework."

"This is more than I signed up for."

He ignored me.

"I want you to think about your former relationships and your current relationship with Hannah. Think about your actions during those times, the books you wrote—your career—and your stability levels and sexual satisfaction. Compare and contrast."

"I see what you're getting at."

"I'm not 'getting at' anything." He smiled and handed the notebook to me. "You're trying to analyze and manipulate my motives."

"And you're shrinking me. Stop." I gestured with the notebook. "So what, you want me to make a Venn diagram? Be prepared for a quiz next week?"

"Actually, no. In that, I want you to write about your worst."

"My worst," I deadpanned.

"That's right. Whatever it is that you feel Hannah doesn't know about you, write it down. You need to have dialogue, if only with yourself. And I won't ask you to share the notebook if you don't want. That's your personal space. No self-critique."

"Easier said than done." I let myself out of the office.

As I rode the elevator down to the first floor, I flipped through the notebook. Page after page of emptiness and pale blue lines provoked me. It has always been that way.

I drove back to the condo and went directly to my desk. *Last Light*, my work in progress, lay open before me. I frowned as I considered it, remembering Mike's words.

Think about your actions during those times, the books you wrote—your career.

Since I'd met Hannah, I wrote only about Hannah. That beautiful woman . . . my sweet little bird. Love is hysteria, and summer makes it worse. Heat spreads the fever. Madness.

I pushed aside *Last Light* and opened my new notebook from Mike.

At the top of the page, in cramped, slanting caps, I wrote:

EXHIBITIONISM

Chapter 3

HANNAH

Pam wanted to see me after lunch.

I worried a nail as I carried my salad out of the Mediterranean deli.

If Pam wanted to see me, I'd probably done something wrong. *Shit.* What could it be?

I sat at the last empty table outside and started stuffing forkfuls of lettuce into my mouth. I ate mindlessly, concentrating instead on how I might have pissed off my boss. Hm. No contract negotiations were under way. We had no new authors. Was I reading too slowly? Did I discard a promising manuscript?

A shadow fell across my table.

I looked up at a pretty, petite woman with fawn brown hair.

"Oh!" she said. "You're Hannah Catalano."

I nodded. Since our TV appearance, Matt and I were pseudo-celebs in Denver. Now everyone who recognized Matt also recognized me. He was "that crazy author who faked his death" and I was "the adorable girl he loves." *It could be worse,* we joked.

"Do you mind?" The woman glanced at the chair across from mine.

"Go for it," I said, and she set down her tray. "It's so busy today."

"Must be the nice weather." As the stranger sipped her drink, I noticed a delicate gold band around her ring finger, encrusted with three diamonds. My chest tightened.

The woman caught me staring and she blushed.

"I just got engaged. And so did you, right? You and that author?"

"Uh . . . yeah." I pushed an olive around my plate.

"This is the craziest coincidence." The woman squinted and glanced over her shoulder, then leaned toward me. "My friend used to date him. Can you believe that?"

"Huh?" A gust of wind rocked the umbrella above our table. It shifted and a shaft of sunlight pierced my eyes. *Friend . . . dated Matt?*

"I know, right?" The woman laughed. Her earrings flashed like fishing lures. "The stories I have heard. You are so *brave* to be marrying him. Is he really into all that weird stuff?"

"I—" I shielded my eyes. Jesus, I needed to see this woman. Was her friend Bethany Meres, Matt's evil ex? And what did she mean by "weird stuff"?

"God, I probably shouldn't have said that. I'm sorry." She lifted her tray. "A table just freed up over there, so I'll give you some peace. Nice meeting you."

The woman hurried off and I sat there staring after her.

I wanted to march over to her table and demand more information, but my lunch break was up. I pictured Pam waiting in her office with an executioner's ax. *Fuck . . .*

I got one last good look at the woman—straight, fine hair to her shoulders, a small, fit body, and a brightly printed Coach purse—and carried my tray back into the deli.

Pamela Wing and her partner, Laura Granite, awaited me in the office. I rarely saw Laura around the agency and the sight of her stopped me in the doorway.

These women looked severe.

Laura beckoned, her perfect eyebrows arching. Pam nodded at me.

Okay . . . I knew this scene. They would feed me some lines about a gap in my skill set, or disappointment with my progress, their hope for more growth. *This isn't working out, Hannah.*

"Great to see you, Hannah," said Laura. Laura was a leggy brunette, in her fifties at least and alarmingly attractive.

My boss, Pam, looked stern as usual.

I perched on the edge of the offered chair.

"Nice to see you as well," I said. *Be brave. Go out with dignity.* I tried to smile at Laura, though I think I grimaced. "How was New York?"

"Same old," she drawled, her city accent thick. Though the Granite Wing Agency was Denver-based, Laura spent weeks on end in New York City. "I got you something."

"*We* got you something," Pam put in.

They laughed together.

A small turquoise box with a white ribbon sat on the desk. I lifted it and read the lid: TIFFANY & CO. "Oh . . . thank you," I managed. My stomach gurgled and my hands shook as I untied the ribbon. *Stupid fucking nerves.*

Inside the box was a long felt pouch, and inside of that a classic Tiffany T-clip pen, all sterling silver except for a thin blue accent.

The pen lay cool and heavy across my palm.

I stared at it, dumbfounded.

Then I stared at Pam as she said, "Hannah, Laura and I would like to bring you on as an associate agent here. What do you say?"

I looked between Pam and Laura, back and forth, blinking owlishly. I wasn't getting canned. I was getting the promotion I'd coveted for months.

"Do you think I'm ready?" My fingers closed around the pen.

"I've been very impressed," Pam said. "You've been with us for almost a year. You learn fast and your dedication is obvious. Excepting your recent absence—" Pam sniffed. Oof, my *absence.* She meant the three weeks in April when I broke up with Matt and hid at an Econo Lodge and drank way too much gin. "You've shown great aptitude for this work."

"This is what I want," I said.

"Then congratulations, Hannah." Laura shook my hand.

I stood and shook Pam's hand. I hoped my expression looked halfway professional, because inside I was screaming and lighting fireworks.

We talked about my contract, expectations, and even "building my client list," a phrase that thrilled me. By the time I returned to my office, I had forgotten entirely about the woman outside the deli and her "weird stuff" comment.

My God . . . I was an associate agent at the Granite Wing Agency.

The workday sailed by in a rose-colored haze.

I left at six and rushed home, but my energy fizzled as I climbed the stairs to the condo. Matt and I hadn't had sex, much less kissed, since his cryptic announcement five days ago.

You don't really know me. Hannah, I want things that . . .

Things that he wasn't willing to discuss, apparently.

I let myself into the condo and found Matt looming in the pantry, a cup of noodles in hand. Freshly showered and shaved, wearing only loose gray sweats, he looked like sex itself. Seriously—my boyfriend, Matthew Sex Sky Jr. Or was it Matthew Asshole Sky Jr., who viewed everything from death to marriage as a game?

"There you are," he said, smiling tentatively.

I pried my eyes off his naked torso.

"Ramen for dinner?"

"I was considering it. I could find something else to eat." He moved into my personal space. I breathed in the scent of his clean skin and aftershave. "Little bird . . ."

"Hi." I stared at his chest. *Something else to eat.* His suggestion wasn't lost on me.

"How was work?" He tucked my hair behind one ear, then the other, the pads of his fingers brushing my cheeks. I resisted the urge to nuzzle his palms. I knew how persuasive those hands could be, and I wasn't in the mood.

"Fine. Good."

"Yeah?" He stroked my neck and I shivered.

"Uh, yeah. Look at this." I shifted my purse between us and displayed the Tiffany pen. Of course I'd Googled the pen in the privacy of my office. It cost nearly two hundred dollars and sold as a "writing instrument." An instrument! How luxurious. But the high price and fancy name meant nothing to me. To me, the pen was priceless. It seemed to embody the elegance and profession-alism I associated with Pam and Laura, and when I slid it across a page for the first time, writing my name in smooth blue script, I felt the beginnings of a story inside me.

My story.

"How chic," Matt murmured. "Is Pam trying to seduce you away from me?"

"She promoted me. I'm . . . an associate agent." My voice sounded dreary. I knew my expression matched. This should have been exciting news—we should have celebrated—but everything felt wrong. *Matt isn't sure he wants to spend the rest of his life with me.* That was the essence of his announcement on Friday, no matter how I looked at it.

And I wanted to spend the rest of my life with him.

I wanted him more than he wanted me.

I winced as that knowledge cut into me again.

"Babe, that's fantastic news." He wrapped me into a hug, crushing my body against his. I stood still for a while, perplexed by his tone, and then I leaned back and eyed him.

"Did you already know?"

"Hm?" He trained his dark green eyes on a cabinet. After a beat, he disentangled himself and wandered over to inspect the knob.

I huffed. This, I forced myself to remember, was progress: Matt acting like a child instead of immediately resorting to lies.

"So you already knew," I prompted.

"Pam and I go way back." He opened the cabinet and pre-tended to tighten the knob. "You know, she called to ask—to tell me. Sure, she mentioned it in passing."

"She asked you?" *Ouch.* That took me down a notch.

"Told, asked. I don't know." Matt turned and gave me a dour look—one I was starting to recognize. The *I'm about to tell you a hard truth* look. "Baby bird, when it comes to the agency, you need to think of me as a majority shareholder, okay? Yes, I'm your boyfriend." A smile tugged at his lips. "But I'm also M. Pierce. Please remember how you got this job."

I glared at him. "*You* got me this job. What has that got to do with anything?"

"Pam and I just want to make sure everything is aboveboard, okay? Things get a little complicated when you have an author dating his agent's assistant, the assistant becoming an agent and working with new authors." Matt gestured vaguely. "We want everything to work."

"I don't see the problem." I clutched my new pen.

"That's because there is no problem. Darling . . ." He returned to me, taking my face between his hands. This time, I pulled away.

"I wish you'd told me, that's all. I feel stupid."

"I wanted it to be a surprise for you." He gave me an anguished look. "And it's great news. We should—" He stepped toward me, I stepped back, and his voice faded.

"I have a ton of work to do." I walk-jogged to the bedroom, my pride stinging. Matt sure was good at making me feel dumb lately—first with the fake TV engagement, now with my job. The job he got me, to be exact. Just when I was starting to feel confident . . .

I curled up on our bed and opened my MacBook. Maybe I'd catch up on *The Vampire Diaries*. Yeah, I had *a ton of work to do.*

My breath hitched when I heard Matt moving down the hall. I half-hoped he would come in, but the shadow of his feet passed.

"Bird?"

A strong hand moved my shoulder.

"Nngh."

"Love, you fell asleep."

The hand slid down my side, over my hip, onto my thigh. I

sighed happily. A familiar form settled behind me. I nestled into that shape where I fit, shoulder to shoulder, back to chest, my rump finding an expected hardness and nuzzling it.

"Mm, fuck. Hannah . . ."

My eyes opened a crack. A button on my blouse—the shirt I'd worn to work—dug into my side. The room was dark.

"Hm?" I mumbled.

"I've missed you. God damn." Matt climbed over me, his narrow waist parting my thighs. My skirt slid up until he pressed against my panties. His breath tickled at my ear. "I've missed your tight little pussy."

In that groggy space between dreams and wakefulness, I forgot my hurt and savored his touch. The firm shape of him ground between my legs. He kissed my throat and my body arched to meet his. *Home.*

My eyes opened fully.

Matt, his expression dazed with desire, hovered over me. I actually pitied him for a moment. It would have been easy to give him what he wanted, because his longing was simple. My longing was difficult, extensive, and unsatisfied.

"Stop," I said with a sigh. I wriggled away. He let me go, dropping onto his back and scrubbing his face.

"Jesus, Hannah."

"S—" I clenched my teeth. No, I didn't owe him an apology for not wanting sex.

We lay side by side, staring at the ceiling. Matt radiated frustration. I wondered if he felt my sadness. After a while, I sat up and smoothed my skirt over my thighs.

"Is this how it's going to be?" he said.

"I don't know." I hugged my knees to my chest. Another long silence stretched between us. "Did you really think I wasn't serious when I said marry me?"

"We've been over this."

"But couldn't you see how happy I was on the show? How much I believed it?"

"No." He sat up. "I couldn't see anything except an audience that wanted to crucify me. I was scared, okay?" He shook his head. "I was freaking out, I was alone, and then you appeared and said marry me and you were my only friend in the building. And once I said that to the audience, everything changed. Hannah, you threw me a lifesaver. Of course I used it."

"But you used me, too."

"I thought you would understand. That was a talk show. This is reality. Marriage, even engagement, is a big fucking deal. And you don't—"

"Know you?" I pressed my fist into the bedspread. "I have seen you drunk, depressed, paranoid, um, jealous, crazy. I mean, what are you so worried about?"

"I don't know. God. Things we might not even"—he touched my shoulder—"know about ourselves. We haven't given ourselves time . . ." He turned me toward him and leaned in. Our lips met. *Easy*, this kiss. And I missed his mouth, his body, which I had pushed away for days.

I yielded briefly, curling my fingers in his hair. He moaned against my lips. The sound vibrated down my spine and desire hummed through me.

"God, you—" I pressed him back.

"Oh, fucking fine," he hissed. "Let's do it."

"What?"

"You want to get engaged so badly? Is that what you need to believe I love you? Fine. Marry me." His eyes burned into mine.

"No," I snapped.

"The hell?"

"Are you serious? Jeez, that was such a heartfelt proposal. Really, it's like your dick just proposed to me." I flicked a meaningful glance at the swell in his boxers.

"No, I fucking proposed on behalf of my dick, which apparently gets nothing until I agree to marry you. Do you see how messed up that is?" He grabbed his pillow and stalked out of the room. The door slammed. My comeback died on my lips.

I crumpled, scooting over to the warm spot left by his body.

No tears. No tears. I squeezed my eyelids together, but I

couldn't silence my thoughts. Was Matt right? Was I giving him an ultimatum, marriage or nothing? We were fine—well, fine in a really dysfunctional way—until my stupid off-the-cuff proposal.

But God, it hurt, being all in while he was hedging his bets. It hurt . . .

I uncurled and undressed, changing into my pajamas—boy shorts and one of Matt's big T-shirts. The clock read 11:04. He really wasn't coming to bed. I shuffled down the hall to the bathroom, brushed my teeth and washed my face. On my way back to our bedroom, a small sound from the family room caught my attention. I peered into the dark.

"Matt?" I whispered.

Silence.

I crept toward the family room, feeling along the wall. I jerked to a stop.

The only light in the room came from Matt's laptop, which stood open on the coffee table. He sat on the couch, his bare shoulders and head visible. His arm moved rhythmically.

On the laptop screen—I squinted—a woman knelt on a broad bed. She was naked, her dark hair tumbling across her back and her breasts hanging down. Behind her, a male figure plunged into her body. Another man—my mouth dropped open—knelt in front of her. She licked and sucked his length eagerly; he thrust into her mouth.

"Oh," I peeped.

Matt glanced over his shoulder. Blood rushed to my face.

"You all right?" he said, his arm still working steadily.

"Uh . . . um . . ." I inched forward, craving a better look at the screen.

"Sorry. I didn't feel like"—his voice caught and he shifted on the couch; he glanced at his cock—"being uncomfortable . . . in the office. Not many options . . . in this place."

I couldn't look away from Matt's porn. Two guys, one girl. The blush drained from my face. Tiny moans and grunts emanated from the laptop.

Hannah, I want things that . . .

"Is this what you want?" I gasped.

Matt gave a tense laugh. His hand stilled, then resumed, and my gaze panned over his lap. Dear God, he was rigid. This stuff excited him. A lot.

"No," he managed. "Just something . . . I like to watch. Fantasy . . . there's a difference." He clenched his teeth and refocused on the screen.

Shit, I was throwing him off his game—after denying him sex.

"Sorry, I'll—sorry!" I fled to our bedroom, my heart thumping and my skin fever hot. Two guys . . . I could never. I climbed under the covers and hugged myself. The image replayed in my mind. The girl had even looked like me—pale skin, dark curls, large breasts. Matt *had* to be thinking about doing that to me. *Sharing me.*

My face burned hotter.

The men in the video had been enjoying their plaything, clearly. They'd looked at her and at one another and moaned in pleasure. And she took it; she let herself be used.

I pressed my thighs together. "Just something I like to watch," Matt had said. I struggled to believe that. Was he telling the truth?

I breathed deeply and evenly. As the minutes passed, my embarrassment cooled and my horror faded. *I know that man in the family room,* I told myself. He was my lover, my night owl, my Matt, and he would never force me into something I didn't want.

I shifted on the mattress and gasped.

With my heart rate settling and my temperature normalizing, I realized I was feeling something else. I eased a hand into my panties. *Whoa.* Was it the video, or was it catching Matt pleasuring himself? Arousal coated my fingertips.

I was turned on.

Chapter 4

MATT

EXHIBITIONISM

I want to fuck her with an audience. I both do and don't want to share her. I want to reveal her like a possession, to draw off her clothes the way one might unveil a painting. She is no object, and yet I want to objectify her.

I want to see her embarrassment. When I bring her out, when I expose her to strangers, I want to feel her tremble and watch her blush. The thought makes me hard. (If the thought excites me this much, what would the reality do?)

I want to make our most private act a spectacle—not often, maybe not more than once, but I need this. Why do I need this?

I want to talk to her while we do it. I want to remind her that they are watching, to arrange her so that they have a good view, and to tell her that they are going to see her come. And when she comes, I want to call her a good girl and then send the watchers away, because she is mine . . .

Hannah and I walked side by side through Larimer Square. It was Sunday evening, warm and windy, and shoppers milled beneath the canopy of lights. A stranger recognized us. Hannah was civil while I bristled in silence.

Strangers . . .

Automatically, I recalled my first entry in the journal Mike had given me.

When I bring her out, when I expose her to strangers . . .

I shivered in the warm night and my dick stirred in my slacks.

"You okay?" Hannah took my hand.

I stopped, startled by her touch. We hadn't been touching much these days. Whether it was catching me jerking off to a threesome or my failure to propose, I didn't know, but Hannah had rebuffed me every night since—until I quit trying. I went to bed late and didn't reach for her. I showered alone after she left for work.

"I'm fine." I brushed my thumb across her fingers. Even that small touch was intoxicating. My breath came faster.

"Can we please act normal tonight?" she said.

"I wasn't planning on making a scene."

"Matt—"

"If you feel the need to prep me, I should probably stay home."

We stared at one another. It was Father's Day and Hannah had insisted that we visit her family. She'd dragged me to a salon that morning to get the black dye trimmed out of my hair. I had "Frankenstein hair," she'd said, and she didn't want to "freak out her family." Though she had tried to laugh it off, I knew what she really meant: my hair was an unsightly reminder of the faked death fiasco, and her parents didn't need extra reminders about my insanity.

We had spent the afternoon combing Larimer Square for a gift for her father. Exasperated and out of options, we'd stumbled into John Atencio, of all fucking places, surrounded by engagement and wedding rings. "Cuff links," I'd growled at the saleswoman.

It was getting dark by the time we were ready to go.

"I want them to see you," Hannah said. She squeezed my hand. "I want you to . . . get to know my family better, and for them to see how amazing you are."

"Don't you mean how sane I am? How well-adjusted I've become?"

"You're hurting me," she whispered. "That's not how I see it and you know that."

"We need to get going."

I dropped her hand and walked briskly to the car. I carried a small black bag from the jeweler—sterling silver cuff links—extravagant, admittedly, but Hannah wanted to make a good impression tonight. I'd also bought two bouquets of peonies for her mother and sister.

I drove slowly through Denver, past my old apartment and past Lot 49, past that patch of green space where Hannah and I had touched for the first time, and down the familiar roads toward the house where she grew up.

I parked at the curb. Hannah's fingers curled on my leg.

"Here." I passed the John Atencio bag to her. She took it and replaced her hand on my thigh, rubbing gently. She knew what that touch did to me . . .

"Mm." I gazed at my lap. "I feel like a well-behaved dog being rewarded."

"You're nervous. I get it now."

"Did it take you all night to figure that out?" I exhaled softly, controlling my desire. "Do you think I don't want your parents to like me—that I'm indifferent to their opinion?" I gazed at the lawn stretching toward the house, all the windows dark. I pictured a much younger Hannah playing on the grass. I also thought about giving Hannah a home and making her happy there.

"You're smirking," she said.

"I'm having unsettling visions of domestic bliss. Remembering, too . . . the first time I drove out here, and you came running across the lawn." I pointed. Ghostly sadness gripped me. "God, I can still see it, the way you looked. I can smell that night, taste it. I know that . . ."

She touched my inner thigh. "Go on."

I kept pointing, searching for words.

"I know that I'll die with those memories in me. I know those are the kind of memories . . . that last." I focused on Hannah. Her face was vibrant, her expression unlike anything I had ever seen. I knew that whatever had been left unsaid, she understood. I also knew that the old cosmic trick was playing itself on me. The greatest cynics fall in love.

I pulled away from the house.

"Matt?" Hannah's hand stilled on my leg. "Uh, my—"

"We'll go back. I'm not ready." I expected her to protest, but when I glanced at her, she was smiling. "Something funny?"

"You." Her finger dragged up the seam of my pants. "You think I don't know you, but I do. This is how you always get when you're nervous. Rude, agitated."

"Mm, one of my many ch—" I groaned. Hannah's hand brushed my cock, which was starved for her touch. I floored the accelerator. "*Fuck.*"

"Matt!" She giggled. "Slow down."

"*You* slow down." I laughed, really laughed, for the first time in days. I didn't know why Hannah had suddenly deigned to touch me and I didn't care. It felt good. Her fingers strayed over my thigh and I drove east, out into the prairie. We had taken this same nighttime drive almost a year ago. We were strangers then, but not anymore.

I parked beside a country road and we walked. The night smelled clean, like wheat and earth, and it felt good to get away from anything man-made.

"The way you look out here," Hannah said, her face tilted toward mine, "makes me want to say I'd leave Denver and move to the middle of nowhere with you."

"How's that?"

"You look happy."

"I like the freedom. It gives me peace. But you're not leaving your job for me, bird. Someone's got to pay the bills."

She giggled and I smiled down at her.

With the road far behind and nothing in sight but stars and grass, I pulled her to a stop.

"I don't have a ring," I said.

"Wh . . ." Her expression went blank. "What?"

"I don't . . . have a ring." I looked away, out at nothing. It seemed incredibly stupid to be without a ring when not one hour ago we'd stood in a jewelry store. It also seemed incredibly stupid that I had been afraid to engage myself to Hannah, when I knew as well as she did that love comes along less than once in a life-time. Once if you're lucky, and I'm not.

"W-what happened to"—her hands were limp in mine, her voice breathless—"'you don't really know me' and . . . and want-ing things that—"

I touched her lips.

"What happened to not touching me? Maybe you don't know me," I said, my thoughts forming as I spoke, "but engagement isn't yes, forever. It's . . . maybe, forever. So . . ." I got down on one knee. Jesus, she looked beautiful. Her eyes filled with tears. "Maybe, forever?"

"I—" She blinked rapidly.

"Hannah, say yes. Marry me. Please."

She nodded—a small, rapid motion—and found her voice. "Yes. Yes . . ."

Rather than rising, I pulled her down. I held her against me and we grasped at one another. "Finish . . . what you started in the car," I hissed. Her hand went straight to my cock. I moaned as she gripped me through my slacks.

We undressed one another frantically, tearing at zippers and buttons, and stretched out together in the grass. I hovered over her, pressing kisses to her nipples, caressing her breasts with my hands and face, and savoring the feel of her body beneath mine.

I needed this. I was burning for this. The tip of my cock traced cum along her belly and every muscle in my body tightened. God, I wanted to make this one count.

I closed my eyes and moved down, resting my forehead against her stomach. She touched my face and stroked my hair. I focused on the sweet-smelling night . . . and Hannah, my fiancée. She was soft below me, still and mysterious, not belonging to the city.

When I thought about the life I wanted to give her, and how

I might put aside my wishes and make her happy, pride tempered my lust. I fit my hands to the curves of her body. I kissed the milk-white skin of her thighs and the softness between her legs.

Twice I brought her over the edge before I entered her. Then I let her ride me. Her pert, round bottom filled my hands. Her steady pace dragged sighs from me.

Finally, the ache of my need became acute. The tight heat of Hannah's body turned from sweetness into slow torture, and I moaned into our kiss.

"Do it to me," I gasped. A plea and a demand.

And she did.

Chapter 5

HANNAH

We pulled up to my parents' house (for the second time) around nine. Matt killed the ignition and braced his hands on the wheel.

"It's okay," I said. "Don't worry."

"I hope to hell they didn't make dinner." He glanced at the house. The porch light cast a yellow cone over two old wicker chairs. Moths bumbled against the bulb.

"They didn't, I'm sure. They eat early. Besides, I told Mom not to do anything special. I said we just wanted to stop by and say hello."

"Maybe we should do this another n—"

"Love, it's Father's Day. There is no other night . . . until next year."

"How do I look?" He fiddled with a button on his cuff.

"Honestly?" I grinned and thumbed a smudge of dirt off his cheek. "A bit like you just had sex in a field."

"Oh, for fuck's sake."

"Baby, relax. I'm kidding." I unbuckled my seat belt and leaned over to kiss his cheek, and he hauled me onto his lap. *"Mmph!"*

"The fucking things I feel when I look at this house. It frightens me, I swear."

"I don't understand."

"Neither do I," he said, "but I see this house and I want to give you a home, somewhere we can . . ." He trailed off.

Have a family, I thought. *A little night owl. A little, little bird.*

As soon as the thought entered my mind, I shoved it out. Violently. I wanted a career, success, love, but not some Martha Stewart vision of happiness. That wasn't me.

So why was I picturing a small girl with blonde curls and a little green-eyed boy?

"What's the matter?" Matt scanned my face.

"I—" I swallowed. "I want you to myself. I mean we just . . . just got engaged."

"You have me to yourself. You know I'm all yours."

"But . . . kids." My voice cracked.

"Oh, bird." He chuckled and nuzzled my cheek. "Is that what you're worried about? We won't start a family right away. Hell, we haven't even set a wedding date. There's no rush."

"Well, what if I—" *Never want kids?* The words withered in my throat. I pulled back to look at Matt. He cocked his head, a touch of confusion dimming his smile. God, I couldn't stand to disappoint him. "Um, what if I can't . . . have kids?"

His smile faded completely.

"We'll cross that bridge when we get to it."

I traced his lips. "That bridge" indeed. It wasn't fair to charge into marriage without telling Matt that the thought of pregnancy made me queasy. But we weren't exactly charging into marriage. We were charging into engagement. *Maybe* forever. My shoulders drooped.

"There's always adoption," I mumbled.

His mouth twisted.

"I don't want someone else's kid. Is there something you're not telling me?"

"No! No. Matt, just . . . kiss me." I pressed my mouth to his spontaneously.

His fingers sifted through my hair. He gripped my jaw and

tasted me deeply. I felt dizzy when he broke the kiss, oxygen starved and hungry for his mouth.

"More?" he whispered.

"Yes . . . please. Er—" I shifted back on his lap, my head spinning. Engagement, talk of children—things were happening too fast. Maybe Matt had been right in wanting to delay our engagement. Why mess with a good thing? *Fuck, Hannah, make up your mind.* "We should probably go in. It's getting late."

We crossed the lawn hand in hand. He passed one of the bouquets to me.

"For your sister," he said. "You give it to her."

Guilt nettled at me as I inhaled the flowers' perfume. I hadn't seen my sister since my birthday, over a month ago. She'd looked out for me after my breakup with Matt, but Matt and I had repaired things, and I'd barely given Chrissy another thought.

The front door swung open and my mother beamed at us.

"Hey, Mom." We hugged.

Daisy's bark resounded from the hallway. The spaniel whooshed out and lunged at Matt, then at me, panting and whining.

"Mrs. Catalano, it's lovely to see you again." Matt hugged my mom and gave her a kiss on the cheek. He offered the bouquet and Mom buried her nose in the blooms.

"So gorgeous. Thank you. You should be calling me Helen by now. It's good to see you all in one piece." She patted Matt's cheek and he smiled graciously. I wanted the earth to swallow me. "You two are just in time for dessert. Do you like ice cream, Matt?"

He gave me a dark look.

"Uh, we already ate, Mom. Sorry. Is Chrissy around?"

"In her room."

Matt took his cue. His social graces never failed to surprise me. "When was I here last?" he said, escorting my mother down the hall. "Thanksgiving, wasn't it?"

I watched them turn the corner. A goofy grin pulled at my mouth. How nice to bring home a man and not a boy.

I bounded up the stairs to Chrissy's room. I knocked once on the door.

No answer.

"Chrissy?" I called.

After a moment, a small, dry voice replied, "Han? Come in."

I let myself into the bedroom. My nose scrunched at the smell of incense and cigarette smoke. I squinted in the dark.

"Shut the door."

"Sure." Frowning, I closed the door and walked to the bed where Chrissy lay, a cigarette between her fingers. She blew a stream of smoke out the window. "Mom and Dad let you smoke in here?" I peered around the room. An ashtray stood on the windowsill, an incense holder on her cluttered desk. Heaps of clothing covered the floor, along with soda cans and junk mail.

"Eh, sorta." Chrissy pushed herself up and coughed into her hand. Her face was sallow, her body hidden beneath an oversized T-shirt. I perched on the edge of her bed.

"Flowers," I said. "From me and Matt."

"Oh, sweet." She accepted the bouquet with a half-smile. "Thought I heard him."

I edged closer to my sister, trying to get a better look at her.

"I bet he'd like to see you, if you feel like venturing downstairs."

"I'm . . . not really dressed," she said. "Some other time."

"So what's . . . going on with you lately?"

She smashed out her cigarette and stared at the peonies. Her expression puckered. I hadn't seen my sister cry in years, and for a moment I didn't know what was happening. Two slivers of light appeared in her eyes, tears brimming.

Then they broke and streamed down her cheeks.

Chapter 6

MATT

"This thing is priceless." I plopped Hannah's baby album on the counter and flipped it open. Small Hannah looked so sweet: childish round cheeks, wild dark curls, and a look of mischief that I knew well.

"I really wish Mom hadn't given you that." She shrugged off her purse.

We were back at the condo, having spent less than an hour at her parents' house.

"Technically, she lent it to me." I grinned at a glossy page of birthday pictures. There was one-year-old Hannah with frosting all over her face. "Mm, messy even in your youth . . ."

My innuendo flew right over her head. She gnawed on a nail and stared off in the distance.

"Hey, your dad seemed to like the cuff links."

"Hm? Yeah."

I began to unbutton my shirt. I felt jittery, like I'd had too much coffee or sugar.

"I'm not sure how much use he'll get out of them, but they're damn nice. Not to imply that your dad isn't a classy guy." I laughed.

"He's pretty cool. Down to earth. We had a good chat while you were talking with Chrissy . . ."

Hannah barely stirred.

"You want to go out for a drink or something?" I tugged her into my arms. She moved listlessly. "I did just propose. You drink for both of us and I'll take advan—"

"Another night. It's late and tomorrow's Monday."

"Mm, true." I kissed her forehead. "I want to tell you something."

"Hm?"

"When I was talking to your father, I asked him—"

"What?" Hannah's eyes narrowed. "Please tell me you didn't, like, ask for his permission to marry me or something."

"Was I not supposed to . . . do that?"

"God." She pushed out of my arms and rubbed her face. "So you told them we're engaged? You could have asked me first."

"I did ask you. In the field. What's the matter?"

"It's just silly. We're not living in the eighteenth century. You don't need his permission. And honestly, we're not even properly engaged yet."

"We're not?" I white-knuckled the edge of the counter. "That's news to me."

"Yeah. No. I don't know."

Women are the most confusing creatures on earth.

Exhibit A: my maybe fiancée.

"Bird, talk to me." I moved behind her and massaged her shoulders. "Is it about a ring? I'll get you one tomorrow. Tonight even. I'm ready to—"

Hannah turned abruptly and kissed me. I froze. What the hell? Her kiss was ravenous, steel-edged. Her hands scoured my chest and she yanked at my slacks.

"God," I gasped, breaking the kiss.

Her intensity pulled me out of my worries and into arousal. Fuck, I loved this woman. Her desire went toe to toe with mine.

I stiffened rapidly and ground my erection against her hip. She gripped my ass and I lifted her breasts.

And just like that, it was over.

"Sorry, I—" She backed into the counter.

My hands fell. I was already panting.

"Hannah, what . . . is going on with you?"

"Nothing." She eased away from me. "Sorry. I must be wound up."

"Yeah, join the club." I tried to get a better look at her, but she moved toward the living room, keeping her back to me.

"I don't feel great. I'm sorry. I should probably try to sleep."

I glanced at my watch. Sleep at ten? That was early for me, but Hannah lived on a normal schedule. I sighed and dragged both hands through my hair. If I had learned one thing about women in my twenty-nine years, it was that they never talked until they were ready.

I waited a minute, hoping for some clue about her mood, but she remained silent.

"Okay," I said. I trailed her to the living room and kissed the top of her head. "Whatever you need. You want company?"

"No, I'll just sleep. Go do your thing." She patted my chest and shuffled down the hall. I wandered into the office.

My body ached with doused excitement. My cock felt cumbersome in my slacks, half-hard and hot. I debated jerking off at my desk.

I typed a tweet.

The burning debates of the twenty-first century. To get off or to write.

I backspaced the tweet immediately. *Fucking hell.* Social media really catered to my special breed of narcissism.

I browsed the Net in a mindless circle—Facebook, Gmail, *Colo Real Estate* . . .

Arousal and anxiety mixed in me strangely.

I unlocked the drawer where I kept my writing papers.

My work in progress, *Last Light*, filled three notebooks. It was nearly complete. I found myself holding off on finishing it because I had no new project. Not even a ghost of an idea.

Beneath *Last Light* lay my notebook from Mike. I fished it out and reread the first entry. I expected to feel revulsion. Instead, my excitement heightened. *Exhibitionism* . . .

On the second page, I began to write:

HUMILIATION

Writing this without judging myself is impossible.

What's wrong with me?

I'm ashamed of myself. Confused by myself. But I know what I feel. Even as I think about this, my body is . . .

I love to see Hannah blush. I love to embarrass her during sex. I know she likes it, too.

When I mock her for coming early, when I toy with her and call her names, it gives me the strangest, deepest pleasure.

I want to see her at the end of a leash. I want to tell her what to wear—tiny, strappy, revealing things. I want her begging, struggling, and

Midsentence, I dropped my pen.

"God damn," I whispered, my hand shaking.

Erotic images flooded my mind—Hannah, the star of every scene. I flicked open my slacks and my cock swelled into my palm. I closed my eyes and gripped the desk. How could I be unfathomable to myself? Dark water. Disturbing things beneath. I didn't want to see.

I jerked off quickly, hunched over the desk and gasping.

When I came, I felt a surge of shame, which crowned my pleasure. If only Hannah could see me now, and see into my mind. She was an innocent accomplice to my passion.

I cleaned up and stripped down to my boxers.

In the long, lucid moments after orgasm, I gazed at the print on the wall—*A Street in Venice,* 1880. The woman in the painting stared back at me. Her subtle smile unnerved me. She was caught in the act, or she had caught me in the act.

Hannah gave me that same smile and dark-eyed look.

I was the fool, mesmerized.

Around midnight, I climbed into our bed. I moved as quietly as possible, but as soon as I stretched out alongside Hannah, she rolled to face me.

She nuzzled her features into my neck and kissed my throat.

I fit her body to mine.

She sighed—sadly, not contentedly—and said, "My sister is pregnant."

Chapter 7

HANNAH

I scanned the tables outside the Mediterranean deli, searching for my sister. She was supposed to meet me on my lunch break. And she wasn't here.

My phone chimed with a text from Chrissy.

Running late. Be there in 10.

I huffed.

My sister and I needed to talk—properly. Last night at home wasn't the time or place. Chrissy didn't want Mom and Dad to hear, and I didn't want Matt to know everything . . . yet.

A flash of gold caught my eye, the accent on a stranger's handbag. My gaze focused. Bright interlocking *C*'s . . . *Coach.*

I sucked in a breath.

She was here.

The brown-haired woman sat alone at a table, preoccupied with her phone.

Matt's proposal, my promotion, and Chrissy's news had put the woman out of my mind completely. Now the memory rushed back.

You are so brave to be marrying him. Is he really into all that weird stuff?

I approached her table and she blinked up at me.

"Hi," I said.

"Oh, hey." Her face relaxed into a smile.

"Could we talk for a moment? I'm expecting someone, but—"

"Of course." Her eyes swept my left hand. No engagement ring, still.

"Thanks." I took a seat across from her, fiddling with my phone and trying to organize my thoughts. I had ten minutes, more or less, to grill her about Matt. Where to start? "Um . . . sorry to interrupt your lunch . . ." I gave a meaningful pause.

"Katie," she said.

"Katie. Thanks. I can't stop thinking about what you said last week. About Matt and . . ." I forced a laugh. "The weird stuff he's into?"

Katie's brow rumpled. Her smile tightened and she took a sip from her drink.

I hadn't ordered any lunch; Chrissy's news had killed my appetite.

"I probably shouldn't have said anything," Katie murmured. "I thought you knew."

"Is your friend who dated Matt . . . Bethany Meres?"

She nodded.

I dug my fingers into the edge of the table. *Stay calm. Milk this stranger for info. Then forget about her forever.*

"I know you must hate her," Katie said. "That's understandable, but she's not the witch that book makes her out to be."

"I just want to talk about the 'weird stuff.' I know Matt's a little kinky." My face heated and I lowered my voice. "I think anyone who's read *Night Owl* knows that."

"It's more than that."

"Could you tell me?"

"I don't even know if it's true." She chewed on her straw. "Beth's pretty bitter about how things went down with Matt.

Maybe she's mouthing off, you know? I wouldn't worry about it. You two seem really happy, and I—"

"Please, just tell me."

Katie swallowed and stared at the top of her soda cup.

"Okay. She said he went . . . too far sometimes. Wouldn't stop when she asked, got too rough. Like he'd hit her when they were, you know. And he . . ."

I leaned forward, willing my posture to relax. She might stop talking if I looked too tense, and I felt poised to snap.

"Go on."

"I guess he wanted to do things she didn't want. He'd get angry about it."

"Like what?"

"Weird stuff. Too crazy for Beth."

"Come on." I gave a feathery laugh. "Like . . . threesomes?"

"God, no." Katie smirked. "That's tame."

"Uh, true . . ." I shrank in my chair.

"He wanted to do some really hardcore stuff with her. Think *whips.*"

Whips? I searched for any memory of Matt mentioning whips. He'd mentioned riding crops, half-jokingly, and plugs . . . and last fall he took a belt to my bottom. Nothing about whips, though. Katie was right. Whips definitely fell under the "hardcore stuff" category.

An image surfaced in my mind: Matt standing at the foot of our bed, shirtless, a whip coiled in his hand.

Scary, or hot? I clenched my thighs beneath the table. *Both.*

"Whips," I repeated dumbly.

"Crazy, right?" Katie yawned and covered her mouth, which was lined with pale pink lipstick. She looked perfectly put-together—the type of girl I always envied—hair straightened and highlighted, designer clothes, flawless makeup.

I was about to ask what other "really hardcore stuff" Bethany had mentioned when a pale-faced Chrissy touched my shoulder.

I jumped in my chair.

"Oh, hey." I stood, but curiosity tethered me to the table. "Sorry, Katie, I have to go. Could we maybe talk again sometime?"

"Well, we seem to keep bumping into one another."

"Yeah. Maybe we could—" *Get drinks this weekend*, I wanted to say, *and talk more*. Was that too forward? I couldn't tell what sounded normal right now. Visions of whips and Matt filled my mind. Rough sex, the way we liked it. The fine line between pleasure and pain. Passing that line, obliterating it.

"I need to sit down," Chrissy said. She moved away and I lingered.

"I hope I see you again," I said to Katie. "I'd like that."

Katie smiled and nodded.

Too rough . . . he'd hit her . . . whips.

My thoughts swirled as I took a seat across from my sister.

The things Katie said hadn't frightened me. If anything, I missed Matt and I wanted to hold him and remember how real he felt. I had hurt him last night when I questioned our engagement. God, how stupid could I be? First he had cold feet, now it was my turn.

"Thanks for coming," I said to Chrissy. "You look better today."

She did look better, but only because she was wearing real clothes—a loose gray T-shirt dress and flip-flops. Her hair was growing out, the black mop stiff with product, and silver hoops lined her ears. She lit a cigarette. I snatched it from her fingers and put it out.

"What the hell?" she growled.

"Uh, you're pregnant?"

"Yeah, like I fucking forgot." Chrissy rolled her eyes and started to light another.

"If this is how you're going to be, I'll leave."

"So leave." She took a drag. "You're the one who wanted to talk to me."

"What, you don't want to talk to anyone?"

She slanted her gaze toward the deli. Last night's vulnerability was gone. Today, she'd tucked her concerns behind a snarky exterior, and suddenly the pregnancy was no big deal.

"It's not like I plan to keep it anyway."

"So you've definitely decided on an abortion?"

"I hate that word," she snapped, "and I don't know."

"Okay. Well, shouldn't you . . ." I took a deep breath. *This* was what I didn't want Matt to know. "Shouldn't you tell Seth? I mean, if you're sure he's—"

"It's him. There hasn't been anyone else for a while."

I closed my eyes and chilled in the late spring heat. Seth Sky, Matt's brother, was the father of my sister's child? How completely fucked-up.

"Do you know how far along you are?"

"About eight weeks."

"Okay . . ." I tracked back mentally to the end of April. It was a bad time, and because of that, I remembered it well. I was hiding at the Econo Lodge, separated from Matt. Chrissy kept me company some nights. She'd tried to cheer me up. She'd even . . .

My eyes widened swiftly.

Two months ago, Chrissy had coaxed me out of my motel room and took me to a suite at Four Seasons, where Seth and his bandmates were staying. Chrissy had a thing with the bass guitarist. But she also had a huge crush on Seth.

That was the night I gave Seth a hand job.

Then I left.

I left my sister with those deadbeats, in that drug-ridden hotel room.

Cue imagination.

Seth exits the bedroom, depressed, prowling. He sees Wiley and Chrissy. Wants me. I'm gone. Maybe he offers her coke, the way he offered it to me. Maybe she tries it, the way I tried it. Whatever really happened, I know how that night ended.

It ended with Seth and my sister having sex.

"At Four Seasons," I whispered.

Chrissy frowned. "Yeah, that night. How did you know?"

"Good guess. And you haven't talked to him since?"

"No," she said. "It was a one-night kind of deal."

"Are you still dancing?"

"Dancing"—that's how we referred to my sister's job at the Dynamite Club, a strip club in Boulder. The job suited her well. She was wild and exhibitionistic.

"Yeah, but the morning sickness is messing with my sleep. Plus, I can kiss my job good-bye if I blow up with a baby. I'm kind of screwed."

"Well, don't let that influence your decision. Do you need money?"

"I've got some saved. I mean, not enough to pay for . . ."

The abortion. She couldn't or wouldn't say it. And, obviously, she still lived without insurance, as she had for the last several years.

"I'll pay," I said, "if you decide to go that route. Or if you keep it. I'll help you no matter what. Don't worry about anything."

My sister straightened in her chair.

"Do you even have that kind of money?"

"I do." Reflexively, I pulled my left hand onto my lap. "We do."

"Oh, God. You mean Matt's money?"

"Why not? His money is mine. He said so."

"Han . . . it is too beyond fucked-up for me to get handouts from the brother of the guy who got me pregnant, okay? And—" She frowned. "Wait. Shit. Did you tell Matt?"

"No! God. I told him you're pregnant." I held up my hands. "That's it. Not, like, who."

"You *can't* tell him."

"Trust me, I won't. I think he'd kill Seth." *I* wanted to kill Seth. Matt really might. I shuddered. "Look, I need to get back to the office, but let's meet again. This weekend, maybe?"

"Sure, whatever."

"Okay. I'll call you. And please—" In the movie of my life, I would touch my sister's hand and look earnestly into her eyes, and tell her everything would be fine. In reality, I fumbled with my purse and frowned at her cigarette. "Quit smoking until you've made up your mind."

I hurried back to the office. A fine, cold sweat gathered on my brow. The spare aesthetic of the agency seemed ominous that day, the air laced with guilt.

My instincts told me to run home to Matt. Now was not the time to start hiding things from him. I was already dodging the Children Discussion.

But I couldn't tell him about Seth. *Seth, of all fucking people . . .*

I popped my head into Pam's office.

"Yes?" She glanced over her computer.

"I read the full manuscript I requested, and I'm interested in representing the author."

"Great. I'd like to take a look at it, if you don't mind. We can discuss it."

"Of course."

"And you're good to go this weekend," Pam added.

"Excuse me?"

"You needed Friday off?"

"Uh, no."

"Well, you've got Friday off. Matthew called. Something about a trip."

Heat spread across my face. My fists tightened.

"Oh, right . . . the trip. I forgot. Thank you, Ms. Wing."

I returned to the condo later than usual, around seven.

Matt hovered by the door.

As soon as I let myself in, he tugged me into his arms.

"Missed you," he whispered. I stiffened in his hold, but he didn't seem to notice. "I made dinner. Mexican . . ." He padded over to the kitchen table and gestured to a plate of *taquitos*. I grimaced. As usual, he'd made the whole box—all twenty-four—and half of the rolls looked suspiciously dark. He saw me eyeing them.

"I did this half in the oven. Then I did this half in the micro-wave, since—"

"I'm not hungry." I plopped my purse on the counter.

Normally, Matt's pitiful cooking attempts melted my heart, but not tonight.

"Oh." He shifted the plate. "Well, they got cold anyway."

"And you really need to stop making the whole box. Make, like . . . half."

"Oh. Yeah . . ." Out of the corner of my eye, I saw his shoulders sink.

"It's too many." I slapped the counter. "It's a waste. We can never eat them all, and then they sit in the fridge getting stale, okay? I feel like that's common sense."

"You're right. I . . ." He began to pile taquitos in his palm, as if he could somehow salvage them. He paced across the kitchen, frowned, and then returned the rolls to the plate.

"And you need to stop going over my head at the agency," I snapped.

"What?"

"Don't play dumb." I whirled toward him. "You called Pam and got me Friday off with your stupid M. Pierce influence and I am *tired* of you Sky men trampling over my life and clearing my fucking work calendar like I'm a child who can't—"

Matt snagged my wrist. With one terse tug, he reeled me into his arms.

This time, I crumpled against him.

"I'm sorry." His soft voice thrummed through me. I listened to his heart and smelled his clean, strong body. "I wanted it to be a surprise."

"Oh . . ."

"Hannah, I want you to meet my family, too. Properly."

I hid my face against Matt's chest. I had definitely not met Matt's aunt and uncle *properly* at his phony memorial.

"And I thought we could fly east a day early. I want to show you some things."

"What things?" I peeked up at his smooth jaw.

"Surprises, little bird."

Simply standing in the circle of Matt's arms eased away the rough edges of my day. I let myself forget about Chrissy and Seth . . . and Katie. Anyway, I didn't plan to ask Matt about the things Katie had said—not until I heard more and determined how much I believed.

I kissed his throat. He sighed and I trailed the tip of my tongue up his neck.

"Hannah . . ."

"I missed you today." Through the fabric of his shirt, I brushed a thumb across his nipple. He responded impulsively, his groin pressing my belly.

"Babe." He cupped my face. "Are you okay? Lately you . . ."

My poor sweet Matt. He struggled, and failed, to articulate my crazy mood swings.

"I'm fine now." I raked a hand down his spine and slid it into the back of his shorts, my nails teasing over his ass. A tense moan sounded in his throat.

"Mm, I just"—he got a handful of my backside—"don't want to repeat last night."

"What do you mean?"

"I mean me jerking off at my desk." He laughed reluctantly and I giggled.

"Is that what you did? I'm sorry, baby." Except I wasn't *too* sorry. I loved driving Matt to touch himself; it was ridiculously hot.

"Not your fault. I got too worked up."

"Yeah? Are you getting too worked up now?" I stepped closer to Matt, crushing my chest to his, and reached between his legs from behind. I palmed his balls and he growled.

"Fuck, yeah." His head rolled back. He rubbed the sides of my breasts.

"Do you always watch porn . . . when you do it alone?"

"Sometimes," he said—no hesitation. "Not always."

I massaged him gently and watched his neck cord and relax with pleasure, his chest rising and falling slowly. I eased back enough to let him play with my breasts, which seemed to please him. I moaned as he squeezed them.

"Want to feel those against your wet cunt," he panted. "My balls."

Unf . . . the dirty talk. My toes curled on the hardwood.

"Do you wanna . . . maybe . . . watch porn with me?" I gasped as soon as I said it. Where did *that* come from?

Matt was right; in some ways, I didn't know him. But I wanted to know him—his habits, his likes and dislikes. I wanted to know all of him.

His head sank and his eyes floated open. He smiled thinly, head cocked.

"Hell, yes . . ."

Chapter 8

MATT

I pulled off my T-shirt and dropped it by the door. Hannah slid her hand out of my basketball shorts, her hot little touch leaving my balls. *God damn . . .*

The girl had a way of distracting me.

Tonight, distracting me from dinner, and some vague plan to sit down with her and talk about Chrissy's pregnancy. It troubled Hannah deeply, and a little more than seemed reasonable.

I eased my dick out of my shorts.

"Oh," she whispered.

She always stared. It always surprised her.

Heavy-lidded satisfaction uncoiled inside me.

"Was getting uncomfortable." I took her hand and led her to the office, collected my MacBook Pro, and tugged her toward the bedroom.

"I really don't watch much of this stuff . . ." I pushed off my shorts and sat on the bed, booting up the laptop. Hannah was curiously quiet, as if she'd exhausted all her courage for the night. "You sure you want to?"

"Yes."

"You watch porn?" I raised a brow.

"Um. Some. Sometimes. Not . . . since I met you, really."

I grinned and stretched. "No need, am I right?"

"Oh my God." She laughed. "So vain."

I hummed a bar of "You're So Vain" and browsed the videos I'd bothered to download. I didn't have many; it was all online anyway. "You should get undressed."

I glanced at Hannah and caught her staring at my dick. Again. She flushed and my grin faded, something darker replacing it.

"Don't be shy. You're going to be my wife. I want you to look at it."

Her mouth fell open. Her eyes strayed over my cock and abs as she undressed, peeling off her polo dress, shimmying out of her thong and unclasping her bra.

In turn, I gazed appreciatively at her body, which she revealed for me without pretense. Her full thighs and curved hips, her heavy breasts . . . the simple exposure made me harden completely.

She joined me on the bed.

She began to stroke my length; her leg pressed alongside mine.

"That's nice . . ." I glanced at her hand. Nice? My control slipped. I slid under. Not for the first time, I thought, *I could die like this, in this dark water. Gladly.*

"Did you pick something?"

"Mm." I opened one of the files. The media player filled the screen. "It's the threesome you caught me watching. You seemed intrigued." I leaned over and bit Hannah's shoulder, then kissed it, my tongue sweeping her warm skin. She shuddered. "Am I right?"

"Um . . . yeah."

"You sure?" I clicked on the progress bar, skipping the preamble—the producer's sad effort to give the porn some plot.

"Yeah, yes." Hannah didn't sound too sure, but she glanced at the screen, where a dark-haired woman knelt on a bed. The room looked like all porn rooms: modern, anonymous, too clean. A man stood behind the woman, his erect cock touching her thigh. He stroked her ass. Hannah stroked my arousal.

I reached between her legs and found her wet. *Perfect.*

"Get on your hands and knees," I said. "I know you like that."

She obeyed quickly, transitioning to her hands and knees on the bed. I knelt behind her, rubbing my head against her glistening cunt. When she tried to slide back onto me, I slapped her ass. The sound sent a tremor of pleasure through me. The sight of her quivering made me twitch.

"Stay still. Be a good girl. Watch."

When the man on the screen penetrated the woman, I slid into Hannah. Slow . . . so slow. One torturous, lazy stroke.

Hannah was panting by the time I buried myself.

We fucked like the couple in the video. When he drilled into her, I moved harder against Hannah. When he pulled her hair, I tugged on Hannah's curls.

"How do you like it?" I gasped.

"Nn . . . good." She struggled to keep her eyes on the screen.

The second man stepped into the frame, casually undoing his jeans.

Hannah inhaled. Her pussy clenched and I moaned.

"You're making me feel so good. Keep watching." I slid out of her—she whined at my absence—and climbed off the bed. The air of the bedroom felt cool against my body.

I disappeared into the closet, returning with Hannah's vibrator—the LELO I bought for her last summer.

"Look." I nodded at my laptop. The second man knelt on the bed before the woman. She got him hard with her hand and mouth. I watched for a beat, my pleasure intensified by Hannah's bright blush and shy gaze. "You remember where this is going?"

"Y-yes . . ."

I dropped the vibrator between her knees.

"Do it, then," I said, and we did. *She* did. Trembling exquisitely, Hannah pushed the toy into her body while I knelt in front of her and slid my member down the back of her throat—again and again. She took it all. Her eyes rolled toward the laptop, where the woman on the bed got her mouth and pussy fucked. I asked if Hannah liked it, being full. She nodded as well as she could. Saliva dripped from her lips.

And cum. My cum.

I gripped her hair and groaned as her tongue flickered against me.

"All you need . . . is something . . . in your ass," I panted.

Hannah shuddered, convulsing on her toy.

I barely noticed when she dropped the LELO and dampened her finger with arousal. Her hot mouth, its tight vacuum and instinctive constriction, dragged me down. Had she come? Was she coming? I didn't know.

Hannah wrapped a hand around my dick and let me thrust into her mouth. "Good," I told her. "Close. Soon. Take it."

She gripped my ass and her slippery finger pressed against my anus.

That sensation . . .

No woman had ever dared.

Drunk with pleasure, I grasped the headboard and bucked against her mouth.

"Is th-that . . . what you want to do?" I hissed.

I bowed over her and arched back.

"Then do it," I said. Her finger pierced me. *Ah*—it was something strange—an intimate feeling beyond reason.

I poured myself into her mouth.

Pearlescent in her afterglow, Hannah lounged on top of me. Her sweet-smelling hair rolled across my chest. Her nipples, still hard, pressed into my skin. Excited me.

That is the state of desire, I guess. A state of imperfect satisfaction.

I slid my laptop onto the bedside table.

We hadn't spoken for several minutes. I was savoring my orgasm—a powerful, jagged release—and playing it over in my mind.

"Did you come?" I said, wincing subtly. Usually I could tell.

"God, yes. Way too fast. I don't know what got into me . . ."

I grinned. "I think porn got into you."

"Matt." She propped herself on my chest and frowned at me. "Did I hurt you?"

I shook my head, my smug expression fading.

Her hand browsed my side, from my thigh to my ribs. She leveled me with her stare. This was Hannah the woman—mature, confident, and patient. A force to be reckoned with.

"What?" I shrugged against the mattress.

"I don't know. You tell me."

I knew what she wanted to hear. I felt a phantom touch where she'd slid her finger.

"It didn't hurt," I said.

"Did it feel good?"

"I came, didn't I?"

"Stop being silly. Silly boy . . ." She began to finger-comb my hair. She nuzzled her cheek against mine and whispered in my ear, "You liked it. Tell me."

A dull throb between my legs reminded me how well I'd liked it.

"You like it when I finger your ass. I imagine it feels the same."

"I *love* it," she said.

"And I love you. Don't make me spell it out."

"You make me spell everything out." She twisted one of my nipples—gently. I hissed. Fuck, she was feisty tonight.

"Didn't know you were into sexual torture." My breath caught as I snickered. Impossible to play it cool with her curves fitted to my body, her pussy so close to my cock.

"Hm, who knows what else I'm into?" She twisted harder. A twinge of pleasure-pain traveled straight to my dick. I rolled— Hannah squeaked at the sudden motion—and pinned her to the bed. I dragged my fingers over her mouth, her breasts, her cunt.

"All mine," I whispered. "My fiancée."

She closed her legs, trapping my erection between her velvet thighs.

"My husband to be," she murmured. "All . . ." The muscles in her legs tightened, gripping me harder. "*Mine.*"

I tilted Hannah's chin and made her look at me.

"I liked it," I said. "What you did. No one's ever . . ."

"No?"

"Just you." I hesitated, my body aching. "I want to give you something."

Beneath me, Hannah softened, a sweet smile spreading on her lips.

"All right," she whispered.

Without climbing off her, I felt around in the bedside drawer until I found what I wanted: a small square box. Maybe because of what it contained—a platinum engagement ring, size six, with a one-carat diamond and two eight-diamond swirls around the band—it felt heavier than I thought it should. The ring was thick and modern in style; I had noticed Hannah admiring it the day we bought her father's cuff links.

I propped myself on my elbows and opened the box.

"This is the ring—"

"I know," she said. Her eyes were wide. "You remembered."

"Mm. Will you wear it?"

Hannah held out her hand. Fucking adorable; she could never speak when she got emotional. She nodded and smiled unsteadily.

I worked the ring onto her finger, over her knuckle, and straightened it. Then I laid her hand across her chest and admired it.

"Perfect," I said. I searched her face. "Now let me"—she moaned when I moved—"in."

Chapter 9

HANNAH

We flew east on Thursday night, my second flight with Matt. I clung to his arm as our plane rose and shuddered in the atmosphere. He stroked my hand and smiled at me.

Oh . . . that warm smile.

I didn't fuss about our first-class seats. In fact, I secretly enjoyed the luxury.

Matt looked gorgeous, semi-casual in dress slacks and a pale button-down. I wore black leggings and a loose boat-neck sweatshirt. When we reached cruising altitude, I relaxed enough to peer around the cabin.

Wow, everyone here looked like Matt. The high-end clothes, the easy elegance, the unmistakable air of privilege.

When our flight attendant introduced herself—*Jane, and welcome to the friendly skies*—Matt rattled off a list of requests, his smooth voice and snowy smile dazzling her. "An extra pillow and blanket for her"—he touched my hand—"and wine, please, white if you have it. None for me." He pressed a twenty into her hand. She dithered, then accepted the bill, and fawned over us for the rest of the flight.

I'd never seen anyone tip a flight attendant, but Matt tipped his way through existence—a twenty for the man who helped with our bags, a twenty after dinner, a fifty for curbside check-in—and we coasted effortlessly across the country.

We could, I realized, coast effortlessly through life. No jobs . . . nice meals . . . world travel . . . *ease*. Why did I buck against it? So many people would kill for that life.

"If we tell her about our engagement"—Matt's voice snapped me out of my daydream—"she'll announce it over the PA system." He questioned me with a glance.

"No! Er, no . . . thank you."

He chuckled and shrugged. "Suit yourself."

"I feel underdressed," I mumbled.

"Hm?" He studied my outfit as if seeing it for the first time. It wasn't the first time, though. That morning, when I'd stepped out of our closet wearing skintight black leggings, Matt spent a good ten minutes circling me and admiring my ass. *Hands-on* admiration. "Bird, you look fine." He rubbed my thigh. "You look comfy."

He dozed and I drank a second glass of wine. The flight attendant kept them coming.

I looked *comfy*. Right. And Matt looked like he belonged in first class. This was his world, and he'd stepped down from his world to live in a tiny condo with me, surrounded by walls he painted—for me!—in ludicrous colors. Surrounded by cheap knickknacks the likes of which I'd never seen in his former apartment.

No wonder he wanted to buy a mansion for us, a home where he might feel comfortable.

I studied his sleeping profile.

The cabin jostled, a tremor of turbulence. Matt's brow furrowed and smoothed.

Behind me, a woman purred about her home on Lake Geneva . . . *Switzerland*.

I drained my glass and felt small.

We landed at Newark International a little before midnight and emerged into a haze of humidity. I toddled after Matt, rubbing sleep from my eyes. He'd had nothing to eat or drink during the flight except coffee. He walked too fast, just like Nate, and glowered at everything.

A dark Mercedes—almost black, but with a ruby undertone—waited for us at the curb. Matt signed some paperwork, tipped the delivery driver, and asked if I was hungry . . . for the third time.

"No," I said. "I promise."

He adjusted his seat while I gazed at the car's interior. LEDs cast lines of soft purple light on leather upholstery. Thick, perfect stitching followed the car's sexy curves. Yes, this car was the definition of sexy. No wonder Matt had rented it.

"I've been thinking of getting one of these," he said. I jumped. He was staring at me, his dark eyes narrowed. "Do you like it?"

"Oh, uh, yeah. For sure. It's . . ." My eyes swept the palatial cabin. "Nice."

"'Nice'?" His mouth twitched.

"Er, supernice. Beautiful. It smells great." I shoved my nose against the leather. Matt laughed and touched my cheek.

"Wine puts such a pretty glow on your face."

That glow brightened, I'm sure.

The Mercedes glided like a yacht into the night. I remember Matt's hand adjusting the rearview mirror. I remember admiring his hand, his wrist and the creamy cuff of his sleeve, and then sliding awake at the sound of his voice.

"Baby bird," he said. "We're at the hotel."

I pressed the heels of my hands into my eyes. Ugh, all that wine on the plane . . .

"Sorry . . ."

"Don't be sorry. Let me carry you in."

I wanted to put up a fight, but Matt's arms felt so good, so secure, and he smelled like soap and clean leather. I laid my head against his chest and watched the world through barely open eyes. I saw light splashed on white stone, a great glass conservatory that looked like a greenhouse, and inside, warm wood paneling and ornate area rugs.

The elevator tolled. We rode up and Matt carried me to our room. His strides were smooth. How long had it been since someone had taken care of me like this? I felt like a child—in the best possible way.

And this was the man who wanted to marry me, to care for me for the rest of his life.

The man I wanted to take care of for the rest of my life.

He laid me on the bed and drew a thin quilt over me, and then he settled behind me, fully clothed. His chest to my back. His groin against my bottom. One long leg draped over mine and a hand cupping my breast.

"I love you, Hannah." His words whispered through my hair. "I love you so much . . . I love you . . ."

I woke with a headache.

The sheets were cool, the AC thrumming.

No Matt.

Two Tylenol and a glass of water stood on the bedside table. I smiled and swallowed the pills. Sweet night owl.

Again, a giddy surge of delight bubbled in my chest. Matt . . . taking care of me. Who knew he could be so tender?

I tiptoed to the doorway and peered into the sitting area.

He sat in a deep red armchair, leaning over his lap and scribbling in a notebook. A look of consternation crossed his face. He tousled his hair, hesitated, and continued writing. And fuck, he looked hot in nothing but low lounge pants.

I savored the vision of sunlight in his golden hair and on his toned, bare torso.

Until he saw me.

His eyes flickered to mine and he snapped the notebook shut.

"Bird, you're up."

"Yeah." I smiled hesitantly. What was that expression on his face? Alarm?

"I didn't hear you. How do you feel?" He came to me and half-hugged me, kissing the top of my head.

"Little headache. Thanks for the Tylenol. How long have you been awake?"

"Not long. Watched you sleep for a while."

I ran my fingers through his hair—he smiled—and flattened my palms on his chest. Sometimes, touching Matt made me feel so shy—especially when he watched me.

I swallowed and trailed my fingers down his abs.

Okay . . . okay. Too early to get him turned on.

My hands swerved away from his waist. I tapped the notebook he held.

"Working on *Last Light*?"

He yanked the book from my touch.

"Yeah. *Last Light*." He turned to the desk and slipped the note-book into his laptop case, zipped the case, and clicked a tiny pad-lock through the zippers. I frowned and jiggled the lock. He ruffled my hair. "Old habits, little bird."

We drank coffee together at the kitchenette. Matt said it was *our day* and he scooted his chair close to mine.

In the shower, he pressed me against the tiles and slid into me. His cock was rigid, insistent. "I've wanted you all morning," he hissed. "I got hard just watching you sleep."

Tender Matt was gone, demanding Matt taking his place.

I moaned long and low as he enjoyed me. He asked me how I liked it, and how much harder I thought I could take it, and then he gave it to me. When I was on the cusp of release, he pinched my clit and twisted. I came in a shaking rush.

He refused to give me our itinerary that day. Each time I asked, he flashed a smile at me. "Places. We're going places."

He plugged in his iPhone and let me pick music. I played "From Finner" and patted my thigh to the beat. *Far from home . . . so happy.*

Matt barely looked at the GPS as he drove.

He skirted the interstate highways, choosing winding country roads instead. We cruised through one small town after another. I lowered the window and smelled sweet grass and summer, and he held my hand.

What I'd seen of New Jersey—Newark and the area around Trenton where Nate lived—looked nothing like this. "So many trees," I said. "It's beautiful here."

"Isn't it? A well-kept secret, this state."

Something stole over Matt as he drove. He released my hand and gripped the wheel. The levity faded from his expression. He grew quiet.

I monitored his mood without comment. Were we going to see his aunt and uncle? Doubtful, with Matt in a T-shirt and jeans. Maybe a cousin? Some unsavory relative?

We entered another town.

A roadside plaque read, WELCOME TO HUNTERDON COUNTY.

"This is Flemington," he said. He stared ahead, eyes dark, arms braced. We swung around a circle and passed a large white barn with a gray roof, and a sign: DVOOR BROS. STOCK FARM, DAIRY COWS, HORSES.

He slowed the car almost to a stop as we crossed an old stone bridge.

MINE STREET.

I blinked rapidly, trying to take in everything.

"It's really . . . cute here," I whispered. Then I clamped my mouth shut. He glanced at the creek below the bridge—flashing water, flat brown rock. He swallowed and I watched the powerful play of emotion on his face.

Half a block from the bridge, he turned into a neighborhood across from a sprawling sandstone church.

"Saint Magdalene's," he said.

We passed several small homes and stopped at the curb beside a blue house with a red door. An oak loomed in the backyard, a flowering tree on the small front lawn. The grass looked neatly kept, as did the shrubs around the stairs, but a pile of trash clustered near the garage door: crates, beams, a garbage can, a sack of cement.

Despite the sunlight, I felt sad and unmoored. Why were we here?

I looked at Matt.

Pale-faced, he stared intently at the house.

"I grew up here," he said.

My lips parted; I sucked in a thread of air.

Jesus. How hadn't I considered this possibility? Matt . . . showing me the home where he grew up. Matt letting me into his life.

I gulped down my instinctive response to the house—*it's tiny!*—and took his hand. He flinched, but his fingers tightened around mine.

Here. He grew up here. Before his parents died, presumably. I pictured a towheaded boy on the front lawn. *Little Matt . . .* Tears shimmered in my eyes.

"I—I want to . . ." I dug through my purse. *Get a fucking grip!* "Take a picture . . ."

He said nothing.

Was this tasteless? Cruel? Weird? My thoughts flashed around wildly as I snapped pictures on my phone, framed by the car window. Little blue house. Lost blue boy.

"Y-you grew up here," I stammered.

"Mm. For the first nine years of my life, at least."

Nine years. Sure enough. When Matt was nine, his parents died in a bus accident in Brazil, and his uncle and aunt whisked him into a different life. Maybe a better life, by the look of this house. I swallowed the questions I wanted to ask. So much I burned to know. Matt was showing me this—giving me something, the edge of the map—and I sensed that I needed to be patient. Time, not wild curiosity, would illuminate his life.

"Do you want to knock? Go in?"

He shook his head.

"Okay." I rubbed my thumb over the top of his hand. We sat in silence, watching the house. He sneered subtly, pulled forward, and nodded.

"That's an addition." He pointed to the extruding back half of the home. "All that. And they cut down the pine tree. There was a big tree—right there by the window. I climbed up one time, looked into my parents' bathroom, and saw Nate doing push-ups, like, against the sink. Admiring himself in the mirror. He was big into his looks."

I pictured boy Matt in the missing tree, and boy Nate with his dark hair. My thoughts strayed to Seth and I grimaced.

Finally, we pulled away from the house and drove through the neighborhood, which was small and T-shaped with two cul-de-sacs. Matt made a few comments. *My friend lived here. These people had a dog that bit Nate. Everyone used to say a Mafia family lived there.*

I saw the place through his wondering child eyes. The menacing dog. The alleged crime family. Cracked streets where Matt maybe rode his bike or trailed his big brothers.

"I'd like to see pictures of you as a kid. I've only seen a few." *Online*, I thought guiltily.

"I'm sure Aunt Ella and Rick can help with that."

I stroked his thigh as we turned out of the neighborhood. Tense muscle under denim. My heart pulled strangely as the blue house vanished from view. *Leaving the past behind*—there's no such thing. I wrapped my thoughts around each question I wanted to ask my future husband, and my desire to know him—to know him to the marrow—turned to steely intention inside me.

Chapter 10

MATT

I cruised around Flemington—down the main street
with its quaint Victorian architecture and pastel-colored homes,
through the winding lanes of St. Magdalene's, past Mine Brook
Park—and Hannah peered out her window like a child.

"Mine Brook," she said. "The title of your book."

"That's right. There used to be copper mines around here.
Dad—" I stumbled over the word. Hannah's curiosity shone in her
eyes, and I wanted to give her the answers she deserved, but how
could I do that if I could barely talk about my parents without my
voice catching?

Ridiculous, these old rags of emotion. I scowled.

"Dad wouldn't let us play in certain woods. Every once in a
while, an old mine shaft collapsed. Of course that made it all very
exciting. We used to play by that creek you saw."

"Yeah? I like that. It sounds . . . happy."

"I was very happy here. Unconditionally happy." I glanced at
Hannah. Her wide, bright eyes locked on me. "Am I boring you?"

"Not at all. I want to hear everything." She looked painfully
earnest.

"We had money, you know. Plenty of it. We could have lived

anywhere, in any way, but my parents insisted on living humbly. And they worked hard. Real saints, you know?" We drove past a stretch of outlets. "Like the prophets. 'They were too good for this world.'"

Her eyebrows bunched together and I frowned.

Right, she won't catch your biblical allusions. Stop that.

"Anyway." I turned onto Highway 202 and stepped on the gas. *"Mine Brook* and *The Silver Cord* are my love songs to this place. I don't know exactly what my parents were trying to accomplish with the small home and public schooling, but I—" Emotion weighed on my chest.

"Go on."

I yanked a hand through my hair.

"I loved my life here. I remember." Thick, dumb tears gathered in my eyes. "The creek, the parks, everything. We were happy . . . with this happiness so cosmically unfair . . . I was nine and I remember thinking, 'My life is perfect.' And Hannah, I *knew* it couldn't last . . . that somehow I would have to pay for it, that happiness."

I blinked the tears from my eyes. Not one fell.

"Matt, that's—"

I heard shock in her voice and I raised a hand to silence her.

"It's not ridiculous. It's true."

She let it go, but I could feel her disapproval rumbling—her dislike of my deeply held belief that the price of pleasure is pain.

"We'll be different," I said. "I see no point in disguising our wealth from our children." I glanced at her. She stuttered out a few "um"s and "well"s. "Bird, I know . . ."

"You do?" Her eyes widened.

"Of course. I know you want to live simply. And we will, somehow. But it would be a farce, to force a small home and public schooling on our children. Not that we'll spoil them, but we'll give them the best possible footing for a good future . . ." I rambled about my plans, expecting Hannah to interrupt. She didn't, though, and I wondered again if she was keeping something from me. Maybe she knew she couldn't have kids. Maybe she was afraid to tell me.

But if that was the case, why the IUD?

I smirked and shook my head, dismissing my heavy thoughts.

I drove to the Fudge Shoppe, a chocolate store owned by an old family friend. I had fond memories of the place—the smell of cocoa, Easter rabbits taller than my nine-year-old body, dipping strawberries in deep silvery vats.

A boyhood friend ran the shop now. He'd bulked up, got a sleeve of tattoos and shaved his head, but we recognized one another immediately.

We embraced, and I introduced Hannah as my fiancée.

"Nothing's changed," I said, looking into the glass cases.

"Well, we're making chocolate from bean to bar now." Stephen took us to the back room and showed us around. Hannah dipped a strawberry, giggling as she did, and I dipped another and fed it to her. I kissed the warm chocolate from her lips.

"Is your dad around?" I was hoping to see Stephen's father, a white-haired man even when I'd known him, who used to show up for church with chocolate stains on his suit. He was a good friend to my father.

"Not today. He's out with Lisa and the kids."

"Your kids?"

"Yup. I got married, oh, seven years ago now. Got two little girls."

"Well, hey, congratulations." I flashed a smile at Hannah. She looked pointedly at the ground. "How is all that?"

"It's good, man. Really good." Stephen folded his arms and nodded. The bells on the front door jingled, announcing a shopper. "I better get out there. Help yourself to anything."

"I was actually hoping you had a key to the church," I said. "Wanted to show Hannah."

"Oh, yeah, of course." Stephen dashed upstairs, his feet thumping overhead, and returned with a key chain. "Front door and back. That's just the shed."

I promised to return the key before five and I drove Hannah over to Three Bridges Reformed Church. I parked in the side lot and led her to the front of the building. We held hands and admired the classic clapboard steeple, the whitewash and red door.

Large trees shaded us.

"I remember playing on this lawn between services," I said. Hannah pressed against my side. "Nate would sit in the church, up near the pulpit, and like some wizard"—I laughed—"order Seth and I to find random things for him. A dry leaf. A broken stick. We'd run down the aisle and come out here to search. We sort of worshiped him."

Inside, the church smelled musty. Cool air lay still on my skin.

We sat on a pew and I closed my eyes and remembered for a while.

Hannah held my hand in both of hers.

When I was ready, I told her the rest of my story. I told her how Mom and Dad traveled to South America with a mission group once a year and provided free medical care to people living in the favelas—the slums of Brazil. I breezed over the accident: a bus crash on a winding mountain road. My parents instantly killed.

Aunt Ella and Uncle Rick came into our lives then. Childless, they happily spirited Nate and Seth and me to their grand colonial-style home in Chatham, and we stopped going to church and playing in muddy creeks, and we learned instead how to play tennis and ride horses.

"'My little gentlemen,' Ella used to call us." I chuckled, my eyes drifting open. "Only Nate really took to that."

"Will we see Nate this weekend?"

Hannah had been so silent while I spoke, her hands so still, that I flinched at her voice.

"If you want. I'm sure he'd love to see you. Would you like that?"

"I think so, yeah." She wiped her eyes quickly and stared toward the front of the church. Shafts of light came in through the single remaining stained-glass window. "I think they hate me, your aunt and uncle. It'll be nice to have someone on my side."

"Hate isn't in their repertoire. And they have no reason to believe you knew I was alive last year. They'll believe what we told the papers—that I masterminded my fake death, that you had no knowledge. No one knows you were visiting the cabin regularly except Kevin, Nate, and Seth. They've all agreed to keep quiet, and I believe them."

I did believe them. Kevin, who owned the cabin, was my first and best friend in Colorado. Nate's loyalty was unquestionable. As for Seth, little though I liked him, I trusted his word. I also knew he had no desire to drag Hannah deeper into my mess.

Hannah squinted at the podium, then at her feet. After a while, she said, "I just want your aunt and uncle to like me. The way they looked at me, at your memorial . . ."

"That was different. Everyone thought you wrote *Night Owl* then. Hannah—" I took her hand and led her out of the church. It struck me as strange that I'd shared my story with her and all she wanted to know was if we might see Nate tomorrow. "I'm marrying you. We're only here to tell them, not to get their approval."

"But you wanted my dad's approval."

"These people aren't my parents." I pulled her toward the car.

"How can you say that?" She dawdled, gazing over her shoulder at the church. I felt myself freezing up inside. Chilling toward her. "It's so . . . ungrateful, Matt."

"Am I supposed to be grateful that my parents died? My *parents* would have loved you, and you're what I want. A simple girl—" The words tumbled out without a thought, and I gaped.

Hannah's hand stiffened in mine.

"What?"

"Nothing," I said, but I couldn't take it back.

The dull impact of my words receded. Hannah swallowed and trailed me to the car.

I'd turned to ice inside. No meaningful emotion could pass from me to her. We drove back to the Fudge Shoppe in silence. I ran the church key in to Stephen and bought a little bag of toffee and chocolate brittle. I plopped the candy on Hannah's lap; she mumbled a thank-you.

Fuck. I could see her pulling away from me—wondering who the hell I was, to call her "a simple girl." But I'd meant something different . . . something better.

We returned to Morristown.

I'd envisioned a day spent in Flemington, and me opening up to Hannah completely. So much for that. We got back to the hotel by two. Hannah went straight up to the room for a nap, insisting she wasn't hungry. I sat alone in Rod's, the hotel restaurant, and ordered a cup of crab bisque and a glass of Coke.

I stirred the soup and broke the crab cake into tiny pieces with my spoon.

Hell, I wasn't hungry either.

A simple girl . . . what I wanted. Couldn't Hannah understand? I didn't want the affectation surrounding my aunt and uncle. I also didn't want the middle-class life on which my parents insisted; I didn't share their humble values. I wanted something uniquely ours—something natural for us.

I shoved away my soup. It had been a mistake to go to Flemington—to see that old sunlight and remember. *Stupid.*

I drank my Coke, paid the bill, and stalked out across the hotel lawn.

God, I despised this blanket of humidity.

I gave Nate a call and asked if it wouldn't be too much trouble for him to drive to Ella and Rick's tomorrow. "Hannah asked for you," I said. "Moral support or something."

"Does she need moral support?" Nate sounded affable, as always, and I sounded half-unhinged, as always.

"Hell if I know," I snapped. "She thinks they hate her."

"What's the matter?"

"I called her a simple girl. God, I said that today." I leaned against a tree.

"'Simple'?" Nate chuckled. "Well, she is very sweet."

"Mm, but how could I *say* that? She's hurt. Pissed. I don't know."

"I'm sure. Give her time. Apologize. Be good to her, Matt. She's a gem."

"I know she's a fucking gem. I *am* good to her. I'm the best I can be."

"Better than this, I hope." He yawned in my ear and I glowered at the grass. "I'll see if Val feels up to visiting Ella and Rick tomorrow. Either way, I'll drive up."

"Thank you."

"Not at all. It'll be great to see you two." Again, he urged me to apologize to Hannah—he was the nettling good angel on my shoulder—and said good-bye.

I returned to our hotel room with every intention of apologizing, but Hannah was still asleep. I rummaged through my suitcase. There, among the shirts, was my little surprise for Hannah: a stainless-steel plug with a sapphire on the stopper. Desire rippled through me.

That morning, Hannah had caught me writing in my journal from Mike. *Matt's Black Book,* as I had started to think of it.

The entry was rambling, lust-fueled.

I wrote about pain. Her pain, my pleasure. Restraints. A riding crop.

Violent desire . . .

Sometimes, I could almost convince myself that Hannah might like my "aberrant desires." She'd let me spank her in the past, after all, with my hand and a belt, and I'd used clamps and other toys with her.

Then, when I was sneaking between the mountains and our condo, we'd indulged in a weekend of rough sex. Struggle and force. Pleading, overpowering. A dark role-play. But I never really knew if Hannah liked those pleasures on the fringes of normalcy, and that fierce sex seemed localized in a riskier time.

Too anxious to rest, too tired to write, I sank into the armchair with my laptop and browsed the Net: Twitter . . . Facebook . . . Gmail.

I had one new e-mail from an unfamiliar sender, krazybaby88. I opened it.

Subject: (no subject)
Sender: krazybaby88
Date: Friday, June 20, 2014
Time: 9:20 AM
I know something you don't know. Your girlfriend knows, too. I wonder why she hasn't told you. Christine Catalano is pregnant. Who's the proud daddy?

It's Seth Sky!

Chapter 11

HANNAH

Matt's aunt and uncle lived in a townhouse in Moore Estate, a bucolic luxury community minutes from our hotel.

I woke up alone that morning, which didn't surprise me. Matt was in one of his moods.

We'd spent the rest of yesterday in the hotel, skirting each other. I watched HBO and ordered room service. He hit the exercise machines, showered, and left for half a dozen smokes. I couldn't get a word out of him.

What the hell was that about? *I* was the injured party here. He'd called me "a simple girl." Yeah, a regular country bumpkin compared to the great Matthew Sky.

Unrefined. Uncultured. Untraveled.

Good to know how you really see me, Matt.

And today, I would meet more of the snobby Sky clan. Hooray.

I rolled out of bed and shuffled into the sitting area. A note lay on the couch.

Having coffee downstairs. Meet me in the lobby. Bought these for today. M.

Even his use of the letter—not Matt, my fiancé, but M., the great author—irritated me.

What he'd bought added insult to injury.

It was an outfit. Not just a necklace or shoes, but a complete outfit—suitable, I presumed, for wearing around the elite Aunt Ella and Uncle Rick.

I opened a Neiman Marcus box to find a cream-colored Herve Leger bandage dress—beautiful, of course—with eyelet trim, short sleeves, and a ruffled hem. A pearl necklace pooled in a crease of fabric. There were matching earrings, small, tasteful.

In a shoebox: powder-pink Fendi flats, the leather smooth as satin.

Pleased to meet you, Mr. and Mrs. Sky. I'm a cupcake.

I dressed in a huff, pissed at Matt's elegant taste, pissed at his effort to control my appearance, and finally pissed at how stunning I looked in the mirror. A rosy blush completed the look. I fingered the pearls resting on my collarbone.

Matt had easily dropped three grand on this ensemble . . . not to make himself more comfortable, I guessed, but to make sure *I* felt comfortable.

I spent a few minutes unwinding, applying makeup and styling my hair, and I was smiling by the time I stepped into the elevator.

So what if he'd called me a simple girl? He'd obviously meant something else, or said it by accident. I was ready to bury the hatchet.

And Matt . . . was not.

Somehow, his mood had worsened overnight.

He took one dark look at me in the lobby. I knew that look, and I shrank from it: distrust.

"Very nice," he said icily. His eyes flickered over me inventory-style: shoes, dress, jewelry, check, check, check.

"Th-thank you. You too . . ."

He had dressed to match me in cream-colored slacks and a blazer.

We drove to Moore Estate—tense, silent. In the driveway, he

said, "Nate agreed to join us today. When he arrives, I'll have to abandon you for a while."

"Abandon me?"

"I have some business in the city."

I shot a pleading look at Matt—he couldn't leave me here!—and met his dispassionate, chilly profile. Oh yes, he could, and he would.

Ella and Rick greeted us at the door. They looked exactly as I remembered them from the memorial: Ella, a petite, crepe-paper-skinned woman with a thick black wave of hair; Rick, a barrel-chested man who stood as tall as Matt. A signet ring winked on his pinky finger. Ella's bracelets jingled endlessly, a fine chime of wealth.

"Your hair!" she gasped, clutching Matt's face.

He smiled at her with real warmth. I shivered.

"What do you think?" he said.

"Well, I—" Ella laughed, a quaver of sadness in the sound. "I heard you dyed it black. Black hair on my golden boy. We should have had you committed."

Matt hugged his frail aunt gingerly. "My fiancée, Hannah." He touched my shoulder.

Ella's eyes dusted over me.

Rick pumped my hand and grinned. "Great to meet you, Hannah. Great. You gotta keep this boy in line."

And that's how the visit went. Ella ignored me as much as civilly possible. Rick pretended we were meeting for the first time and that the phony memorial service never happened. He tossed out words like "gotta" and "hafta" as a stand-in, I think, for a down-to-earth attitude, and he traipsed through the house in golf shoes.

We settled in the living room, which was small but opulent. Hanging tapestries, ambient light, and oil paintings with antique gilded frames filled the house.

Ella directed all her attention at Matt.

Rick, who must have long ago given up trying to control his wife, periodically threw me a bone. *How d'ya like New Jersey, Hannah? How d'ya like Colorado? Ski much? No?*

I wanted Matt to rescue me from this stuffy situation, or at least to acknowledge my existence, but he was oblivious—and blameless, laughing, charming. He chatted with Ella about cousins I didn't know. With Rick, he spoke about stocks, soccer, and cars.

Who was this guy, and where was my fiancé?

Around one, I heard a knock at the door.

Nate let himself in and I sprang from the couch and launched myself at him, with Matt, Ella, and Rick all looking slightly appalled.

Nate, thank God for him, laughed and opened his arms. "Hey, stranger."

I hugged him hard. He hugged me back just as hard. Whatever lingering grudge I held against Nate—last year, he'd known Matt's death was faked, and he and Matt had kept me in the dark—dissipated on a wave of gratitude.

"Get me *out* of here," I whispered.

Nate's expression never faltered. He greeted Ella first—she clung to him and kissed his cheeks—then Rick and Matt. Two quick man-hugs.

"Hey, this looks better." He ruffled Matt's hair. "Golden boy again."

Ugh. Fucking golden boy . . .

I could think of more appropriate nicknames.

"Yeah." Matt shrugged. "Got rid of the black. Was Hannah's idea."

"Oh? She's a keeper."

"Sit with us," said Ella, patting the couch.

"I'd actually like to take Matt and Hannah out for ice cream. You want to join us?" Nate glanced between Ella and Rick. He must have known they would say no.

Ella's nose wrinkled. "I don't think we will." She gripped her husband's knee.

"Just the kids, then. We'll be back soon."

"You and Hannah go on," Matt said. "I'll stay. I have some things to discuss with Rick."

Again, a round of appalled looks—this time from Nate, Ella, and Rick.

I edged toward Matt. He smiled and kissed my cheek (a frosty smile and a chaste kiss).

Outside, I slid into Nate's familiar Cadillac sedan. *Secure*, I thought. Being around Matt made me feel wild. Being around Nate made me feel safe. I filed away that information for my . . . book? My short story?

My project.

Nate pulled out of Moore Estate and drove slowly toward Friendly's. Mottled sunlight scrolled over the windshield. I studied his face—handsome, black-haired, without a trace of fatigue or resentment. Matt's tireless dark angel. Maybe mine, too.

"Thank you," I said.

"My pleasure, Hannah. I know Ella and Rick can be a little . . ." He gestured.

"Yeah . . ."

"They'll come around. She'll come around. Matt's her baby. She worries."

"Matt is everyone's baby, apparently." I clenched my teeth, then let out a hissing sigh. Is this what marriage to Matt would be like—him descending into fickle moods, me biting my tongue or sniping at him behind his back?

No. I wouldn't let us become that couple.

I expected Nate to ask what was the matter, but he only said, "Yours, too, I hope," and then, with an absent glance at my ring, "Congratulations, by the way. I should have said that to both of you back at the house. Thoughtless."

"I wish you had. No one's talking about it, the engagement. Like it's not happening."

"Oh, but it is happening. Did you know he called me about it? He's excited. Nervous."

"Nervous?"

Nate nodded. "Who do you think ordered him out here? He's just as nervous as you are, if not more."

I blinked three times, rapidly, and tried to imagine Nate coaxing

Matt to visit his aunt and uncle. The story made sense, actually. Matt would have avoided this situation. Too formal, too social. Nate had more tact than both of us put together.

At Friendly's, he ordered a small vanilla cone for me, nothing for himself, and we sat side by side at a lumpy red picnic table. He watched me indulgently as I worked on the cone. Again, I got the distinct impression that I was a child to the Sky brothers—a cute thing, like a knickknack. Quaint. *She's a keeper.*

"Our parents used to get us ice cream," Nate said. "On vacation. Sort of a family ritual."

"Oh . . ." I licked a big dollop from the cone. More Sky family revelations. This trip was turning into an emotional wringer. "I'm so . . . sorry about what happened to them."

He sat up straighter and shrugged. He undid the top button of his collar and, with a dry sigh, smoothed a hand down the back of his neck. I cringed inwardly. Over the past year, I had taken countless amounts of comfort from this man . . . and given back none. I didn't know how to begin to comfort someone who seemed so well-adjusted.

"Thank you." He laid his cheek in his palm and resumed watching me, and I enjoyed the rest of my ice cream in silence.

Afterward, I said, "Do you have any advice? You know, since . . ." I wiggled my ring finger. "Your marriage seems great."

Nate didn't hesitate.

"Be honest. About things that happen, about how you feel. Small lies and secrecy may not seem like a big deal, but"—he gazed down at me, and his gaze went through me—"you know how water gets into rocks, freezes . . ."

I imagined the slow, aching crunch of ice fracturing stone, and I knew I had to tell Matt that Seth got my sister pregnant.

I also knew I had to tell him that I never wanted to be pregnant. I nodded swiftly.

"All the same"—Nate chuckled—"I'm sure Matt needs to hear that more than you do. Strange that he didn't join us. He's usually so . . ."

Possessive. Jealous.

"I know," I said. "He probably wanted to make his escape. He's being cryptic today . . . something about business in the city."

"The city?" Nate's eyes jolted to mine. His terse tone, his rigid posture, sent a ripple of alarm through me.

"Um, yeah. Probably book stuff? His editor is in the city."

"*Seth* is in the city," Nate said. "Matt called me last night, asked where Seth was staying. I wouldn't tell him at first, but—*goddamn it.*" He rubbed his face. "He insisted he wanted to smooth things over, send a bottle of champagne or something."

He rose, yanking out his cell, and strode toward the car. Soon he was jogging.

All at once, my day clicked into clarity.

Matt's bad mood last night and this morning. His "smoke breaks." Avoiding me. Ignoring me. And that look he gave me in the lobby this morning, a look of pure mistrust . . .

I sprinted after Nate, yanking at his sleeve when I caught up. He held the phone to his ear. His gaze flashed across my face.

"Seth got my sister pregnant," I stammered. "And I think . . . Matt might have found out somehow. He's been acting weird all day. Bad weird."

Nate's jaw didn't drop. It tightened almost spasmodically. He lowered the phone and thumbed the screen.

"Well, fuck," he said.

Chapter 12

MATT

The train from Convent Station takes about an hour to reach New York City.

I chose a seat on the top level of an empty car. I wanted to be alone.

I closed my eyes and listened as a garbled voice announced each stop. I knew this route well. Growing up, I used to ride the train from Chatham into the city. I had like-minded "friends" there. We drank and went crazy together.

And nothing has changed, I realized as I emerged into the crowds of Penn Station. For me, the city still rumbled with madness. A sea of tourists. The end of the line.

My phone rang for the seventh time—Hannah and Nate were alternating calls—and I shut it off. They knew what I was up to, clearly. Hannah must have mentioned my "business in the city," Nate must have remembered my desire to "smooth things over" with Seth, and together they must have realized . . .

I caught a cab to the Plaza Hotel, where Nate had told me Goldengrove was staying.

As the cab inched through traffic, I stoked my anger. *Seth got*

Chrissy pregnant. Seth fucked Chrissy. Seth pursued Hannah. Seth fucked Hannah's hand.

Seth came in her hand.

Seth tried to sleep with her.

Last month, when Hannah and I got back together, I'd made her explain what happened with Seth—in great detail. Then I wrote the scene into *Last Light*. Then I asked her to tell me again and again, until she lost her temper. *You're obsessing,* she'd said. *You're scaring me.*

She was right—and no matter how many times she painted that scene in the Four Seasons suite, describing her agency and guilt, I saw her as a victim. She was my sweet little bird, addled by our breakup, drunk, drugged, falling into Seth's clutches.

A victim of circumstance.

Just like Chrissy.

"Happy summer," said the cabbie as I climbed out of his car, and I registered vaguely that it was the first day of summer. I shrugged off my thin blazer and slung it over my shoulder. Hannah and I should have been celebrating summer together. Good wine for her, a nice meal for both of us, outdoor sex. I wasn't upset with Hannah for keeping the truth from me. Not very upset, at least. She must have been worried about my reaction.

She was right to be worried.

My brother seemed to be waiting for me, standing by the Pulitzer Fountain. His hair looked lank, disheveled. He wore torn jeans and a T-shirt. I drew closer.

Tourists shuffled around, taking pictures and heading toward the park.

I watched sunlight shimmer in the fountain.

I watched Seth.

He scanned the crowd, missed me, and checked his phone. He was perspiring lightly.

"You're high," I said.

His eyes jerked to mine. Cocaine, I guessed, because New York is a blow town, and because Seth had the jagged, jittery look of one-too-many mornings spent getting high before coming down. He pocketed his phone and shrugged.

"Mm, you can't really hide that from me." I stood close to him so that no one else could hear us. I took him by the shoulder—gently, kindly—and turned him toward the fountain, buying us time. How long before someone recognized M. Pierce, the author, or Seth Sky, the lead singer of Goldengrove?

"Were you high when you fucked Chrissy Catalano? When you got her pregnant? No protection handy, or were you too far gone to care?"

My voice came out soft and sickeningly warm. My fingers tightened on his shoulder.

"I know," he said. "Nate called me. I just found out. I know she's pregnant."

So it was true—or it might be true—that mysterious e-mail I received yesterday. *Who's the proud daddy? It's Seth Sky!*

"Why couldn't you stay away from them? Hannah, her sister."

"You're no fucking saint." He tried to jerk his shoulder from my grip, but I held on tight. And he was weak. He'd lost weight since I'd seen him last, three months ago. Even his anger was diminished. I smiled and rubbed my mouth. I let him go. I tried to unbutton my cuffs, with some passing idea of rolling up the sleeves, and then I hit Seth in the face.

He sank, catching himself on the edge of the fountain. Bystanders danced away like startled pigeons. *Get the fuck out of here*, I thought, and I hit my brother again.

This bastard. This fucking bastard. He twisted and scrabbled at my neck, sputtering. He kicked my legs out from under me and the ground rushed up. My cheekbone grated on stone.

Get the fuck out of here.

This fucking bastard.

With one powerful hand, I grasped Seth's hair and dunked his head in the fountain. I leaned my weight against his body and held him under. His arms surged wildly. He tore at me and at the fountain ledge. Bubbles billowed around his face.

I should kill you, I thought. *I could.* Adrenaline welled in my body. My face throbbed; something wet dribbled down my cheek. Water splashed my shirt, my hair, and it felt good.

Seth's body went slack slowly.

My rage grasped at thin air.

If I summoned the image of Hannah and Seth, the way I did sometimes when I wanted to feel angry, I might have held him under too long. But I wanted a fight, and the fight was gone. I dragged his wiry body back. He gasped and crawled away from me, over the heated stones. Just like an animal.

I left before I could feel pity.

I jogged away from the hotel, tasting iron and salt, turned onto Eighth Avenue and ran all the way back to the station, back into its cement belly, into a crowded train.

Chapter 13

HANNAH

Matt returned to the hotel at five.

I was there, sitting on the couch, watching the door.

I heard the metallic slip of the key card. The mechanism unlocked with a clack.

"Fuck," I whispered as he stepped into the room.

Dark blood congealed around a gash on his cheek. His shirt was halfway untucked, clinging to his torso, his blazer nowhere to be seen. Sweat matted his hair.

"You're back," he said.

"Yeah . . ." I stepped closer to him. He eyed me warily, as if he might run. "Nate, um, drove me back. We've been calling." Another step.

"Mm."

Another step, then another. Matt let the door fall shut and smirked. Despite his disheveled appearance, relief coursed through me. *He's here.*

I cupped the undamaged side of his face. A muscle jumped in his jaw.

Wild Matt . . . he filled me with excitement, even now.

"Baby." I stood on tiptoe and kissed the skin near his wound. "What happened?"

"Don't you know? I think you know."

I slipped my arms around him, and after a moment he returned the hug. He exhaled, then fit my body to his in a way that was classically Matt. Possessively, impatiently. With a touch of irritation. Cupping my ass, bringing my groin against his thigh. Pressing the small of my back, making my spine flex and my belly nuzzle him intimately. He curled my shoulders into his chest. He cradled the back of my neck and pushed his fingers through my hair.

I shivered.

That hand in my hair . . . could bring pleasure or pain.

"What am I going to do with you?" he said with a sigh.

"I'm sorry." I clung to his shirt. I desperately wanted to know how Matt had found out—*Seth got Chrissy pregnant*, the unspoken bombshell—and what happened in New York, and what Seth looked like right now, but those questions could wait.

"Why didn't you tell me?" he said. "This new honesty thing goes both ways."

"I was afraid. Look at you. I knew what would happen."

He gave me a wry look. I winced at the sight of his injury.

"And did you stop it from happening, little bird?"

"No," I mumbled.

He tilted up my chin. I swallowed and flushed like a guilty child.

"It would have been better to hear it from you." He held me awhile longer, and I waited for him to tell me how he *did* hear it, and finally he said, "I'm tired. We'll talk about it later. I need to—" He frowned, thumbing a smudge of his blood from my brow. He started to unbutton his shirt. I brushed away his hands.

"Let me."

He glared, but he let me undo his shirt and lead him to the bathroom, where I cleaned the gash on his cheekbone. New blood dampened the washcloth.

"Crazy boy," I whispered. I kissed his knuckles. They were red.

"Your crazy boy." His strong hands enfolded mine. We stood like that for I don't know how long, touching one another tenderly, a counterpoint to violence I could only imagine. If I thought about Seth, my mind flashed over images of a body strewn across the floor. Blood. Stillness. So I didn't think about him.

My fiancé wasn't violent by nature . . . *right?*

He kissed my ring finger.

"You still want to marry me?" he said, half-smiling and half-serious.

"Always."

He took a quick shower and I changed into one of his T-shirts, which was voluminous on me. I removed my new pearl earrings but kept on the necklace. I felt pretty with those heavy spheres resting against my throat.

Mrs. Hannah Sky . . . I lay on our bed and mouthed the words.

Our engagement should be a magical time. *Would* be a magical time. I refused to let Seth or my sister's news overshadow our happiness. Now that Matt knew everything, we could handle the situation together.

He strolled into the bedroom, a towel banded around his waist. I licked my lips and sat up. *Damn . . . that body.*

"I like your shirt, bird."

I plucked at his shirt and smiled shyly. Matt's eyes were dark, his expression unreadable. Serious-discussion time.

"Matt, I—"

He silenced me with a gesture.

He sat on the edge of the bed and beckoned. I crawled to him, suddenly hyperaware of my naked body beneath his T-shirt. The way Matt looked at me told me he was aware, too. His gaze lingered on my nipples, which stood stiff against the thin cotton.

"I bought you this," he said. "We'll use it now."

My gaze dropped to his hands. My mouth formed a small, speechless O.

Matt held a metal plug—large, teardrop-shaped—with a sapphire gem in the stopper. He tipped it into my hand. It was heavy and cold. Intimidating, yet pretty.

Okay . . . he wanted sex. Now. After whatever had happened in the city. And he wanted to put a plug in my ass. I returned the toy to his hands.

"Chrissy is pregnant. Seth is the father." He spoke calmly. "And you've known that, haven't you, Hannah?"

I nodded, flushing. What the hell was this? Sexy time, or serious-talk time?

"I want to punish you," he said.

"Punish me?" I spluttered.

"Mm. Bend over my lap." He patted his thighs. When I hesitated, he cupped the back of my neck and guided me down.

I spread my arms across the sheets and lay there quivering. He brushed the T-shirt off my bottom. I tensed, expecting pain, but he only stroked my skin lovingly.

"Gorgeous," he murmured.

Something cold and blunt touched my sex—the plug—and he dipped it into me, then drew it out, in again, out again. I groaned.

"Lubricating it," he explained. "You're very wet."

I tried to relax when he slid the plug up my crack and began to apply gentle pressure. I'd taken *him* there, after all; I could take the plug. But my mind refused to cooperate. I kept picturing the raw gash on his cheek and remembering the things Katie said: *Too rough. He'd hit her. Really hardcore stuff. Whips.*

The plug popped into my bottom and I gasped. The stopper nestled against my skin. It felt . . . foreign, full, but pleasant, a cool and heavy pressure.

Matt moaned and kissed the tail of my spine. I felt him hardening beneath his towel.

I am not afraid of my fiancé, I told myself. *I love this man. I know this man.*

But I didn't know this new bedroom etiquette—at least, not in the context of punishment. I'd hurt Matt by keeping a secret from him. Now he wanted to hurt me . . . physically. How did I feel about that?

He slapped my backside, jarring the plug. I jumped.

"Matt!"

"Shhh," he crooned. "I had to, Hannah." His touch immediately turned gentle—caresses, a finger inside of me, one on my clit. I sighed and panted, giving myself over to those sensations. Then he spanked me again and I yelped.

He moved me off his lap and left me sprawled on the bed. He stood and stared down at me. "Play with yourself," he said. "Make sure I can see that plug while you do."

I fumbled onto my knees, my ass in the air. Matt made an appreciative sound. Out of the corner of my eye, I saw his towel drop—a flag of surrender spiraling to the floor.

He can't resist me.

Feminine pride bloomed inside me and I spread my knees. Let him get a good look at my sex. I began to finger myself, grinding on my hand, and I rubbed my clit in a slow circle.

"Ah, Hannah . . ." His voice was strained.

I stripped off the T-shirt and glanced over my shoulder.

Matt stroked himself—a sight that made my body clench—and stared wantonly at my backside, at the skin between my legs. There, I felt an acute ache for him. Arousal slid down my fingers. My blood turned to fire.

"Please," I whispered.

He shook his head.

"Don't come, Hannah."

I balked, my hand going still. *Don't come?*

"Keep going," he snapped.

The edge in his voice made me flinch. My fingers resumed their motion, my body trembling. What is it about denial? I suddenly wanted—needed—to come.

Matt pleasured himself at a leisurely pace. Once, he grasped my hips and brought his mouth close to my sex, his breath fanning over the heated skin. I felt incredible tension in his hands. The strength of restraint.

"You're hard to resist," he hissed. He climbed onto the bed and flipped me over. Wild for release, I spread my legs invitingly and lifted my body, but he pressed me down. With one hand against my abdomen and the other stroking his length, he came.

He never entered me. He didn't even moan. His dark, angry eyes raked my body, his cum wet my sex, and then he backed away.

I lay on the bed panting as Matt picked up his towel and ruffled his hair.

He glanced at me. "Don't. Come."

I swallowed and sat up. The plug shifted inside me, making me moan.

"Oh, and you can take that out," he murmured. His gaze loitered on me. I knew how I looked—my lips slightly swollen, skin flushed, wearing nothing but a string of pearls and a plug—and I made one last play.

"Please," I whispered, lowering my eyes. "Fuck me, Matt . . ."

"Hannah." His voice was a growl. He kissed me swiftly, devouring my mouth, then pulled back and stalked out of the room. I whined, reaching after him. Was this my punishment? It was the worst, the best punishment. The most affecting punishment. His absence.

I fell asleep without Matt—he stayed up late, a soft light emanating from the sitting area—but I woke beside him, his body curled around mine.

Morning sun spilled over his back. I stroked his golden hair.

I'd gone to sleep confused and a little angry—but when Matt's eyes opened and he smiled at me, I knew we were going to have a better day.

The hell with yesterday. A bump in the road.

I fluttered my lashes against his cheek and pressed the gentlest kiss to his wound.

"Mm, I'm"—he touched the scabbing gash—"I'm such a fucking idiot," he grumbled.

"Oh, baby, no."

"Yes. I am." He climbed onto me and settled down. I stroked his bare sides, reveling in the way his body pressed into mine. Every morning with Matt, I felt the same giddy thrill. *Is he really mine? Yes, he is.* "Shouldn't have fucking . . . gone to see him . . ."

"Why did you?" I whispered.

"Some weird e-mail. I got some weird fucking e-mail from an address I didn't recognize." He nuzzled my chest as he spoke. He was feeling good and communicating, so despite the chill I felt— *Weird e-mail? From whom?*—I played it cool.

"Oh yeah? What did it say?"

"I'll show you later. Basically it said your sister was pregnant and Seth got her that way. Strange fucking tone, kind of taunting." He seemed less disturbed than I felt. Then again, he probably got a lot of odd messages. "I should have talked to you about it, but I think I've been waiting . . . for an excuse to hit him. Nate told me Goldengrove was at the Plaza Hotel, and I went there and . . . we fought. He's fine. He's lucky. I could have fucking killed him . . ."

I kissed the top of Matt's head and cringed. I really, really didn't want to talk about Matt's anger with Seth, because I was to blame.

Seth getting Chrissy pregnant was just the cherry on top of Matt's towering rage.

"How was the city?" I hedged.

His head came up. He flashed a boyish smile at me. "Same old. You ever been?"

"No." I curled my toes under the sheets. "You know me, simple Hannah . . ."

His smile dimmed. "Bird, I didn't mean that. Not like that. Simple is . . . good."

If simple is good, then why do you want us to live in a mansion? I bit my tongue.

"What you are is perfect for me." He kissed my forehead. "I love you. You're so intelligent, gorgeous, intuitive. You're sensitive. You're—"

I touched his lips, shushing him with a grin.

"That'll do. You're out of the doghouse . . . for now."

"So easily? And I was ready to kiss ass for the next hour. Literally . . ."

I blinked and flushed. "Okay, you're back in the doghouse."

We clambered out of bed at ten. I felt thoroughly satisfied, and I tabled my concerns about last night. I got room service to bring up Matt's favorite breakfast (the only actual breakfast he'd eat)—two grapefruit halves doused in sugar and coffee, black.

Our flight back to Denver was uneventful, but as we were taxi-ing toward DIA, Matt turned to me and said, "Is she going to have it?"

The question stunned me into silence.

"The baby," he prompted. "Is your sister going to have it?"

"I don't know. She's thinking about it."

"You would be an aunt. Auntie Hannah." He grinned.

I giggled. "Uncle Matthew."

We smiled at each other stupidly for a moment, then simulta-neously frowned. *What the hell?* Chrissy's pregnancy was *not* a happy situation, and we were not having a baby conversation right now. My overloaded mind couldn't fit family thoughts.

"Ah, we"—Matt whisked a hand through his hair—"we'll help her. Financially."

I hugged his arm. "Sweet night owl."

He gazed resolutely out the window.

"It seems like the right thing to do. We'll plan for Seth staying out of the picture. I don't think he . . ." Matt hesitated.

The seat belt sign went off with a ring and he hurried to re-trieve our carry-ons.

End of discussion, apparently.

On our way to the baggage claim, I dragged Matt into Hud-son Booksellers. I have a weakness for airport bookstores.

"Really?" He glowered at the store. "Our bags . . ."

Matt navigated air travel the same way he drove, with glares all around. If he had his way, we'd march everywhere and never enjoy anything.

"Really." I smiled sweetly at him.

I drifted about the store, stopping at the Moleskine display and flipping through a pretty, overpriced little journal. It was the sort of small luxury I'd denied myself all my life. I frowned as I moved to return the journal to the shelf. I could buy this now, guiltlessly.

"You like it?" Matt tucked a curl behind my ear. He leaned down and kissed my temple.

"Um. Yeah, I . . ." His words pinged in my mind. *Simple girl.* Was this a silly indulgence? He wrote bestselling novels in plain marble notebooks from the grocery store. To him, this probably seemed so . . . gratuitous. So nouveau riche. "It's stupid. Never mind."

I hurried away, hiding in the magazine section.

There, I found myself face-to-face with a gorgeous bride in a lacy gown, standing with her groom in a field. *The Knot* magazine. I swallowed and plucked it off the rack. God, she looked beautiful. The magazine promised "10 stylish outdoor weddings YOU can do" and "5 simple steps to an intimate evening wedding."

"Bridal magazines?"

I jumped. Matt loomed at my shoulder, his eyes round.

He was following me around the store like a puppy dog.

"No! No, uh—" I dropped the magazine and bolted out of the store, my face inflamed. Shopping with Matt: epic mistake. I barreled toward the baggage claim, forgot to check the monitors for our claim number, and ended up slumped against a wall, watching lumpen suitcases orbit on the belts.

Stupid, stupid, stupid. First the almost baby conversation, then the bridal magazine. If I wasn't careful, I would freak Matt right out of our engagement.

I waited for him to find me.

And he found me.

He always does.

He came striding along with our luggage, mine a fat blue duffel, his a sleek silver Tumi case. Now that we were really living together, I noticed our varying tastes. I liked cheap, cute, cluttered. Matt liked expensive, elegant, spare. But he let me decorate our condo like a circus . . .

Maybe there was hope for our future home.

Mmph, home. No more domestic thoughts today.

"There you are." He smiled brightly. "You gave me a scare."

"Sorry." I looked at my feet.

"You dropped your magazine." He thrust a Hudson Booksellers bag into my line of vision. "I got you a few others."

"Huh?" I took the bag—*oof, heavy*—and flipped through the magazines: *Premier Bride, Wedding Style, Town & Country Weddings, Get Married,* and, of course, *The Knot.* Tears glazed my eyes. *Oh, Matt . . .*

"And these," he said, withdrawing a stack of Moleskine notebooks from another bag. He added them to the pile of magazines in my hands.

A tear slipped down my cheek.

I hugged the magazines and journals.

"Bird, why are you crying?"

"I'm just . . . happy," I whispered. "So happy."

He hugged me tight. I pressed my face into his chest and let another tear fall. Did he know what these magazines meant to me? They were Matt's permission to think about our wedding—to plan and anticipate it. Sweet joy spread through me.

My phone chimed and I plucked it out of my purse.

I stayed in Matt's arms as I read the text.

It was from Chrissy.

R we getting together this weekend or what?

Shit. I'd forgotten about my plans to check up on Chrissy this weekend. I glanced at Matt, who watched me patiently, and tapped out a quick reply.

Stuff came up, so sorry. Let's get together Friday night.

I hesitated, and then I added:

& I'm bringing my fiancé.

Chapter 14

MATT

PUNISHMENT

She lied to me—withheld information from me—and I punished her for it. I spanked her. I used her. I denied her orgasm.

I've wanted this for a while, and now that I've had it, I want more.

When she's bad, I want to tell her so. I want to take out my anger on her gorgeous body. She doesn't understand how it provokes me, the sight of her.

I am constantly aching.

Mike's lips thinned into a line as he read my notebook.

Matt's Black Book of Aberrant Desires, I'd written inside the cover. Mike didn't crack a smile at that. I cleared my throat and he glanced at me.

"Yes?"

"Nothing," I said. I wished I hadn't let him see the book. By the same turn, it felt good to share those strange desires with someone.

He flipped a page and continued reading. "Your trip was good?"

"Yeah. Uneventful . . ."

Again, Mike glanced at me.

"How did you cut your face?"

"Hm?" My hand rose halfway to the wound. *The fountain. Seth.* "I fell."

He watched me a moment too long and frowned.

"All right. You fell. Maybe you can tell me more about that sometime. For now, let's talk about this." He gestured with the notebook. "Desires for control, ownership—physical and emotional possession, I think—and a shame fetish."

"Don't fucking put it that way." I stuck an unlit smoke between my lips.

"Erotic humiliation," Mike said.

"Whatever." I glared at the floor. "Fine."

"No need to get defensive. I'm not horrified, Matthew. Just a discussion. Looking at this"—he handed the notebook back to me—"my immediate question is, how would you feel in Hannah's position? Would you be comfortable if she felt this proprietary about your body? Would you allow her to humiliate, dominate, and punish you? To expose you to others?"

I smiled slyly at Mike.

"She has tied me to the bed," I murmured. *Put that in your pipe and smoke it, Mike.* My eyes swept the family photo on his desk. I couldn't picture Mrs. Mike getting that freaky.

"I'm aware. I read *Night Owl.*"

"The fuck?" I gaped.

"I read everything you publish. You're my client. It's part of my job. You know this, Matthew. Holistic mental health."

I rubbed my face. *Good God.*

"Look, to answer your question . . ." My mind traveled back to Hannah. Last week, she'd put her finger in my backside, then made me confess to liking it. And before our brief breakup, she'd asked me to jerk off for her viewing pleasure. On my knees. On the floor. "She, ah . . . she sometimes . . . has the upper hand, yeah. I don't mind."

"You enjoy it?"

I shrugged.

"Well." Mike tapped his desk, soliciting my attention. "It's one thing to have these desires, and to explore sexuality with your partner, and quite another thing to punish her in bed for problems within your relationship. Can you see that?"

"Nope." I twisted the lighter in my pocket.

"I think we'll end this appointment early then."

"Huh?" I glanced at the clock, which said we had twenty minutes to go.

"You're closed off, embarrassed, defensive. We're getting nowhere. Spend a week remembering that I am on your side, trying to help you. Get comfortable with the idea that I know about all that"—he pointed to my notebook—"and come back on Monday ready to talk."

"Fine." I pushed out of the armchair. Getting dismissed by my own shrink kind of sucked, but I wasn't about to turn down freedom.

"Homework, Matthew."

"What?" I snarled.

"If you feel so inclined, try asking Hannah how she felt about the punishment. And if you won't do that, at least try to imagine Hannah striking you in bed, or withholding your orgasm or even sex, with no explanation or verbal contract, based upon an argument—"

I stepped out and slammed the door while Mike was still talking. And I lit my goddamn cigarette in the elevator.

When I got back to the condo, I sprawled on the couch and texted Hannah.

Sweet bird. I need a fix.

She replied immediately.

Little Bird: Hi you.

Matt: Hi.

Little Bird: What happened to your appointment?

Matt: I left early.

Little Bird: Oh . . .

Matt: Mike sent me home. Said I wasn't cooperating or some shit.

Little Bird: Bad boy.

Matt: Mm, exactly. Are your office doors shut?

Little Bird: Yes . . .

Matt: Touch your breasts for me. Just a little.

Little Bird: Matt . . .

Matt: Are you wet?

Little Bird: I am now.

Matt: And your pussy. Slip a finger into it. For me . . .

Little Bird: God, Matt. Want you . . .

Matt: I could drive over.

Little Bird: No! Not at work.

Matt: In my car then. Don't you want me in you? And my cum.

Little Bird: Matt. Jesus.

Matt: I want to put it in you. Make you take it. Come in you.

Several minutes passed. I gripped my dick through my slacks and sighed. All that skeevy talk in Mike's office had done a number on me.

And Hannah . . . lately, she was more adorable than ever. When she cried over the damn bridal magazines, I wanted to drag her into the nearest bathroom and have my way with her. What gave? I couldn't keep my hands off her.

At last, my cell buzzed.

Get over here Matt.

I grinned and slid off the couch. "That's my girl," I murmured. I parked a block from the agency, which was desolate that day.

The slap of my sandals echoed around the lobby. At the top of the stairs, I tousled my hair and checked my reflection in a glass case.

Golden boy, I thought spontaneously. What had I ever done to earn that nickname? Behind my pretty face was a consummate jerk.

Hannah leapt from her chair when I breezed into the office.

God damn, she looked good. She wore her hair in a high, messy bun. Her blouse hung open enough to give me a view of her cleavage. She pushed her glasses up her nose and shot a look at Pam's office door.

"Matt!" she hissed. "What happened to . . . the car?"

I lifted a finger to my lips. *Silence.* I locked the door behind me, then locked the door between Pam and Hannah's offices. My erection strained against my jeans. I slid smoothly into Hannah's chair and pulled her onto my lap.

Mm—there.

I exhaled against the back of her neck. I gripped her hips and moved her bottom over my lap, letting her feel my hardness. She shivered.

As I hiked up her skirt, her hands fumbled between us, undoing my fly and freeing my cock. I shifted her thong and she sat, impaling herself. I inhaled swiftly. "Hannah," I gasped.

She reached back at an ungainly angle and covered my mouth with her palm. *Fuck, yes.* This forced silence would drive me mad.

She bounced on my lap—I bucked to meet her motions—and when she gave a reedy moan, I sealed my hand across her lips. My free hand traveled her body, cupping her breasts through her bra and rubbing her clit.

I began to yank her down onto my cock, forcing a fast tempo. Pushing her over the edge.

She came moments before I did, her hand braced against the desk, our bodies pinned and shuddering together. Ah, the things I wanted to say to her . . .

Her hand fell, streaking sweat and saliva over my jaw. I wiped my cheek on my shoulder and whispered in her ear, "You have the tightest pussy I've ever fucked, Hannah Catalano."

We adjusted our clothes hastily.

She perched on the desk opposite me. A beautiful flush gilded her cheeks. Her chest surged with hungry breaths; her eyes glittered with excitement.

"You look very pleased with yourself, Mr. Sky." She grinned.

"Oh, I am." I chuckled and stroked her leg.

Absently, I scanned her desk. A magazine lay atop a stack of manuscripts, and when I reached for it, Hannah snatched it.

I recognized the cover immediately. *The Knot.* I laughed.

"Babe, are you playing on the job?"

"No, I . . ." Her voice hitched and she glared at me. Fucking hell, was she *trying* to be cute, or was my Hannah addiction in overdrive?

Sticky notes protruded from the magazine.

I smiled—encouragingly, I hoped—and tilted my head. "Show me."

"No, just . . ." She played with the magazine. "I'm not, like, planning. I . . ."

"Then start planning." I cupped her cheek. Her eyes widened.

"The—the wedding?"

"Why not? God knows I'm not going to plan it. Have you got some little-bird ideas?" I hauled her back onto my lap. Her flimsy office chair swayed. She swiveled sideways and plopped the magazine on her thighs.

"You make me feel like a little girl," she whispered.

I frowned. "I do?"

She touched my lips. "In a good way, Matt." She squinted at the magazine—a nervous tic of hers—and flipped it open to a page displaying "do-it-yourself string accents and lanterns." She pointed to a nighttime photo of a large, sprawling oak with dozens of mason jars hanging from its branches, tea lights shining in the glass.

I kissed her shoulder.

"That's lovely," I said.

"Yeah?" She searched my expression. "It's . . . simple and . . . intimate."

"Mm. Great atmosphere."

Hannah practically vibrated with happiness on my lap. This side of her—the feminine "ooh"ing and "aah"ing over bridal magazines—surprised me, but pleasantly. I wanted to make her happier. I would give her anything. A fucking fairy-tale wedding. A cake ten stories tall.

I opened to another tagged page displaying more candlelit nighttime scenes. Jars filled with glass beads and lights, papier-mâché luminaries.

Hannah peeked at me continually.

"An evening ceremony, then," I said.

She plucked the magazine from me and tossed it onto the desk. "Oh, I don't know. Whatever you want. Something . . . simple."

"I want what you want." I slid her off my lap and stood. "You know I love the evening. The night." I moved to lean against the door. Now I needed a little distance from Hannah. If she kept giving me those coy looks through her long lashes, we'd have to go another round.

She scooted up to her desk.

"Cool," she said, her eyes downcast. Her fingers danced over the keyboard. She straightened a pile of papers.

"Work."

"Hm?" Her head shot up.

"I want to watch you work."

"Um. I can try."

"Forget I'm here."

"No chance of that," she said with a giggle. After some dithering, she began reading from the computer screen and typing. She glanced at a paper, typed some more. Licked her lips. Looked at me. I smiled and shook my head.

With a huff, she refocused on the screen.

I stood very still, and Hannah's work finally absorbed her. Calm confidence came into her expression. She reclined in her chair as she read, then leaned forward to jot down notes.

The future Mrs. Hannah Sky, working the job she'd refused to give up for me. *Good for her.* I felt clean, happy pride watching her, and Mike's questions passed back through my mind.

*Would you be comfortable if she felt this proprietary about
your body?*

Would you allow her to humiliate, dominate, and punish you?

I slipped out of the office while Hannah wasn't looking.

I just might, Mike. I just might.

Chapter 15

HANNAH

I ate lunch at the Mediterranean deli every day that week, but I didn't see Katie.

Maybe I'd freaked her out, or maybe she'd had second thoughts about tattling on Bethany. Either way, her disappearance—and the questions she'd spawned—unsettled me.

On Friday evening, I swung by the deli after work. The outdoor tables were empty, plastic tablecloths fluttering in a warm wind.

I strolled along the sidewalk, humming.

The universe seemed to be telling me to make my peace with Katie's absence. Plus, I did feel a little guilty listening to potential lies about Matt. I should have told him about Katie, just like I should have told him about Seth and Chrissy. But now Katie was gone, taking her weird claims with her, and I didn't need to tell Matt anything.

And anything I wanted to know about Matt, I could ask him. *Right?*

I tucked my hands into my jean pockets—casual Friday.

Asking Matt questions . . . easier said than done.

I turned a street corner aimlessly, enjoying the summer evening.

I shot a text to Matt as I walked.

Doing some shopping, might be home a little later than usual.

He replied quickly.

Buy yourself something nice. Isn't your sister coming over tonight?

We'd decided to have Chrissy over to the condo rather than going to meet her someplace. My parents' house was out of the question, and almost any public place was out of the question. We had private matters to discuss.

I replied to Matt's text.

Maybe I'll buy you something nice. Yes, she's coming over at 7. Plenty of time. Love you.

I hoped Matt had gone for a run today, or at least sat out on our crappy little balcony for a while. This evening felt too good to miss.

My cheeks heated as I considered the balcony. He deserved something nicer. I made a mental note to re-raise the house-shopping issue.

I passed a narrow hole-in-the-wall shop—HORSE TACK AND WESTERN SUPPLY—and stopped in my tracks. I backpedaled a few steps.

A tooled leather saddle stood in the storefront display. Cowboy boots lined the bottom of the case, and against the wall, wound around a peg, hung a whip.

Holy shit. The whip looked innocuous enough, until I considered Matt wielding it.

No . . . way. No way. He couldn't possibly want to use that on someone, could he?

I stepped into the store, bells announcing my entrance. My eyes adjusted to the low light. The pleasant scent of leather and polish filled my nostrils.

"Can I help you?" said the woman behind the counter.

"I was"—so glad for the semidarkness hiding my blush—"interested in the . . . whip. The one you've got out front."

"Sure, hon. We've got more of those back here." She led me to a slice of wall flanked by big western belt buckles and pocket-knives. "All our whips are David Morgan. Here's the model from the front case. You whip-cracking at the fair?"

"Excuse me?"

"The Boulder County Fair. They're doing a whip-cracking show this year. We've been getting a lot of customers looking at whips for that."

"Oh, no. But . . ." I edged closer to the whip, touching it tentatively. I shivered. The black plaited cord felt rough and merciless. A snake coiled to strike. "My husband does. He . . ."

Smelling a potential purchase, the woman launched into a speech about the virtues of the whip, which, I learned, was a six-foot bullwhip—*the perfect length!*—handcrafted, all leather, no stuffing, with replacement fall and cracker included, a bonus pot of leather dressing, and a one-year warranty—a real steal at . . . seven hundred bucks!

"Whoa," I mumbled.

By the time the woman stopped talking, she'd removed the whip from the wall and unwound and wound it several times, and finally she laid the looped leather in my hands.

I swallowed and stared at it.

Matt and I were getting to know one another. Finally. Last weekend, he opened up about his parents and his upbringing. Was this whip another piece of the puzzle? Did Matt want things he was afraid to tell me about?

"I'll take it," I said.

I paid for the whip with my personal debit card, not our shared account, and the saleswoman packaged it in a flat velvet-lined box. I bought black ribbon from a gift shop across the street and tied it around the box. With a bow. Then I sat in my car gazing at it.

Did I seriously just buy a whip . . . that might get used on me?

Is this sexy, or totally messed up?

I got back to the condo and scurried to the bedroom before Matt emerged from his office. I shoved the box in our closet. Definitely something to deal with later.

"Bird?" His voice drifted down the hallway.

"In here! Changing!" I wiggled out of my jeans and threw them on top of the box just as he appeared in the doorway.

He grinned wolfishly at me.

"Changing into what? I could recommend something . . ."

"Pfft. My sister will be here soon." I tugged on sweats and a tank top. Matt admired me as I sashayed past and bumped my hip against his.

"Tempting the devil," he mumbled, trailing me out of the closet. *Whew.*

He hovered in the kitchen, watching me closely. I smiled and he narrowed his eyes. Yikes, what was he thinking?

"Hungry?" I said.

"Not very. You?" He stepped closer to me.

"Er, no. I had a late lunch. Kind of a big lunch." I backed into the counter and peered up into his somber green eyes.

"How was shopping?"

I sucked in a breath. "Fine. Didn't find anything . . . but it was so nice out."

He folded his arms and sighed through his nostrils. His lips twitched. *Shit, what was that look on his face?*

"Hannah, I'm sorry I withheld your orgasm with no . . . verbal contract."

My mouth fell open, my mind racing to grasp his meaning.

"Oh," I whispered. Right. He meant last weekend, the "punishment" in the hotel room. I'd wanted to discuss that with him, but I never plucked up the courage.

In fact, I'd never asked to see the weird e-mail he got.

I'd willfully forgotten all of it.

"How did you—" He sneered.

"Baby, what is it?" I wrapped my arms around his neck.

"How did you feel about that?"

"Um . . . confused, I guess." I stroked his neck. "You've never done that before."

"Mm."

"What do you mean, 'verbal contract'?"

He frowned and folded his arms around me. "No idea. It's something Mike said."

"Mike?" My stomach somersaulted. "You told him about that?"

"Not exactly. We've been—I—"

Three loud knocks interrupted him. *No!* Matt disentangled himself and stalked over to the door. *Fuck, I wanted to talk about this.* I glared at his back as he greeted Chrissy.

For one weird, paranoid moment, I wondered if he timed this—planned this discussion on the cusp of Chrissy's arrival so that it couldn't actually become . . . a discussion.

"Hey, Chrissy." I hugged my sister. She looked cute in leggings and a purple-to-white ombré tank top. My eyes darted to her stomach, then swerved away. "Come on in."

We sat in the TV room, Chrissy in an armchair and Matt and I on the couch.

Hm. What now?

Matt was giving Chrissy an intense, scrutinizing stare, and Chrissy looked embarrassed for the first time in her life.

"Do you want something to drink?" I offered.

"Yogurt?" Matt said.

I blinked at him.

"Matt . . ." I patted his thigh. "We don't have yogurt."

"I bought some." He moved briskly to the kitchen. "It's low-fat," he added. "Did you know that one cup of this is better than milk? More calcium. You need calcium, Chrissy. And protein, too. You like blueberries?"

"Uh, sure," Chrissy said.

I twisted around on the couch and gaped at Matt.

Who was this guy, and who body-snatched my fiancé?

"Good. I threw a few on top. Berries are"—his brow knit as he returned with the yogurt—"a good source of fiber and vitamin C. All stuff you need right now." He handed the bowl to Chrissy and returned to the couch. I grasped his hand.

"Can we talk for a moment?" I whispered.

"Sure." He gazed at me evenly.

"In . . . private?"

My sister spooned yogurt into her mouth and watched us. *The Matt and Hannah Show.*

"Why? Aren't we supposed to be getting things out in the open?" He gestured to our tiny living/family room.

"Fine," I muttered. Apparently I should have prepped him for this conversation. "The thing is, Chrissy isn't sure"—I smiled apologetically at her—"she wants to keep it yet."

Matt scowled. "Could we avoid that phrase? 'Keep it.' Sounds so fucking inhumane. 'It'? Is it a boy or a girl?"

"She's only eight weeks. We don't know yet."

"Well, then." He stood and paced beside Laurence's hutch. The rabbit, who was as sensitive to Matt's moods as I was, darted into a corner. "I don't see why we can't be *prepared* for the *possibility*"— oh boy, Matt was getting irritated—"that she *might* want to have the child. I bought you some groceries." He addressed Chrissy, ignoring me now. "Frozen salmon filets, some whole grain bread and cereal. You need eggs in your diet. I read about it."

My mouth hung open, jaw unhinged.

Matt . . . researched pregnancy? Bought food for my sister?

And, oh my God, was he against abortion? *No fucking way.* We *had* to talk—about a lot of things. Why the hell did we never talk?

"Thanks," said Chrissy. "I am actually . . ." She popped a blueberry into her mouth. "Going to have it. I mean, the baby." She cleared her throat.

Matt shot a look at me. An "I told you so" kind of look.

"Seth called me," Chrissy went on. "He wants to take a paternity test, be a part of things."

"What?" Matt and I spoke in unison.

"He *is* a part of things already." Chrissy lifted her chin.

"You are not to speak to him." Matt advanced, towering over

my sister. She folded her arms across her stomach. His eyes widened. *Holy shit.* I couldn't be sure what I was seeing, but Matt seemed more than concerned for the baby. He seemed almost . . . proprietary.

"I'll do what I want. You can't railroad over *me*." My sister gave him a saucy look.

I leapt off the couch and hugged him from behind. Chrissy didn't know that look on his face, that tension in his arms. I knew. He was about to blow.

"Just who do you think will be paying for this child?" He spat the words. "Paying your exorbitant medical bills. Providing you with housing if your parents kick you out. Day care. Food. Schooling. *We* will, you ungrateful little—"

"Matt!" I tried to tug him away from Chrissy. He was a monolith, rooted to the rug.

"Seth has plenty of money," she sniped.

"Seth is on drugs." Matt trembled in my arms. "He was coked up like a fucking whore in broad daylight last weekend. I almost drowned the weaselly son of a bitch."

Oh . . . my . . . God. Matt getting angry was like Matt getting horny. Crazy unpredictable.

"Please," I whispered. "Stop."

Chrissy darted away, heading for the door. "He does drugs socially. Rarely."

"Ah, of course." Matt followed Chrissy. I clung ineffectually to his arm. "That makes it quite all right. A father who does drugs socially, rarely. You do that, too? I wouldn't be surprised. Have you already subjected that poor child to substances? Are you going to be a single mother working at a strip club? You're well on your way to trashiest parents of the year."

"Fuck you! *I've* never done coke"—Chrissy's eyes flickered to me, then back to Matt—"and I'm sorry if you're fucking sensitive about that topic."

"Chrissy!" My voice went shrill. Had Seth told her about our hookup? Was she seriously throwing me under the bus right now? I *did* do a line that night. One line. The first and the last.

Matt stilled. The muscles in his arms relaxed, which somehow frightened me more than his tension.

"Get out." His voice was murderously low.

My sister's insolence faded in a heartbeat; she shrank against the door.

"G-gladly." She glanced at me and flushed. "See why I didn't want to tell him? Get your psycho boyfriend under control. God."

She scurried out of the condo.

The door slammed and I sagged against it.

Who should I follow? Matt, or my sister?

My heart pummeled against my ribs.

Matt returned to the couch and sat there, posed like "The Thinker." His gaze strayed restively over the area rug. I went to him.

"I'm . . . sorry," I said, unsure why I said it. I perched beside him and rubbed his shoulders. "That didn't go as planned . . ."

Mmph, I could almost *feel* Matt thinking about the Four Seasons scene: me doing a line, my hand around Seth's—

"The hell with her," he said.

I pulled back.

"What? She was embarrassed, Matt. Defensive. You laid into her."

"*I* laid into *her*?" He gave me an incredulous look. "She . . . she—"

"She'll come around. Let me talk to her."

"I don't give a fuck if she comes around." Fresh anger darkened his face. "She can come around all she wants. She's not getting shit from me. I bought her *food*. I wrote her a *check*. I was ready to set up a line of credit if she—"

"What the hell? Why didn't you tell me about any of this?"

Matt blinked and tilted his head, as if communication were an alien concept.

"Hello?" I waved my hand in his face. "See this ring? It means we're getting married. It means we have to talk about things. Be a unified front."

"Hannah . . ." He looked appalled. "It's my money. I thought—"

Hot tears sprang to my eyes. *His* money? What happened to *our* money? I'd just dropped seven hundred bucks on a whip that I was prepared to give to this unpredictable man because I wanted to know everything he wanted, even if it frightened me.

I bolted out of the room.

This week . . . this fucking week.

I needed a good, long, loud cry. And tea. And cuddles. But not with Matt. And not with one of the zillions of plush animals he'd given me. God, I missed Daisy.

I whimpered and clapped a hand over my mouth.

As I headed down the hallway, I realized I had nowhere private to go. The office basically belonged to Matt. The bedroom and bathroom were ours. The kitchen and TV room were too open, and he was there. Should I hide in the laundry room?

I remembered his defense when I caught him mansion-shopping.

This place is tiny. You have no real room of your own.

Ugh, he was right.

I locked myself in the bedroom and let my tears fall.

Chapter 16

MATT

Sleeping on the couch is a bitch.

My back ached even after my morning run, even after a round of sit-ups and stretches—and a long, hot, lonely shower.

As I padded past the bedroom, a towel around my waist, I tried the knob once more.

Still locked.

I pressed my ear to the door and frowned.

Hannah had been bunkered in our bedroom all night and most of this morning. It was nearly noon. The AC ticked on and I sighed, roaming back to the kitchen.

"I am definitely in the doghouse," I muttered to Laurence.

A notepad on the counter contained my list for the day.

FIX SHIT

— Talk about things w/Hannah (money, therapy, Chrissy)

— Date (picnic or dinner)

I peeled off the note and wrote another.

Hannah baby, please come out. You can't stay in there forever. I'm sorry. I love you. I need clothes. XO

I knocked gently on the bedroom door before slipping the note
beneath it. Then I retreated to the TV room.

Several minutes later, I heard the door squeak open and clap
shut.

I returned to find it locked, a pair of my socks folded on the
floor beside a note.

Here you go.

Grinning, I turned over her note and wrote another.

Where am I supposed to wear these? Or am I supposed to
use them for something else? Take pity on a half-naked man.
It's getting chilly out here.

I flicked my reply under the door, then sat on the floor and
waited. Soon I heard Hannah rustling in the bedroom. The door
opened a crack and a T-shirt flew out.

She slammed it shut quickly.

Click went the lock.

"Goddamn it, Hannah."

I pulled on the T-shirt and shot another note under the door.

Is this your way of saying you want to see my dick? So coy . . .

A moment later, the door opened and a pair of sweatpants hit
me in the face.

Slam!—click.

"Hannah!" I lunged against the door. "Baby bird?"

No reply.

God, women are fucking mysterious.

I stalked back to the kitchen and prepared for our picnic, jam-
ming things into a daypack. Goober peanut butter and jelly. A

sack of the whole grain bread I'd bought for ungrateful Chrissy. A few pears, a banana. Hannah called bananas "the portable fruit." And her safe word, which she had never used, not even during our roughest play, was "peaches." Jesus, did she have to be so cute?

"What's got you in a huff?"

I jumped and turned. Hannah stood a few feet away, her curvy hip propped against the counter, nothing on but an oversized T-shirt.

"Packing," I mumbled. "For our picnic."

She arched a brow.

"We're going on a picnic?"

"I'd like to." I cleared my throat and gazed into the bag. I plucked out the banana. "I got the . . . portable fruit."

I half-smiled and glanced at her. She frowned, her expression softening.

"Stop being cute," she said.

"Can't help it. Hey, thanks for picking this hot outfit . . ." I regarded my sweats.

"You're infuriating."

"So I hear." I stepped toward Hannah. Makeup sex? She took a step back.

"I'm going to shower. Then we can . . . go on your picnic, I guess."

She flitted away and I stared after her. *God, if her shirt would just ride up a little higher. . . .*

We drove out to Betasso Preserve, where I knew we'd have some privacy. I took the Jeep. In spite of Hannah's aloof mood, I found myself smiling as we hit the trail.

"I haven't been here in a long time," I said. "It's beautiful."

She remained silent.

I reached for her hand and admired her as we hiked. She wore loose, khaki-colored pants that hid the curves of her legs and a tight black tank top that hid nothing. A pink sports bra peeked out from under the tank, clinging to her ample chest.

I am horny as fuck today, I mused as we walked. Did sleeping without Hannah affect me, or was I always this bad? Impossible to tell. The harder I tried to pry my eyes off her, the more lascivious my stares became.

Finally, I tore my gaze free and glared at the horizon. It really was beautiful—the hills dotted with pines, the sky a flawless faded blue. No one in sight. Dry grass, hot wind . . . a harsh beauty particular to Colorado, which I had come to love.

Mm, and Hannah's breasts . . .

I longed to peel that sports bra off them, to free her copious, luscious flesh. Hold her ass while I sucked her nipples. See her cunt, her legs spread—

Fuck! I jerked my stare away from Hannah . . . again.

"Are you . . . okay?" she said.

"Of course." I looked steadfastly at the trail. "Enjoying nature."

"You sure? 'Cause you look like you want to murder nature."

"I can't focus. It's this pace. I'm used to running on these trails."

Briefly, I envisioned myself and Hannah jogging. Hannah jogging. Hannah's tits—

Good fucking God!

"We're dawdling," I snapped. "I'm hungry . . . starved." I picked up the pace, hauling poor Hannah along at my side.

When we lost sight of the trailhead and picnic tables, I plowed off the path, up a hillside. There, in an arbitrary coppice of pines, I came to a halt. I glared around.

"Here," I announced.

She spread our blanket and I set down the pack.

The shade felt heavenly. I stripped off my T-shirt and used it to wick the light sweat from my face and arms. After a beat, I looked at Hannah.

Damn.

I'd hoped to catch her staring at me, but she was focused on unpacking our lunch.

"I need sunscreen on my back," I said quietly.

Without so much as glancing at me, she found the bottle

and held it up. I smirked and took it. So, she wanted to play hardball . . .

"Thanks." I sat on a corner of the blanket and worked off my Merrells and socks at a leisurely pace. I rolled my ankles. I reapplied a film of lotion to my arms, then the back of my neck, my sides around to my spine, down to the small of my back. I stretched forward and gave a soft, content moan as some bone in my back popped.

"I thought you were *starved*," Hannah snapped, glaring into the pack.

"I am. My mouth is watering, in fact . . ." My gaze lingered on her body. I grinned and waggled the sunscreen bottle. "Safety first, though."

I lay on my back and stretched out one leg. As I slathered sunscreen on my chest, I watched Hannah out of the corner of my eye. Ha, she looked tense . . . as tense as I'd probably looked on the trail, trying to keep my eyes off her.

How does it feel, little bird?

I sighed audibly as I spread the lotion across my pecs, down my abs, lower. Hannah's gaze flickered to my hands. I slipped the tips of my fingers under the band of my boxers and circled my waist slowly, lifting my hips.

"There," I murmured. I sat up and smiled languidly at her.

"All done caressing yourself?" She smirked.

"You tell me." I crawled toward her. "I know you like to watch . . ."

Her eyes widened, her lips parting.

"Here." She shoved a sandwich at me.

Damnit.

I sat beside her, staring out at the mountains and chewing on a gluey peanut butter and jelly sandwich. She handed me a Coke and popped open her beer.

"Thanks for packing this," she said.

Finally, finally, she smiled at me.

"Of course. There's a slice of orange in there."

She blinked and fished the small Tupperware out of the cooler pack. I knew she liked orange in her Blue Moon. I watched her squeeze the juice into the bottle, then pop in the rind.

A blush crept into her cheeks.

"You thought of everything," she whispered.

"Oh, I doubt that." I chuckled and took another bite. Warm wind rolled up the hill, fanning over us. My head cleared as my lust cooled.

"Is this . . . the bread you bought for Chrissy?"

"Mm. We might as well get some use out of it."

"We could still give it to her."

"No." I shook my head. "That's an unequivocal no, Hannah. If she's getting help from Seth, we're not helping her."

"Well, I'm not okay with that." Hannah lowered her sandwich and turned to face me. I took a deep breath. This, after all, was what I'd actually intended to do today. Talk.

"And I'm not okay with Seth being in her life. She's in your life. You're in my life. If he's in her life, he's . . ." My appetite disappeared. I tossed the corner of my sandwich to a squirrel. "Then he's in our life. In *your* life. I won't have that."

Hannah stared at me as if I'd grown two heads.

"Say something," I said.

"S-sorry, it's just—it's nice to—" She shoved the remainder of her sandwich in her mouth, her cheeks puffing out. "Nice to talk."

I frowned and cocked my head. Did we not talk enough?

"Um, the thing is . . . Chrissy *is* in my life," she said. "She'll be in my life no matter what. She needs me now, and I don't really want Seth in her life either, but I'm not going to try to control her. I'm just going to help her."

"Do I have any fucking say in the matter?"

"Of course you have a say, Matt." She touched my cheek. Her hand grazed the faint trace of my cut. "I won't do anything without consulting you."

"I don't want you seeing him." My jaw clenched. Cold anger and shame gusted through me. "He touched you . . ."

"Oh, love." Hannah climbed swiftly onto my lap and wrapped herself around me. I shivered—with rage. She stroked my hair and neck and whispered sweet, soothing nothings into my ear. "It's okay. Never again. I love you."

I clung to her.

God, pain is sharp. Even old pain. Past pain. Or maybe that's the worst kind, because it stabs unexpectedly into our present happiness.

"It's my fault he came into your life in the first place. He's my brother. You met him at my idiotic memorial. I should never have—"

She touched my lips.

"No 'what-if's," she said. "This is our reality, remember?"

We shared a soft, slow kiss, and I broke it before I lost myself.

"About last night." I tucked Hannah's head under my chin. It was easier to address the mountains. "I lost my temper. I'm sorry. I should have told you I bought food for Chrissy and planned to give her a check. Bird, I'm not used to this . . . unified-front, joint-decision thing. I've told you my money is yours and I meant it. Bear with me. I'm still getting used to all this."

Her breath on my neck distracted me badly.

Her small hands roamed my torso.

"Okay," she said.

Okay? Too easy . . .

I mentally revisited my "FIX SHIT" list. *Talk about things. Money: check. Chrissy: check. Therapy: fucking hell . . .*

In my ideal vision of this conversation, I told Hannah everything. I showed her my *Black Book of Aberrant Desires*. We discussed the things I'd discussed with Mike. She was amenable, excited, unafraid. And then we had hot, sadistic sex all night.

In reality . . .

This peaceful picnic blanket seemed like no place for talk of pain and shame. Hannah's mood had done a one-eighty. She kissed me and I tasted beer and citrus.

"Hannah, is—" I gasped. She straddled my lap and began to grind on me, rolling the apex of her legs along my dick.

"Is what?" She threw back her head, her curls sliding off her shoulders. Instinctively, I tugged on them, eliciting a moan.

"Is there . . . anything else you want to talk about?"

I gazed down, mesmerized by the motion of her body on mine. My dick rose readily.

"Another time," she whispered.

Fuck, yes. Another time . . .

I groaned and braced my hands on the blanket behind me, letting Hannah do her thing. My lust sprang back to life. I closed my eyes and moved my hips, making damn sure she felt my hardness, and when Hannah scampered up to undo her pants and slide down her thong, I flicked open my pants and freed my cock.

She resettled on me, gripping my shoulders for leverage. Skin to skin. Now, when she ground her body on my lap, the lips of her sex spread desire up and down my cock. But she didn't slide onto it. She pinned it to my belly, an aching hardness, damp at the tip, and glided over it until she was soaked.

"This is fucking good," I hissed.

I tried to angle my hips so that I pierced her, but no dice.

"I know you need it," she whispered in my ear. "You've been staring at me all morning. At these . . ."

My eyes slipped open.

Hannah had yanked up her sports bra and tank. Her breasts hung down, full and bare.

"Ah, fuck. Fuck yeah." They spilled into my hands. As I squeezed them, Hannah changed her motion, tilting her pelvis so that her clit rubbed up and down my dick. I wanted her. To be in her. I wanted to be on top of her, taking her. But this? Watching her pleasure herself on my body? This was so fucking hot.

"You—are you"—I rolled her nipples to stiff peaks—"gonna make yourself . . ."

"Yes," she breathed. She moved faster, harder, and her hand darted between us. She positioned my shaft and slammed onto it.

"Fuck! *Hah* . . . babe." That tight, sudden grip hurt. And then it felt better. And better. I sank onto my back and arched. "God, ride me."

Hannah bounced on me once, twice, and began to quake.

Her climax clenched my arousal. I seized her hips, willing her to continue, but she climbed off of me and collapsed with a groan.

"God, that was good." Her hand twitched on my chest, her fingers grazing my nipple.

"Hannah," I snarled, reaching for my shaft.

"No, no." With a tsk, she batted away my hand and forced my cock back into my boxers. The fabric grated against my head. My whole package throbbed, overheated, oversensitive, damp. I sat up and glared at the ridiculous tent in my boxers.

"What the hell?"

Hannah shimmied back into her thong and pants. She pulled her bra and tank into place.

"I wanted to punish you," she said simply. She knelt and began to do up my pants, imprisoning my hard dick. I moaned and reached for it. *No fucking way . . .*

"Love, please." I grimaced. "This shit is not funny."

Again, she batted at my hand, and when I tried to undo my fly, she pinned my wrists to the blanket. "Don't, Matt." She gazed at me earnestly.

"Fuck!" I flopped onto my back and lay there panting, burning with pent-up desire. God, I wanted to fuck. Hannah held my hand. She brushed her thumb over my wrist.

"Good boy . . ."

"You." I glared at her.

"I know it's not funny. It wasn't funny for me, either. It was confusing and . . . agonizing." She bit her bottom lip. She laid a hand over my crotch and I sucked in a breath. "And sort of . . . a crazy turn-on," she mumbled.

I scowled. Was this a turn-on? Well, in a manner of speaking . . . *A really fucking unfortunate manner.*

I closed my eyes and debated the wisdom of forcing myself on Hannah. Negative, we weren't playing like that right now. She couldn't stop me from jerking off, though.

But that would be a defeat.

"You're so beautiful," she whispered. I opened my eyes and

squeezed her hand. Her gaze strayed over the bulge in my pants. "You're hard to resist. Was it hard to deny me?"

"Very . . . hard." I rolled my eyes and she giggled. "Shush. Your bird giggles aren't helping. Finish your beer."

She scooted away and sipped her beer.

"I need a moment to . . ." *Get a grip. Literally.* "Relax."

And I did relax, after what felt like forever. Hannah watched me, her boldness diffused into timidity, finished her drink and ate a pear. The juice dribbled down her chin. I smirked and looked away. At least she wasn't sucking on a goddamn banana.

My dick settled down and I sighed. Blessed relief. But a touch from Hannah, a certain sort of look, and I'd be hard all over again.

I pulled on my T-shirt and stretched.

Hannah ventured a smile. Cute . . . how shy she'd turned.

"You look mighty pleased with yourself," I said.

She shrugged and busied herself with repacking our picnic.

I leaned over and kissed her shoulder. *Mm, the taste of her skin . . .*

"You know I plan to pay you back for this."

She glanced at me through her lashes. A familiar glow spread over her cheeks.

"I know," she said. "I was hoping you would."

Chapter 17

HANNAH

On Monday morning, I strolled into work feeling like a goddess.

I could hardly believe what I'd done to Matt—what he'd let me do!—and every time I remembered the stormy anger in his eyes, I got a shiver of triumph.

I plan to pay you back for this . . .

Please do, Mr. Sky; I have just the thing for it.

No sooner had I settled behind my desk than I heard a knock.

"Come in," I called as Pam entered.

I shrank when I saw the look on her face: eyebrows in a severe V, lips tight.

Pamela Wing would always be my boss, even now when we were partners at the agency. Maybe that was a good thing. A little authority goes a long way.

Unbidden, the image of Matt with a whip flashed through my brain.

Gah! Not now.

"Hi, Pam." I squirmed.

"Hannah." She nodded and plopped a manuscript on my desk.

I scanned the title page. *LAST LIGHT by Matthew R. Sky Jr. writing as M. Pierce.*

My good mood deflated. *Oh . . .*

So Matt had finished his second novel about us. And sent it to his agent. And said nothing to me.

"Great," I mumbled.

"I wouldn't go that far," Pam said dryly, "but it is what it is. I think it gives him some secret pleasure, being a byword among the critics who adored him. Any idea when this phenomenon will run its course?"

A byword? Phenomenon? I tightened my hands under the desk. I knew Pam wanted Matt to get back to his literary roots—she'd hinted at it more than once—but she didn't have to be so rude. This book, after all, was about us. About me.

A terrible thought jabbed at me. Did Pam blame me for Matt's career shift? And *was* I to blame? Her bestselling author of acclaimed literary fiction—the brightest feather in her cap—had morphed into a bestselling author of erotica.

His style and his voice had changed. His themes. His audience.

The only common denominator between Matt's career prior to me and after me was his unchecked popularity.

"I don't control what he writes," I said, willing strength into my voice. "I never know what he plans to write. We don't talk about it. In fact, I didn't even know he'd finished this." I glared at *Last Light.* "But I'll stand by any decision he makes with his writing."

I met Pam's stare—maybe a little defiantly. What I wanted to say was, *You should stand by his decisions, too.*

Pam cocked her head and smiled frigidly. "So you stand by his decision to tell the world what really happened when he 'died' last year?"

"We already told everyone what happened."

"This tells a different story." She pointed at the manuscript. "No less romantic, though. The two of you plotting his disappearance. You, sneaking out to the cabin to see him. I suppose you're right. It does make for a . . . *great* story."

I froze in my chair.

Oh . . . shit. How had I never considered this? I knew Matt was writing *Last Light*, I knew he planned to publish it, and I knew what it was about. I'd even read a chunk of it in April when I ambushed him at the condo.

Last Light, quite simply, told the truth behind Matt's faked death and my part in it, and Nate's part in it, and . . . oh God, all the stuff that happened with Seth . . .

The drugs. The hookup.

My office teetered. I held on to the desk.

Matt had already fed a standard lie to major magazines and papers, not to mention anyone who saw us on the *Denver Buzz*. Our story was that he orchestrated his faked death alone. No one knew. I believed it was true and mourned him, just like the poor, exploited public.

And in our story, I emerged victorious. I was the girlfriend who loved her neurotic artist so much that she forgave him for doing the unthinkable. Angelic Hannah—love's saint.

Nate looked equally heroic. After Matt reappeared, shocking and disgusting the public, Nate had made several statements in support of his youngest brother. *Of course I forgive him. The loss of him, the grief, was horrible. That he's alive is nothing but miraculous.*

But if *Last Light* got published . . .

It would shine a spotlight on all our scheming and deceit. Matt's aunt and uncle would know I'd lied to their faces. My parents would know. *Everyone* would know. And whatever public support we'd rallied with our "epic love story" would vanish into the ether.

Matt, did you consider this?

"Hannah?" said Pam.

I gazed up at Matt's agent, another person we'd deceived. She'd comforted me during Matt's memorial, and she'd arranged all the interviews and appearances through which we disseminated our lie.

Now she knew the truth—obviously—and I saw hurt under her stony exterior.

"It's . . . fiction," I managed.

Pam laughed, her lips curling. "I'm sure. Whatever it is, it will be a sensation."

We stared at one another in a deadlock. *Oh, Pam.* This woman had been so good to me, so loyal to Matt. She deserved the truth.

My eyes watered and I looked away.

"I'll leave it with you, Hannah. You might as well read it, unless you already have."

"Th-thank you." I touched the stack of papers. I *did* want to read it. I'd only skimmed the book in April, and it wasn't complete at the time. Now I could read every grisly detail.

Pam moved toward the doorway. I listened as her heels clicked to a stop. She spoke with her back to me, her voice softer.

"For six years I guarded his identity. I handled his privacy with the utmost discretion, and kept his secrets, when it would have behooved me and his career to reveal him." She shook her head slowly and turned her face so that I could see her profile. "But he's not right in the head. What I don't understand is how he brought you in on it."

I stayed quiet, knowing I'd break into tears if I spoke.

Pam clicked her tongue. "Well, he's very persuasive. An occupational hazard, I'm sure." She shut the door behind her and my vision quivered with tears.

I had no right to be as happy as I'd been in the past few weeks. My engagement to Matt and the love story we were telling the world stood on a platform of lies. And he . . . my tears dropped onto the manuscript, raising rumpled spots on the paper.

He was fucking smart enough to know that *everyone* would read *Last Light* as truth. No-fucking-body would mistake it for fiction. He'd made a fool of me in front of Pam. *What the hell?* I jabbed out a text message. I didn't feel like blubbering my way through a call.

Pam showed me finished LL ms. I am so ANGRY at u. Thanks for the heads up. She knows everything now. U cannot publish LL.

Matt's reply came promptly.

We'll talk when you get home.

Talk when I get home?

A new surge of tears started, ugly and hot. I hiccuped and blew my nose noisily. I knew Pam could hear me from her office and I didn't care. *Some of us actually know how to show our feelings, unlike Matt-fucking-Sky writing as M.—fucking-Pierce.*

I spent the rest of the workday reading *Last Light.* Why, I don't know, except that I couldn't focus on anything else. My mood vacillated among rage and sorrow and fear. And arousal. Fucking Matt. His books affected me, always.

By five, I'd cooled off enough to drive home safely.

I found him smoking on the balcony.

I carried the tear-dotted manuscript under my arm.

When Matt said nothing, I began to read from a dog-eared page: "'Seth pulled my hand to his dick. My fingertips brushed the overheated skin and he sighed.'" No reaction. I skipped a few lines. "'I wrapped my fingers around his shaft. He hardened fully in my hold. I began to stroke him, my gaze moving between his arousal and his face.'"

Matt glanced over his shoulder.

"That's what happened, no?"

"Matt . . ." My voice shriveled.

"Mm." He turned back toward the city. "You gave me a full and free account of the incident. You knew it was for my book. It's cruel of you to read it to me."

"C . . . cruel? *I'm* the cruel one?"

"When would I touch your sister, Hannah? Not in a million years. What combination of drugs and drink could induce me to fool around with her? None. And not because she isn't attractive"— he spun and loomed over me, his face thunderous—"but because she's your goddamn sister. It would be *wrong*. Revolting. I would never—"

"Shut up!" I shrieked. My arms trembled. "Shut up or I'll hit you, and I don't want to fucking hit you."

"Do it. It would be preferable to your reading from that—"

I shoved him. He didn't move.

"Try harder," he snapped.

I planted my palm against his chest and pushed. *Mmph! This selfish son of a bitch.* He barely wavered. I pummeled his chest with my fist, big tears rushing to my eyes.

"Sometimes I hate you!" I puffed.

He caught my jaw. Fingers like iron drew me up short, wrenching my face toward his. I froze, my eyes going round.

Matt brought his mouth to mine.

His smoky breath touched my lips.

"And sometimes I hate you," he hissed, "for doing it with him. *To* him . . ."

His glare scoured my face—I held my breath—and then he let me go. I staggered back, flattening myself against the deck door. *Holy shit.*

"I thought we were past that," I whispered. A tear dropped from my chin.

"So did I. And now you come to me, reading it to me." He glared hell at the manuscript.

"Because you plan to publish it. How can you be so dense?"

"You knew I planned to publish it all along. What the hell is your problem? You realize *Night Owl* is for sale online, yeah? That the paperback will be in every bookstore in America come September? What the fuck, Hannah?"

"This is different. Matt, the truth." I slapped the chunk of papers. "The . . . the fucking truth about me helping you fake your death, about Nate, about—"

"It doesn't matter that it's *the truth*. It will be sold as *fiction*. As far as I know, unless a book is libel, no court of law can come after you for—"

"What if they can? I lied to the police for you! I gave actual . . . false reports."

"Shall I phone Shapiro and have him confirm that your fears are unfounded?"

Matt gaped at me. I gaped at him. I did not seriously want Shapiro, the Sky family lawyer, embroiled in yet another fiasco with me and one of Matt's books. The *Night Owl* situation had been hairy enough.

"Fine, the . . . legal stuff . . . even if that weren't an issue. What about the rest?"

"Let me just—" He rubbed his mouth. "Let me get this straight. You expect me . . . to refrain from publishing *Last Light* . . . because it's true?"

"Uh . . . yes?"

"Ha . . ." He cocked his head and half-smiled. "Ah—I don't know what to say. I'm sorry. The . . ." He shook another cigarette from his pack. *Ugh,* I really wanted him to quit. My angry text at work probably sent him on a smoking tear, and just when he was tapering down. "The answer is no." His expression grew calm and almost haughty. He turned away again.

I stood there, staring at his back in a daze.

The answer . . . is no? I wasn't *asking* him not to publish the book; I was *telling* him not to. It couldn't happen. Fucking wouldn't happen. All day at work I'd tormented myself with the possible ramifications of *Last Light* seeing the light of day. Legal . . . social . . . familial ramifications. Was Matt suffering some sort of disconnect from reality?

Not to mention the awkward-as-hell situation he'd put me in with Pam.

I threw the manuscript at him.

As I twisted away, I saw a page lick into the air and go sailing out over Denver.

"Hannah," he growled. He snatched at the stray papers.

I stalked inside and locked myself in our bedroom.

That douche-canoe could sleep on the couch. Again. *Fuck*, we needed a bigger place.

I booted up my laptop and sat on the bed, simmering. I expected Matt to come storming down the hall, banging at the door, but I heard nothing.

God, he could be so infuriating! And this wasn't a joke—wasn't up for discussion.

I listened to angry music (Eminem), hopped off the bed and paced, and finally opened Gmail and sent a message to Matt. *Deep breaths . . .*

Subject: Ultimatum
Sender: Hannah Catalano
Date: Monday, June 30, 2014
Time: 5:11 PM
Matt,

I don't know how to reason with you right now. You're being crazy. You absolutely CANNOT publish *Last Light*. Your aunt already seems to hate me. How much more do you think she (and the public) will hate me when they know I helped plan and execute your fake death?

Do you want people to hate me?

And don't tell me people will think the book is fiction, because they won't. Also, don't you DARE compare *Night Owl* to *Last Light*. This is so different. My reputation is at stake here. So is Nate's. The book portrays me doing drugs, hooking up with your brother, and basically letting you risk your life.

You would have to be seriously unfeeling to even THINK of publishing it.

That said, I know full well that I can't stop you from doing what you want. You always do what you want. You're a spoiled brat, do you know that? Golden boy with green eyes. It's really hard to love you sometimes.

If you continue the publication process with *Last Light*, if you're so hell-bent on blowing the lid off everything, I'll finish and publish MY story. Fair's fair.

Hannah

P.S. Enjoy the couch tonight. We obviously need a bigger place, because you need a proper doghouse.

P.P.S. Quit smoking. That's a new stipulation.

Attachment: UNTITLED.doc

Chapter 18

MATT

I sat in my office, reading the first chapter of Hannah's story. *MY story,* she'd called it. I smiled and shook my head.

Mm, my little bird with her very own version of events . . .

How charming. Was I supposed to feel threatened? The poor girl had no leverage.

She'd written only one chapter of her supposed story. It recounted our appearance on the *Denver Buzz,* her anxiety about the proposal, and our argument when she caught me house-shopping. I skimmed the text, remembering, until her words stopped me.

The smile died on my lips.

My desire to carry a child, Hannah had written, *could be described as less than zero.*

"The hell?" I mumbled. I tracked back and reread.

Holy shit. Matt wanted kids?

Again, I reread the chapter. And again. I needed more, but there wasn't more.

I clicked on her Word document and forced a page break. I stared at the new page, my mind tossing and turning. Then I centered the words "Chapter 2, *Matt*" and began to write.

Mike kept a framed picture of his family on his desk . . .

Three hours later, I finished my chapter. I proofed it and replied to Hannah's e-mail.

Subject: Stipulations, ultimatums, lions, tigers, bears . . . oh my?
Sender: Matthew R. Sky Jr.
Date: Monday, June 30, 2014
Time: 9:10 PM
Baby Bird,
"Keep writing with me." Wasn't that one of your stipulations? Yes, I think it was, along with "marry me" and "no more lies" and "see your shrink."

I mean to do all those things and more. I'll add "quit smoking" to the list. I'm trying, you know . . .

When you finish your story (when we finish it?) you will understand the pains of bringing a book into the world. You will understand how I feel about *Last Light*. I'm not publishing it to hurt you. In fact, I don't get where all this apprehension is coming from. You've known for a while that I planned to publish it. Did the possible consequences just dawn on you?

Whatever the case, I'll set up a meeting with Pam and we three will discuss it. Do you like the sound of that?

Love,

Your Night Owl, Certified Spoiled Brat & Resident Golden Boy

P.S. Of course we need a bigger place. I told you so . . .

Attachment: UNTITLED.doc

My cursor hovered over the Send button.

In Chapter 2, my unsolicited addition to Hannah's story, I had described a session with Mike: the day he gave me my *Black Book of Aberrant Desires*.

The chapter ended with the word EXHIBITIONISM.

Maybe this—this story—would be the easiest way to tell Hannah everything.

I glanced at the clock. Nine-ish. She might still be awake.

"Ah, fuck it." I hit Send, then pushed away from my desk and glared at *A Street in Venice*. The painting gave me no peace. I picked the small darts from my drawer and threw them at the board on the far wall. *Thunk*. One hit the double ring. *Thunk*. Outside the triple ring.

Usually I had better aim.

Now I couldn't focus.

No children with Hannah. No family.

I simply wasn't ready to discuss that issue, much less accept it, and so I ignored it.

I waited in my office for ten minutes, expecting a knock. None came.

I emerged into the hallway, paused outside our bedroom, and listened. There was no light beneath the door and no sound from within.

Impatience seized me. I forced a credit card between the door and the frame, and the lock released. The door swung inward.

Hannah sat on our bed in the dark, her MacBook open in front of her. The screen's soft glow lit her face.

She didn't jump, but she regarded me cautiously.

I struggled to read her expression.

Silence.

A stalemate.

"I came for my sleeping bag," I lied. "I don't really fit on the couch."

"Okay."

"And quit locking the door." I walked to the closet and flicked on the light. Maybe she hadn't read my e-mail yet. Maybe she had and was planning her escape. I grabbed my Marmot stuff sack and lingered, compressing the down like a stress ball. How to prolong my time in the bedroom? I moved a few shoeboxes, searching for . . . whatever. A flashlight. A peace offering.

Beneath a bag of Hannah's winter clothes I found a large,

flat box tied with black ribbon. A little tag on the box read, Matt.

I carried it out of the closet.

"What's this?" I shook the box.

Hannah darted off the bed and snatched the box. I tightened my hold on the corner, mostly to keep her close. We played tug-of-war for a moment, me grinning and Hannah exasperated, yanking at the box with all her might.

"You're feisty tonight." I chuckled.

I twisted the box out of her grip and lifted it, my arm stretched toward the ceiling. I raised a brow. She didn't even try to reach for it. Too bad . . . would have been cute.

"It's a gift. But I don't want you to have it yet. Give it to me."

"Pout prettily and I will." I smiled.

"Matt . . ." Her voice hardened with warning.

"Let me hold you, then, and I won't ask about it. And I'll give it back."

She glared up at me, but she nodded. I tossed the box onto our bed. Something inside shifted. I dropped my sleeping bag and pulled her into my arms.

She'd changed into tiny, soft shorts and a cami. A burst of honeysuckle scent rose from her hair. I nuzzled my nose into her curls and sighed, my hands roaming.

"Don't make me sleep in the TV room. I'm lonely for you . . ." I wedged her shorts between her legs and cupped her ass. She trembled and held my hip with one hand.

If only we could talk, I could fix things. Hannah didn't want my children. That was a problem. I could fix it. And she was pissed about *Last Light*. I could fix that, too.

"Hannah—"

"Go," she said.

I woke to the sound of the condo door closing.

"Bird," I mumbled. I tried to sit up and flopped over, stuck in my mummy bag. "Ah, for fuck's sake."

My shoulders ached. My back was stiff.

I wriggled out of the sleeping bag and prowled into the kitchen.

Somehow, Hannah had slipped off to work without waking me. She must have skipped breakfast. I frowned and contemplated the door.

Were we having a serious fight?

She'd upset me last night; I'd upset her. Then I'd barged into the bedroom for makeup sex (or conversation, at least) and she shut me down . . . again.

When did we last fuck, anyway?

I wrote a text—*I need sex*—and deleted it. Stupid. "Grow the fuck up," I grumbled. Still, some fearful little voice piped up in my brain, warning me that marriage was more of this—a creeping siege, a war of attrition. Never before had Hannah locked me out of our bedroom. Now, with a ring on her finger, she'd ordered me out of our bed twice. And I'd rolled over like a well-trained dog. What next?

Tomorrow I could wake up and be that guy who only gets a blow job on his birthday.

I shuddered.

My morning coffee tasted bland. I skipped my run and searched the condo for a note from Hannah, but I found nothing. She'd re-hid the present and made our bed.

I retreated to the office and checked my e-mail.

My mood lifted when I saw a new e-mail from Hannah.

Subject: Camping in the TV room
Sender: Hannah Catalano
Date: Tuesday, July 1, 2014
Time: 6:50 AM
Sweet Matt,

I'm sorry I sent you out of the bedroom last night. I needed alone time . . . to think. Exhibitionism? I have so many questions. I want to know more. I'm not scared; I'm curious. Do you really have a journal?

I'm also sorry I flew off the handle about *Last Light*. You need to understand that you put me in a terrible position by sending the novel to Pam without warning me. (Yes, I would be amenable to a meeting with her. I'll set it up.)

Chapter 3 is attached. I'd accuse you of hijacking my story, but it's always been our story, hasn't it? Let's make it good. You're It, Matt.

Love,

The Bossy Bird

P.S. Ready to start house-shopping when you are.

P.P.S. Snuck out of the bedroom to kiss you good night. You were sound asleep.

Attachments (2):   UNTITLED.doc

TIGER.JPG

I opened the attached image.

It was a picture of me asleep on the floor of the TV room, my body halfway outside the sleeping bag. My bare arms and back sprawled over the area rug. *Tiger?* I replied to the e-mail before reading her chapter.

Subject: Roar
Sender: Matthew R. Sky, Jr.
Date: Tuesday, July 1, 2014
Time: 8:39 AM
Tiger, huh?
Happy July, baby. You mind if we reenact last year's Fourth? Fond memories . . . and I don't mean the fireworks.

Can't wait to read your chapter. I've missed writing with you.

Matt

P.S. I'll look into a realtor.

P.P.S. I need sex.

I typed out a third postscript: *Btw no kids isn't a deal breaker but are you sure?* The cursor blinked steadily, ambivalently. I sneered.

Btw? Deal breaker?

Who the hell was I kidding?

The thought that Hannah didn't want a family with me cut me to the bone.

I backspaced the last postscript and sent my reply, and then I opened Hannah's Word document. Chapter 3. Where would she take this? I craved her impressions.

The chapter began with . . . Hannah's lunch break?

She'd met a stranger that day . . . shared her table at the Mediterranean deli.

My jaw clenched.

Hannah described the stranger as *a pretty, petite woman with fawn brown hair . . . straight, fine hair to her shoulders . . . a small, fit body.*

I didn't need to read the rest, but I did, anyway. The woman claimed to have a friend who once dated me. She dropped an ominous hint. *Is he really into all that weird stuff?*

I finished reading and let the feelings pass over me—anger, paranoia, shades of amusement and admiration. And other feelings. Darker feelings. How many secrets were Hannah and I keeping from each other?

I carried my cell to the balcony and smoked half a cigarette.

Then I dialed a number I knew by heart.

She answered with a breathless little gasp. "Matt!"

"Bethany," I said.

Chapter 19

HANNAH

My goal for the day: not to gnaw off all my nails while waiting to hear from Matt.

Also: Be sort of remotely productive at work.

It was one in the afternoon—Matt could have read my chapter ten times over—and still no word. *Shit.*

I'd set my alarm for five that morning, specifically to hammer out Chapter 3. Matt dropped a bomb in Chapter 2: exhibitionism, and the existence of some therapeutic journal in which he was writing all the stuff I didn't know about him. So, I'd followed his lead and dropped a bomb of my own: Katie, the strange woman with confusing claims about Matt.

Claims that were starting to seem more plausible . . .

I scrubbed my face. Was he freaking out? Did he know Katie? Was he angry with me? And what about my Chapter 1 revelation, that I never wanted to do the pregnancy thing? Matt hadn't responded to that. His e-mails were breezy and funny. Did he miss it?

I sent him a text.

Are you okay? I'm worried. What did you think of the chapter?

No reply.

I shuffled into Pam's office, knocking perfunctorily on the frame as I passed.

"Hannah." She looked up from her computer.

"Matt and I wanted to set up a meeting to discuss *Last Light* with you. Is there—"

"Oh, he already called about that. We're—"

"He did?" I glowered. *Fucking Matt!*

"Well, yes." Pam returned her attention to the computer. "He wanted a realtor referral. I know several. He mentioned the meeting in passing. We settled on Thursday morning."

"Great. That's . . . all I wanted." I slouched back to my desk. *Awesome.* Matt was too *something* to text or e-mail me, but calm enough to call Pam about a realtor and arrange our meeting. And again, he'd made me look like a dunce in front of her. *Ugh.*

I forced myself to finish out the workday.

Then I sped back to the condo.

Matt was sitting on the couch, watching a soccer game. He clicked it off as I shut the door, but he didn't move. I stared at the back of his head.

Why was I suddenly afraid?

"Hey," I whispered. I crept around the couch.

He took in my work outfit with a glance: a pale pink blouse tucked into a nude peplum skirt and matching peep-toe pumps. "I missed you this morning."

"Oh . . . I sorta . . . snuck out."

"I noticed."

"Sorry." I rubbed the back of my neck. "I had a lot on my mind."

"I'm sure." He frowned and dragged his fingertips over his knees, contemplating the floor. Then he stood abruptly and disappeared down the hall, returning a minute later with a black spiral notebook. Was it *the* notebook?

"You asked if I really had a journal," he said. "For Mike. I do."

"Oh . . ." I stared at it.

He stepped closer to me, and closer, until he practically stood on top of me. I felt breathless, that near to him. His particular scent—spicy, clean—his towering height and burning stare . . . completely unnerved me.

"Here," he said, offering the notebook.

I plucked at the corner. He didn't let go. Yikes, this felt familiar. Last night, we'd wrestled with the boxed whip for a good five minutes. I was furious then—he was being pushy—but now? Matt held my gaze, his expression simultaneously hungry and vulnerable.

"Go ahead," he whispered. He released the notebook and I bumped into the wall, clutching it. "Read it."

"Now?" I swallowed. "You're . . . you're kind of . . . intimidating me."

"Yes." He pinned my shoulder to the wall and cradled my cheek in his palm, which felt cool. My face must have been on fire. "Read it now, with me, or not at all."

"Okay. Let me—" I shook my purse off my shoulder. It landed with a loud clunk.

"You're sweating, little bird." His dark eyes strafed over me. *Oh . . . God.* Something about my unease always got Matt hot and bothered. And what the hell? Something about my unease always got *me* hot and bothered.

"It's . . . hot out." My chest rose and fell deeply as I struggled to calm my heart.

"Here." With one hand, he unclasped the top three buttons of my blouse. They sprang open. The cool condo air slipped into my cleavage. Matt's fingers slipped into my cleavage.

"Matt," I gasped.

"Read," he said, "before I change my mind."

Oh sweet Lord . . . I fumbled with the journal, my pulse leaping and my mind reeling. First entry: exhibitionism. Matt bit the cup of my bra and I quivered. My eyes skimmed over the page. Desire—hot and damp—gathered between my legs. *I want to fuck her with an audience . . . reveal her like a possession . . .*

Shock and strange pleasure made my thighs clench.

To make our most private act a spectacle . . . why do I need this?

I flipped the page. Matt forced his hand between my clamped legs and groaned when he touched my thong. It was soaked.

Dear God, I knew Matt was kinky, but I had no idea how deep his depravity ran. *I love to see Hannah blush . . . I want to see her at the end of a leash.*

Pain. Pleasure. Shame.

I want to take out my anger on her gorgeous body . . .

I am constantly aching.

"Constantly . . . aching," I panted, arching off the wall. I dropped the journal.

"Yes," he hissed.

I knew the feeling. When we weren't fighting, and sometimes when we were, I lived with a chronic yearning for his body. The sight of him in anything—a towel, his running clothes, jeans and a T-shirt—had my stomach doing backflips, no matter how often I saw him. And the sight of him in nothing? I moaned at the thought.

"You're turning me the fuck on," he said. He pressed my body back into the wall. His erection pushed against my belly.

"Matt, I—" I danced away. *Oh, fuck*, I wanted to get back between his hard body and that wall. "I'll be . . . be right back. I want to show you something."

I pried off my pumps and dashed to the bedroom. *Be brave. Be bold.* Later, I could think about Matt's kink and how much of it actually appealed to me. Right now—I grabbed the black box from our closet—I wanted, needed him to see my willingness to try new things.

My trust in him . . .

When I got back to the TV room, Matt had removed his shirt. I almost tripped for staring at him. His loose white lounge pants set off the tawny tone of his skin. His arousal was . . .

Oh so obvious.

And for once, Matt didn't laugh when he caught me staring.

He wants me to look, I remembered. I gathered a shaky breath and stared at my leisure as I padded up to him, ignoring my embarrassment. *This is my future husband. I'm allowed to admire his . . . body.* And what a body it was . . .

"This again," he said, accepting the box. With marked impatience, he whisked off the ribbon and overturned the lid. And there was the whip, coiled in its velvet bed. Matt tilted his head and glanced at me. "You're pale."

"And?" I shrugged.

He lifted out the whip, dropping the box. With the coiled leather, he tilted up my chin. My eyes widened; my mouth dried.

"Just an observation, little bird."

He trailed the cord down my throat. I gulped. He nestled it into my cleavage, stared a moment, and then undid another button, exposing the lacy cups of my bra.

He stroked my swelling breasts with the whip. It felt . . . unkind, rough.

I shivered.

Matt stepped away suddenly, unfurling the whip and watching it trail across the floor.

"For the life of me," he said, "I can't guess why you would . . . give me this."

His narrowed eyes landed on me.

Because of fucking Katie! I couldn't say that now, though. Not yet. It would ruin the moment. And we were having a moment, right? The journal . . . the whip . . .

I floundered in silence.

"Unless it's something you've been wanting." He rewound the whip slowly. I focused on his long fingers, his strong hands, working deftly with the plaited cord. "Come." He strolled toward the office. After a beat, I followed him, staring at his back . . . his ass.

Goddamn it, he had me all worked up, and he probably knew it.

"My aunt and uncle owned a stable for several years. They bred Friesian horses. You know the breed?" He stepped into the office and I hovered near the door.

"No." My voice was small.

"Mm. Doesn't matter. Aunt Ella had us all learn to ride. I

swear, she was determined to raise the last Renaissance men . . ." He glared at the ceiling, the walls, the floor, a question in his gaze. What the hell was he doing? "There were always whips in the barn. Seth and I used to sneak them out and mess around with them."

He tested the weight of the whip, snaking it over the floor.

"One of my exes was into this sort of thing," he added. "Whips, that is. Not horses."

"Bethany?" I whispered.

"No, she and I didn't do any of that." He watched me carefully, his expression guarded. "Not for lack of trying on her part. I made the mistake of telling her how I played with other partners. She nagged me about it, pushed for it constantly. But I didn't want that with her."

"Why . . . why not?" I couldn't conceal my shock. Bethany was the one pushing for kinky sex? Katie had lied to me, or she was misinformed. My cold panic turned to a burning blush. *Fuck*. Now *I* was pushing for kinky sex, giving Matt a whip, all because of some stupid misleading remark from a total stranger. *Hannah, you idiot!*

And nowhere in that black journal had Matt mentioned whips. *Fuck, fuck, fuck.* Restraints, yes. Riding crops, yes. Plugs, pain, punishment, shame. But not whips.

"I want it with you," he said.

My mouth fell open.

Before I could sputter out . . . something . . . he nudged me into the hallway.

"Stand out there." He grinned at me like a boy. "Look at the darts."

The darts? My spinning mind took its time making sense of Matt's words. The . . . dartboard. In his office. I looked at it. Two darts protruded from the board. Matt drew back his arm in a tight, controlled motion—the tail of the whip curled into the air—and a loud popping sound filled the office. I yelped and jumped.

When I opened my eyes, Matt was glaring at me.

"You missed it," he snapped. He pointed to the floor. One of the darts lay on the hardwood. "Done right, it sounds a lot worse than it feels. Or so I'm told."

Again, and with a patient expression, he raised the whip.

"Cover your ears and watch," he said.

I did.

I'd always imagined a whip's crack as swift, sloppy, and brutal, but the leather cord became an elegant extension of Matt's arm. It formed a slow helix in the air, flickered out, snapped the dart off the board, and relaxed across the floor. Matt beamed at me. I uncovered my ears and grinned stupidly at him. God, he was so cute, and so . . .

He quirked a brow. "You okay?"

"Yeah." I curled my toes. "You look really hot. Holding that."

"Do I?" His shadow fell over me. There's a little terror in delight. I wanted to run, and he probably would have liked that. "You trust me with it? With you."

I nodded.

He took my hand and led me back to the TV room.

"Keep your skirt on." Matt arranged me against the wall. He lifted my hair and kissed the back of my neck. "Unzip it, though, so you can get a hand inside and play with your clit."

I did as I was told, but haltingly, my brain-to-hand signals slowed by desire and fear. *Done right, it sounds a lot worse than it feels. Or so I'm told.* Matt's words weren't exactly comforting. I glanced over my shoulder.

"So, you . . ." I slipped a hand into my skirt, into my thong, and trembled. "You've never actually been . . . hit with one of these?"

He pressed against my back and ass so that I felt his erection.

"Anyone who can whip a dart off a board"—his whispering voice heated my ear—"has hurt himself many times in the learning process. Practice makes perfect, bird."

I envisioned a younger Matt standing in a field, cracking a whip. And holy shit, he knew how to ride a horse? All this new intel, combined with his kinky journal, had me reeling. I moaned as my fingertip skimmed over my clit.

"Good girl. Keep that up." He tensed as if to step away, but he cradled my cheek and sighed across my lips. "Hannah, you feel how hard this makes me?"

I wrapped my lips around his finger and nodded, sucking softly.

"Fuck." He moaned. *Oh*, I liked that sound.

Matt backed off and I closed my eyes, my nerves singing.

"Tell me when to stop," he said. His voice had changed. Gone was the undertone of recklessness, replaced by calm control. Fear kept my eyes closed, but I longed to look at him: shirtless, aroused, wielding that black whip.

In my mind's eye, he looked . . . beautiful.

Crack!

I yelped, more from surprise than pain. Gradually, I felt a stinging line across my bottom, dulled by the fabric of my skirt.

"*Ah.*" I breathed. Desire and excitement surged through me. We were actually doing this—Matt was whipping me—and it felt nothing like my gruesome imaginings, which involved screams and red stripes along my skin.

No, this was . . . tantalizing.

I wedged my other hand into my skirt and began to finger myself. Matt moaned his appreciation. I wiggled my bottom. *Give me more.*

Another loud pop sounded. The pain followed, subtly delayed. Thunder and lightning. Lightning and thunder. I gasped, desire oozing over my fingers.

Another crack, and no pain.

"You tease," I panted.

"You want it," he growled.

In answer, I pushed down my skirt. It fell around my ankles. Matt didn't hesitate. *Crack* went the whip, I rolled my clit up and down, and a burning slice of sensation fell across my ass.

Violent desire, Matt called it in his journal.

Oh, I was so on board with that.

My legs trembled and I fought to stay upright.

"I'm going to come," I gasped.

I heard the whip slap against the floor.

"Not without me you aren't." He moved swiftly, his body pinning mine to the wall, his fingers sliding aside my thong. Something filled me, and it wasn't . . . him. My eyes flew open. *Fuck*, it was the handle of the whip, the rough knob of it deep inside me.

Matt's mouth captured mine. I groaned and bit his lip. He fucked me with that stiff braided cord—he gave me no choice but to come—and when I did, he took his turn, casting away the whip and entering me, driving us together into bliss.

Chapter 20

MATT

Hannah lay along the floor with her head on my lap.

I sat against the wall, the whip coiled nearby.

Breathless silence.

She was so sweet now, her legs drawn toward her chest and her lovely face pillowed on my thighs. Her bottom glowed with three faint red stripes.

"I wish I could carry you outside, into the evening." I stroked her hair. "Just like this, in your blouse and panties."

Her eyes opened, luminous in the dim room.

What strange power she had over me, looking at me with those eyes.

"Let's buy a home where you can," she said. I stared at her mouth, her plump lips and small pink tongue. I leaned down and kissed it. She came alive for me, folding her arms around my neck and arching up from the floor.

"Were you a witch in another life?" I pressed my forehead to hers. "Witch bird."

She giggled and dragged me down. Side by side on the floor, we nuzzled one another. Nothing had changed with the revelation of my journal. I felt a happiness that was half relief.

The other half was Hannah.

I kissed her throat and hooked a leg around her.

"I want to marry you," I said. Her heart quickened against my chest. Could we actually have this for the rest of our lives?

After some minutes, we stood and stretched. I snagged the whip and grinned, eyeing the handle. "This is going to be fun to clean."

She swatted my arm.

"You kinky bastard."

"You said it." I coiled the whip and tapped it against her bottom. "Go put on something hot. We've got dinner reservations."

"We do?"

"Yeah, at Mizuna. They're holding a table for us. I told them to expect us around seven. Of course, then you had to go and make me whip you."

"Ha!" Hannah bounced on her toes. God, she was so fucking adorable.

"Clothes." I steered her toward the bedroom.

Hannah took her time getting ready.

She paired her nude pumps with a fitted beige and black dress. I dressed quickly—light slacks and a black dress shirt—and watched her apply makeup.

"We match." She beamed at me in the mirror.

"Mm." I loomed at her shoulder, observing her dozens of makeup tubes, pallets, and bottles. For a girl who wore little makeup, she sure owned a lot. "How do you keep track of what's what?" I twisted a tube.

She snatched it and applied the gloss to her cheekbones, making them shine. Mysterious.

"More bird witchery." She grinned at me.

She let me choose her jewelry.

I found a black lace choker among her things.

"This," I said, banding it around her neck. A vivid blush came into her cheeks. "And this." Around her wrist, I clasped the owl charm bracelet I had given her for Christmas.

When we stepped into the empty restaurant, Hannah hesitated. "Is it closed?" The tables were set but barren, varnished wood and overturned glasses gleaming.

I shook my head.

"We wouldn't be able to talk if . . ." I shrugged and led her to a table for two. "I know the owner. They just moved a few reservations." *And offered discounts that I would cover.*

Hannah laughed and rolled her eyes.

"You are ridiculous." She unfolded her napkin. "And adorable."

A single waiter glided out, smiling and gracious, and I ordered for both of us—the lobster mac and cheese to start, a baby-lettuce salad and Chardonnay for Hannah, and for our entrées, the New York strip and roasted duck breast.

"We'll share. Ever had duck?" I twisted my fork on the tablecloth and stared at Hannah. She kept glancing around and fidgeting.

"Um, no."

"You'll like it. All dark meat, even the breast." I slid my foot forward until my shoe bumped hers. She jumped.

"Sore bottom?" I murmured. "You're restless on that chair."

"Matt!"

"What?" I chuckled. "We're alone."

"Quite . . ." She peered around again.

"Is it making you uncomfortable? We can leave."

"No, no. It's just . . . strange for me."

I reached for her hand. She squeezed my fingers and I smiled, but the smile faded rapidly.

"Next time someone approaches you making claims about me," I said, "please, tell me."

She shrank in her chair. "Well, I did tell you. Sorta."

"Yes, sort of." I stroked her knuckles. "I'm surprised it hasn't happened before, to be honest. People are so fucking crazy. But I

deserve to know, and I would rather not learn about it in our col-
laborative story, do you understand?"

She nodded and stared at her lap.

"I'm not chastising you. I'm guilty of the same, more or less.
The journal . . ." I shrugged. "We were both keeping secrets. As
it happens, though, your mysterious lunch companion was not a
friend of Bethany Meres. She *was* Bethany."

Hannah jolted, her knee banging the table.

"What?"

"It's all right." I cupped my hands around hers. I let the information sink in, and then I continued, "I knew when I read the de-
scription. Her hair, her physique. It was enough. A quick phone
call confirmed it."

Hannah blanched.

"Yes, I called her. I paid her a visit, too."

"Wh-when? Why?"

"Earlier, while you were at work. And because I like to deliver
my threats personally."

"Threats?"

"Mm."

"Matt, what—" Another shade of pigment faded from her face.
"God, I feel so *stupid*."

"Don't. You know how vindictive she can be. Think about
what she did when I broke up with her." I frowned and glanced
around the empty restaurant. If not for Bethany revealing
M. Pierce's identity—me—Hannah and I wouldn't have to dine
alone to get a little peace. People in Denver wouldn't recognize
us instantly. I would never have faked my death, lived in Kevin's
cabin, and connived to drive Hannah to me with *Night Owl*.

Our story would be so different.

And maybe I deserved Bethany's vengeance, but Hannah didn't.
She was innocent.

I clasped her hands tighter and closed my eyes.

"Did she approach you more than once?"

"A few times," she whispered. She told me how Bethany had

claimed to be "Katie" and reluctantly divulged lies about my sexual appetites. My brutality, my forcefulness. Hannah cringed all through the telling. "She was trying to sabotage our fucking engagement. I get it now. She was planting those ideas, that you wanted other stuff, or trying to scare me."

The server arrived with our appetizers.

"Drink your wine," I said.

Hannah obeyed, guzzling half the glass under my gaze. I kissed her knuckles. I wondered how close Bethany had actually come to fucking up my happiness with Hannah. What if Hannah had found my black journal before I got a chance to explain? My entries, combined with Bethany's lies, could easily have scared Hannah off . . .

I frowned and tilted my head.

"Did you ever mention Chrissy's pregnancy to Bethany? Specifically, Seth's part in it?"

Hannah stared at the tablecloth, brow furrowed. "No, I—" Her eyes widened. "Wait. She was there the day I met Chrissy for lunch, to talk about it. We did talk about Seth."

I stabbed my fork into a chunk of lobster. *Of fucking course.*

My appetite was fading; I fed the bite into Hannah's mouth. She washed it down with a swig of wine.

"She eavesdropped." I leaned my brow into my palm. "That e-mail I received in New Jersey . . . who else would send such a thing, and benefit from sending it?"

We sat in silence, wondering at the depth of Bethany's anger.

I had broken up with her nearly a year ago, but she wasn't moving on—clearly. Maybe our saccharine appearance on the *Denver Buzz* had rekindled her anger. All that talk of love and marriage . . . and *Night Owl*, our passion made a public spectacle.

Throwing our happiness in Bethany's face.

"What if she tells someone?" Hannah plucked at my sleeve. "About Seth and Chrissy. I don't know who would listen, but . . . tabloids? Gossip blogs?"

I shook my head briskly, mostly to allay my own anxiety. "No audience for that shit."

"There's an audience for every sort of shit, Matt. He's the lead singer of a pretty major band. You're . . . you. And Chrissy and I are sisters. *Someone* would find that luridly interesting."

"I told you I paid Bethany a visit. I promised her that if she takes another step in your direction, I will solicit Shapiro's assistance in finding some grounds to sue her out of every penny she's got. You know legal threats are very . . . compelling."

Hannah frowned. I couldn't set her at ease, much less myself, and any pity I'd felt for Bethany began to crystallize into hate.

Our entrees arrived. We picked at the artistically arranged dishes, barely denting our small portions. Hannah drank a second glass of wine.

"We want to see the dessert menu," I snapped at our waiter. He scurried away and returned with it. I barely read the page. "She'll have the stout float. Nothing for me."

"Hey. You're too tense." She massaged my hands.

With two glasses of good wine in me, I might not be so fucking tense.

I winced at the thought.

"I wanted us to have a nice time," I said. "I thought I had control of the Bethany situation. But now, with her knowing about Chrissy . . ."

"Now you don't have control."

"Well put," I muttered.

"But you have me. And nothing Bethany does can drive us apart, especially now that we know her game. So let's have a good time."

Hannah tackled the float valiantly. Chin in palm, I watched her, deep within my dark mood, but after a while I shifted my chair closer to hers. I spooned mascarpone into her mouth. Brandy syrup drizzled down her chin. She licked it away and I kissed her. So sweet, those lips, and the way her mouth worked against mine.

Because we were alone, I gripped her thigh and dragged it over my lap.

Her short dress rode up. Her leg brushed my cock.

We laughed and let go of one another.

"Even I wouldn't try that here," I said, "with our poor waiter hovering somewhere."

"Hovering in terror."

"What?" I licked a daub of cream from her cupid's bow. We got tangled up again, kissing and snickering.

"You were so mean to him!" She shook with giggles. Her brows drew down in mock severity. "'We want'"—laughter bubbled out of her, her faux male voice trembling—"'we want to see the dessert menu! Now! Where is her fucking float?'"

"Ha!" I leaned back and admired Hannah's amusement—the way it lit her face.

"You know, I'm surprised the prospect of a one-man audience disturbs you." She stroked her chin. "I read something somewhere about exhibitionism . . ."

"Not now." I glowered at her.

"Oh, I know. I haven't actually agreed yet."

"Yet?"

She shrugged and sipped her float. Pretty, mischievous Hannah . . . I smiled at her.

"You don't have to agree," I said. "You know, I've never done that with anyone."

She glanced at me quickly. "No?"

"No. It's something I want . . . wanted to try, that's all." I narrowed my eyes. "With you."

The image, the idea of exposing Hannah—and enjoying her in front of others—blinked into my mind. I breathed out slowly. *Fuck . . .*

"Let's go," she whispered in my ear. "It's too warm in here. I'm tipsy."

I left our waiter an exorbitant tip. Hannah approved. We held hands and strolled around Denver, both of us a little drunk. I told her about Marion, the realtor Pam recommended.

"We spoke on the phone. She seems very capable. I gave her our price range and she'll send us some listings before the weekend."

"What's our price range?" Hannah smirked. "One million to—"

"I said two-fifty and up."

"Two hundred and fifty . . . thousand?"

"Mm. The price of your average suburban shanty. Happy?"

"*So* happy." She hugged me around the middle. I lifted her feet off the sidewalk.

"It's heaven to make you happy," I whispered into her hair.

Hannah prevailed upon my good mood, asking if she could deliver the food I'd bought for Chrissy. "And the check, too."

"Sure." I shrugged. "I suppose so. That whole-grain bread is awful anyway."

"Let's get a dog when we have a house." She swung our joined hands like a child.

"Fine," I said, "but no cats. I hate cats. A dog would be all right, so long as he doesn't bother Laurence."

"He!" Hannah laughed. "What if I want a girl?"

We exchanged a fast, alarmed look. Were we still talking about dogs? I quickened my pace, waving a hand.

"He, she . . . I'm fine with whatever."

I felt Hannah's eyes on me, but I refused to look at her.

"Matt, I—"

"Please. Not now." *Children*. I had wanted to talk about this, and now I was afraid to talk about it. What if she said something finalizing and I couldn't change her mind?

"I know what you were thinking about," she said.

She pulled me to a stop. We sat on a bench and watched the nighttime traffic.

"I'm not ready." Her tone was cautious.

"Mm."

"I might never be."

I looked at her. Now it was Hannah's turn to avoid eye contact.

The weight of her words settled on me—*never*—and I sat in silence, stunned by how much I wanted what she didn't. A little Matt-Hannah person. A family. *Fucking hell . . .*

"I only thought . . . ," I started. "Well, I wanted—one day—it's only occurred to me lately—"

"I basically raised my brother and sister."

"What?" I frowned.

"Yeah. Um, Jay is nine years younger than I am. Chrissy is six years younger. Honestly, I thought it was normal . . . until I made friends in high school and realized, well, that it wasn't normal." She shrugged. "Dad worked really hard and Mom had some anxiety issues when we were growing up. She was a stay-at-home mom, technically, but a lot of times she just . . . wasn't around. I knew how to change a diaper when I was seven. I got, like, CPR certified at ten."

"Is that even legal?"

Hannah nodded. "The older I got, the more Mom relied on me. She would come home and I had fed the kids and put them to bed. And they would ask me stuff before even thinking to ask her. Could they go to a friend's house, have a snack before dinner, watch TV?"

"Damn . . ."

"Yeah. By the time I went to college, Jay and Chrissy could fend for themselves, and Mom got some of her issues figured out. She got on medication and started working and stuff. But from ten to nineteen"—Hannah looked at me earnestly—"I sort of had to *be* a mother, and I didn't like it. I don't know if it would be different if the child was mine, or if it would be the same . . . crushing responsibility, total loss of freedom . . ."

"Mm." I reached for her hands, which were knotted on her lap. Hannah's reasoning made sense. And now, her fiercely protective feeling for Chrissy made more sense.

"And pregnancy freaks me out," she persisted. "The idea of something alive inside me? That's scary and weird for me . . . Say something."

"What is there to say?" I released her hands. "I get it."

"Do you? But you're upset. Talk to me."

"There's nothing to talk about." I stared ahead.

"There's plenty to talk about. I mean . . . are you . . . pro-life?" she blurted.

"What? God, no. Why?"

"I don't know. The way you reacted to the idea of Chrissy getting an abortion. And, I mean, I know you're . . . some sort of Christian."

"Oh, yes, let the generalities fly." I scowled.

"Why are you so touchy about your faith?"

"Because I don't have much faith left," I snapped, "and what little I've got shouldn't be used to make me out as some Bible-thumping hypocrite, all right? It's *personal.*"

She wiggled her hand out of mine.

"I am not doing that. Stop ruining our nice night."

I frowned and looked down at Hannah. She was right, as usual. Any time she mentioned my faith, I bit her head off.

"It's . . . her choice," I said. It *was* Chrissy's choice. If Hannah were pregnant, though, I wouldn't be so indifferent, and I knew it. We'd called one another Auntie Hannah and Uncle Matthew, playfully. That kind of play is dangerous. In that moment, I had imagined Hannah with our niece or nephew, and the idea was sweet. If that idea became an impossibility, it would be a loss for me, no two ways about it.

"You look unhappy." She touched my cheek. "What are you thinking about?"

"Nothing," I said, which might turn out to be true.

Chapter 21

HANNAH

I wheeled my chair into Pam's office. Matt sat across from Pam's desk. Pam sat behind it like the presiding judge.

Matt held the *Last Light* manuscript, which looked a little worse for wear since I'd chucked it at him on our balcony.

I bit my lip, fighting inappropriate laughter

"I'll start by stating the obvious," Matt said. "Hannah is uneasy about *Last Light*'s publication—how it could affect our image, my career, et cetera."

"Valid concerns," said Pam. "There will be a lot of speculation with the book. Your detractors will love it—gives them ammo to call you a liar. Your loyal readers will love it, too. It's a bold story. Whatever the case, the response will be loud, which is good for sales."

"I'm not particularly worried about sales." Matt slouched, his long legs extending under Pam's desk. It was fascinating to watch them interact. Matt appeared unconcerned with Pam's opinion, when I knew he cared deeply, and Pam threw her weight around, when I knew how much she valued Matt.

Also, sweet Lord, my future husband in serious mode is hot.

I flushed, dismissing the thought.

When would I get used to being around him? Maybe never.

Matt and Pam bickered lazily and I felt useless. *Ignore me; I'm just here for decoration.* I sighed too deeply. They both went silent and glared at me. I smiled. *Oops . . .*

Their banter resumed.

"All I'm suggesting . . ." Matt was on his feet.

Pam was gesturing. "Could have told me . . ."

"And risk having you tell the authorities?"

"Have I ever told anyone anything?"

"That's hardly what this is about!"

I cleared my throat.

Again, two pairs of irate eyes landed on me.

"I . . . have an idea," I said.

"By all means," Pam said.

Matt's expression softened. He retook his seat and reached for my hand. I smiled and squeezed his fingers.

"I've been thinking about the book," I said, "which, well, I don't exactly want published." I glanced at Pam. She was watching us with a flat "get a room" sort of look. "But I know how important it is to Matt. I also know everyone who reads it is going to think it's true, and I don't think we can risk looking like we lied to the media. Not in such a bold-faced way, without addressing the issue. So, let's publish it with a proviso. An open-ended disclaimer. I mean, something more than the usual 'this is a work of fiction' stuff."

"You don't think that'll highlight the issue?" Matt said. "You know, put it in people's minds that we're worried about the public reception?"

"That's already going to be in their minds," Pam said. "What sort of disclaimer were you thinking, Hannah?"

"Something frank. Really to the point. Um . . . you know, 'the author and publisher of this book are aware that it contradicts the factual account of events.' And we could reiterate that it's a fictitious reimagining of events, for entertainment only."

Pam and Matt regarded me with thoughtful expressions.

"That's . . . not such a bad idea," he said.

Pam tapped her desk. "It would head things off at the pass, for sure."

"And we wouldn't need to say anything more." I shrugged. "Our line would be right there, on every copy of the book, and people could take it or leave it."

After the meeting, Matt stalked around my office, looking gorgeous and trapped. I kissed him and detained his attention for all of five minutes, during which he managed to finger me and lift me off the desk and leave me panting.

The doors were locked, but I broke our kiss and pressed him back.

"No more office sex," I whispered. "That was a onetime thing."

"Mm, I see." He licked his finger clean.

"You!" I tugged his hair. "You're bad."

"The worst."

He held me for a while—I couldn't get enough of being in his arms—and I stroked his back and sides, though I knew I couldn't soothe the restlessness out of him. It was in his nature.

"You impressed Pam in there," he said. "And me."

"Yeah?" I beamed.

"Mm. You're constantly impressing me."

I looked Matt up and down. "So are you." We laughed and I finally nudged him toward the door. "Go write. I know you want to."

"Is it obvious?"

"To me, yeah. Plus, I want to read the next chapter." I scuffed my heel along the floor. "Um, no obligation, though. I know you probably wanna write other stuff, too."

"Do I?" He chuckled and stepped out.

I swung by the condo after work to pick up the food Matt had bought for Chrissy. We ate a quick dinner together—leftover pizza—and Matt reluctantly produced the check.

"Five grand?" I gawked at it.

"That's really not much."

"I don't think she has many"—I faltered at the words "baby-related"—"uh, expenses yet." Matt had gotten weird and moody the other night when we'd almost talked about kids. Then he'd clammed up. I didn't want to upset him again.

I had said my part, though, and he'd heard me loud and clear. *I might never be ready for kids.* Childbearing, childrearing, the whole business freaked me out.

"She should be eating healthy, at least. Organic food isn't cheap. And eventually she'll need those"—he waved a hand—"horrible-looking pants with the stretchy . . ." He trailed off, glaring at the pizza box.

Mmph, adorable. I kissed his cheek. "Do you want to come?"

"In a manner of speaking." He grinned. "Nah, you know I don't. Go on, before I change my mind about helping her."

"You won't change your mind." I nuzzled him. "You're too sweet."

"Only for you."

He helped me carry the grocery bags to the car and then watched me drive off. He always looked so forlorn—when I left for work, an errand, whatever. It was simultaneously heart-melting and heart-crushing.

I watched him grow smaller in the rearview mirror.

Then I turned the corner and started to miss him.

"Be cooler than this," I muttered. From the dashboard, a plush patchwork squirrel observed me with beady eyes. A gift from Matt. *Ugh, Matt, you're turning me into a sap.*

I rode to my parents' house with the squirrel on my lap.

I'd arranged to meet Chrissy out back, avoiding Mom and Dad as much as possible, but no one answered when I tapped on the patio door. I tugged at the handle. Locked.

Fuck, everything would be easier when Chrissy told our parents. *If* she decided to tell them.

I rang the bell and Dad answered. We hugged on the steps. He clung to me a little longer than usual, and a little harder, and I frowned when I drew back.

"Everything okay, Dad?"

"Just missing my girl," he said. Guilt swamped me. I needed to visit more often.

"Is Chrissy around?"

"No." Dad frowned at the floor. Chrissy's choices of dress, oc‑cupation, almost everything, disappointed our father. "I thought she quit that job"—he meant stripping—"but she's off at that *place* with some *boy* doing I probably don't want to know what."

Some boy?

"Dad, I gotta go. I'll visit soon." I gave him a quick kiss and dashed back to my Civic.

I called Chrissy on my way to Boulder.

"Han?" she answered. I heard music and voices in the back‑ground.

"Are you at Dynamite? Seriously?"

"*Yyyup.* Problems?"

"We were supposed to meet at home. I have—"

"Oh, no. Tonight? No, that was Thursday night." A certain smudge around the edge of Chrissy's voice told me she'd been drinking.

"It *is* Thursday night," I hissed.

"I had to go out. Seth came by. Can you believe it?" My sis‑ter's voice radiated awe. When it came to Seth Sky, she was a fan girl, not her usual cynical self.

My hand trembled on the wheel.

I ended the call and chucked my phone onto the passenger seat.

Matt wouldn't like this, I knew, but I had to see my sister. I had to protect her.

I parked on the street and hurried down the alley, flashing my ID as I ducked into the Dynamite Club. The pink-red light, the throbbing music and scent of alcohol and perfume brought back the memory of being here with Matt. I paused in the crowd and closed my eyes. God, I barely knew him then . . . he was a capti‑vating stranger . . . and at dinner and then at the club that night, he'd seemed so capable and controlled.

Only later did I get to know the rest of him. Broken Matt. Sweet Matt. Vulnerable Matt. I loved all of it, the good and the bad.

"You look like you're having a nice dream," someone whispered.

I kept my eyes closed and counted backward from ten.

Then I gazed up at Seth.

"Who needs nice dreams?" I said. "I have nice things in my life."

"Lucky you."

We stared at one another, openly assessing. God, Seth didn't look good. He wore his dark hair in a ponytail, which accentuated the sharp angles of his face. He'd lost weight. Quite a bit of weight. Bruise-blue shadows filled the hollows of his features. I recognized the glassy gleam in his eyes. He was high or drunk, or both.

My gaze raked down to his boots. His clothes—a plain gray T-shirt and jeans—were clean but loose on his lean frame.

"I want to talk to you," I said. "Not here."

Seth shrugged and moved toward the exit, his rangy body slipping through the crowd.

I found Chrissy sharing a booth with a dancer. At least, the girl *looked* like one of the dancers. Three sweating glasses stood between them.

"You're drinking." I frowned at my sister.

"Yeah. One Long Island."

"Hi!" said the friend. I ignored her.

"One is one too many if you're going to—" I pursed my lips, but I wanted to scream: *If you're going to have that baby.* "If you're going to *drive*, Chrissy." I laid ridiculous emphasis on the word "drive." "Even one drink could *impair* things."

"I think a little bit is okay."

The stupid friend chimed in: "Driving? Didn't Seth drive you here?"

"Shut *up*." I glared at the friend.

"What the hell?" said Chrissy. "If you're going to be a bitch, I don't want to talk to you. I'm actually having a good night. Don't come around with your boyfriend's shitty attitude."

Heat rushed to my head.

I vividly imagined throwing my sister's drink in her face, and I stormed out before it came to that. In the alleyway, I gulped down summer air. A twist of smoke burned my throat. I coughed and glared at the offending smoker.

Seth Fucking Sky, of course.

"Rough night?" He raised a brow.

"Like you care." I turned away. It hurt to look at him—to see him hurting. I had played a part in his pain, hooking up with him so carelessly, and that memory was too fresh.

"I do care, Hannah."

I hugged myself. "You look really bad."

"Hey, thanks."

"You know you do. Why can't you just take care of yourself?" I glared over my shoulder, my eyes burning.

He shook his head. "I don't know."

"It is *hard* to watch, okay? I know you and Matt don't get along, but you're the same. Self-destructive and stupidly stubborn. And—" My throat clenched; my voice shook. I can never speak when I get too angry or sad.

What I really wanted to do was apologize for helping Seth hurt himself by hooking up with him when my heart belonged to Matt, but I couldn't make the words come out.

"I would have let you take care of me," he said. Easy for him to say; he was halfway fucked-up. He leaned against the wall and sucked on his cigarette. He watched me, his dark eyes slanted down, and then gestured toward the club. "I doubt that little thing can do the job."

That little thing—my sister.

"She needs taking care of," I said, "not the other way around."

"I'm gonna try."

"Is that why she's in there drinking? God, I want to hate you. I do. I hate you for fucking up her life like this."

"She was well on her way to fucking it up when I came along." Seth exhaled away from me. "If not with me, with Wiley, with some other guy. Girl is wild. And Hannah—" He reached for me, the sarcasm draining from his tone. "She came on to me . . . I didn't—"

"I don't want to know." I sidestepped his hand.

"I want you to know. She did. You left, she came into the room—"

"*No.*" I covered my ears. When he stopped speaking, I lowered my hands.

How long had I been here? I felt for my phone and remembered I'd left it in the car.

A group of people filed into the club.

"We had fun that night," Seth said. "I mean after the memorial, driving out to that bar. Making our escape." He laughed. "It was winter, right? Fucking cold. I really thought he was dead." Sadness, not bitterness, underpinned Seth's voice. "It's hard to forgive him."

I fished the crumpled check out of my pocket and offered it to Seth.

"He wants to help her."

"I heard otherwise." Seth unfolded the check and frowned at it.

"He was angry. He came around."

"Kid's got a temper on him. I should know." After a brief hesitation, he pocketed the check. "I'll see she gets it. We're doing some . . . fancy paternity test. DNA stuff. It's a safe one. We'll put the money toward that, and anything else she—"

"What the hell are you two doing out here?" Chrissy swayed in the club's doorway. Instinctively, I moved away from Seth.

"Trying to figure out ways to help you," I said.

"Yeah, right." Her eyes flickered to Seth. "Give me a cigarette."

"Chris, she's trying to help. Matt wrote you a check—"

"Look at you, defending her." Chrissy's nostrils flared. "I don't want his help. Give me a fucking cigarette, would you?"

"No," he said. He flashed an aggrieved look at me. "I think you should go . . ."

Me? Go? Chrissy was *my* sister.

With stinging eyes, I rushed toward my car, bumping past drunken strangers. I yanked open the trunk and snatched up all the plastic grocery sacks, and I lumbered back down the alley to where Seth and Chrissy were quarreling.

"You don't get to pick and choose who helps you." I set the load of groceries at Chrissy's feet. "Matt bought all this food for *you*, so you and that baby can be healthy."

Her eyes bored into me.

"He's a judgmental asshole, and you're not far behind, all of the sudden." She kicked the nearest bag, hard. Something inside popped. I pictured Matt shopping for those groceries—looming in the aisle, glaring at the selection of whole-grain breads and inspecting each loaf in his angry way—and I dove down, gathering the bags away from Chrissy.

A slippery trail ran onto my shirt.

Broken egg.

I gasped and tears squeezed out of my eyes. I tried to stop them, but as soon as I tried, a torrent followed. I swore under my breath and swiped at my cheeks, smearing egg.

Strong arms closed around me. Seth guided me to my feet.

"Thank you for the food. Leave it; I'll get it. Where's your car?"

I pointed blindly and he guided me away from the light and stink of the club.

"There you go," Chrissy called. "Help poor Hannah!"

Seth deposited me behind the wheel of my Civic. I sat there blubbering, an eggy, teary mess. He strained across my lap and snagged my phone.

"Matt's been calling you," he said. "I think you should call him back."

At the thought of Matt's anger—here I was with Seth, whom Matt had effectively ordered me not to see—a new surge of tears seeped into my hands.

"Hannah, calm down. I'll—" My phone started to ring. "It's Matt." Seth hovered on the edge of my vision, holding out the phone while I sniffled and sobbed. Where was all this emotion coming from? Guilt . . . confusion . . . fear. Oh God, Matt was going to be so pissed.

"Can you take this?" Seth said.

I shook my head furiously.

He turned away and thumbed the screen. He brought my phone to his ear.

"Hello, Matt."

Chapter 22

MATT

I overpaid my cab and launched out into the street.

Hannah's Civic was parked in a metered spot and I could see her sitting behind the wheel. No sign of Seth or Chrissy.

I ran to her.

The driver-side door lurched open and I pulled her out.

"I'm sorry," she bleated.

"Don't be. What the hell happened?" I took in her red-rimmed eyes, dry cheeks, and stained shirt. Seth hadn't given me details on the phone, and I hadn't listened too well. *Hannah is parked outside Dynamite. She's fine, but she's emotional. I think you should come get her.*

I cussed him out for being in Colorado.

I threatened him.

I threw *All the King's Men* across the living room.

I was still shouting into my cell when he hung up.

"I drove to my parents' to meet up with Chrissy," Hannah mumbled into my shirt, "and Dad said she was *here* with some *guy* and I lost it, 'cause I knew it was Seth. She was drinking. She was crazy. Matt, she hates me."

She snuffled loudly and I cupped her face.

"Hey, hey. No more crying. It's okay. Are they gone now?"

"Yeah. Seth"—she dragged her fist across her nose—"wanted to stay with me, but I made him leave, because . . ." She looked up at me with watery eyes.

"Good call," I muttered. "Goddamn it, Hannah . . ." I clenched my teeth.

We held one another, standing on the sidewalk, and I rocked her gently.

"She kicked your groceries," she whispered. At that, she nearly started to cry again, and I whispered in her ear that it was all right, and that it was over.

"She's hormonal and confused. Don't think about it now. Give me your keys." I put Hannah on the passenger seat like a baby. Lifted her in, buckled her seat belt. She didn't protest. She touched my hands and forearms wonderingly, as if my gentleness were a miracle.

Maybe it was a miracle.

I wanted to punch a hole in the nearest anything.

I plugged in my phone and shuffled a playlist for the drive back to Denver. When the Yeah Yeah Yeahs' "Wedding Song" came on, I reached over and rubbed Hannah's thigh. She'd been mostly quiet, looking out her window. She filled me in on some details— Seth seemed high but genuinely concerned for Chrissy, they were doing a paternity test, she gave him the check—and I didn't push her for more.

At the condo, I undressed her and we showered together.

She kept giving me quick, wide-eyed looks.

"It's okay," I told her again and again. I washed her hair. I stroked her body, nothing more. Afterward, we made coffee and sat on the couch.

I blew a curl of steam off my mug and smiled at Hannah. "Coffee at midnight. Sounds like some bad indie band, am I right?"

She smiled back at me and nodded.

"Bird, talk to me."

"I'm . . . worried about him."

I swallowed a mouthful of coffee. It scalded my tongue. Anger, which I had been tempering all night, rumbled inside me. Clouds massing for a storm.

"Because he was high?"

"He looked terrible," she said. "Too skinny, miserable. He's in no way equipped to help Chrissy right now. *He* needs help. And the way she bossed him around, it was—"

"You're preaching to the choir. I want him gone. We're all the help she needs."

"I'm not talking about her." Hannah clunked her mug onto the coffee table. "I'm talking about your brother. The help your brother needs."

"He is not my fucking concern."

"You wouldn't be alive if Nate decided that you weren't his 'fucking concern.'"

"What is this, exactly?" I drew away from her. "Your sister is testing my patience to the limit. I don't understand what you're getting at right now. Are you suggesting that I should be doing something for Seth? Handouts for the two of them?"

"God." She shook her head. "Never mind."

"No, please, illuminate me. I must have a goodwill sign stamped across my face. Tell me just *how* I should help my brother, who assaulted my girlfriend and knocked up her sister."

"He didn't assault me. For the millionth time. You hurt him—terrified him—by faking your death. When are you going to own that? How would you feel if Nate did that to you? Seth lost his parents, too." Hannah stood, visibly mustering her courage. "I saw Seth grieving at your memorial. That shit messed him up. I'm sure he shares all your hang-ups about loss and—"

"Hang-ups." I rose, wanting more distance from her. I moved away and regarded Hannah coolly. "*Hang-ups,*" I repeated.

"Okay, wrong word. Chill. You know what I mean."

"*Chill?*"

She threw up her hands. "Forget it. You're impossible when you get like this."

I leaned against the wall, wishing I had a cigarette. I'd trashed my pack earlier in the day. I needed to quit for Hannah, who summoned my dead parents against me . . . in defense of Seth.

"Go to bed," I said.

"I am going, but not because you say so. I'm not a child."

"No? You're happy to act like one when you need taking care of."

She turned scarlet and scowled at her feet.

"There's no shame in that, little bird." I strolled toward her and took her jaw in my hand. I forced her to look at me. Defiance shone in her eyes, and a little alarm. "Just remember who loves you. Remember who takes care of you." I brushed my thumb over her lips. "Sleep."

I ran that night the way I had run when Hannah broke up with me in April: past the boundary of my stamina, into pain and then numbness.

Anything can become self-harm. Not just sharp objects and drugs and alcohol, but exercise and creativity, ambition, desire. Love. What else is love, if not the power to destroy?

In a moment of carelessness, Hannah could ruin me.

But she is gentle, I wrote, having returned from my run and gone straight to my desk. Sweat dripped down my face. The desire to put Hannah into words, and to understand her, seared me. She spoke about my parents and Seth. I saw their faces in a constellation, meaning nothing. *She is like the little bird I call her. Strong and delicate. I'm out of my depth.*

Chapter 23

HANNAH

On Friday morning, Matt and I acted as if we'd never argued.

I could almost believe we hadn't.

Last night, I'd set foot in that no-man's-land topic—his parents—and he locked up like Fort Knox. End of discussion. End of the evening.

"Happy Friday," he said as we toweled off after our shower.

"Same to you." I hugged him tight. Matt communicated through physicality, something I'd learned, and a hug meant more than a dozen apologies.

His semihard cock pressed at my belly. *Oh Lord.*

If I dress in a hurry . . . maybe we could quickly . . .

I tugged off his towel and he laughed reluctantly.

"Hi," I whispered, wrapping my fingers around his dick.

"Ah, fuck." He locked his hands behind his skull. I tugged at him gently. Would I ever get tired of the way he responded to this? Like a gun to his head.

I shook off my towel and pressed my sex against the cold marble corner of the sink.

"Go on," he said, fixated on the V of my thighs. "Get wet on that."

He liked a little show, and despite my sometimes crippling shyness, I liked putting it on for him. I jerked him off and rolled my body against the blunt corner, soaking it. Soon he was bucking into my grip, pulling me away from the sink and taking over with his expert hands. Hands I loved, long and veined. Fingers that thrummed my clit at perfect pitch. Fingers that entered me boldly, possessively, and almost carelessly. As if this part of me were his.

I watched us handling one another in the mirror, and coming; Matt first, in a thick pale jet against my belly, and me a moment later, my pleasure dripping over his hands.

I carried that memory with me to work.

Matt forwarded an e-mail to me at noon.

Subject: Fwd: Listings
Sender: Matthew R. Sky Jr.
Date: Friday, July 4, 2014
Time: 12:08 PM
Who the hell works on the Fourth of July? Only my workaholic wife-to-be.

Thanks for the helping hand this morning.

Okay, that was pretty bad . . .

Marion sent the listings just now. I like the look of a few. She can start showing us around as early as Monday. Thoughts?

Also, please find attached Chapter 4, for your reading pleasure.

Matt

Attachment: UNTITLED.doc

I started to read Matt's chapter before I even glanced at the listings. Priorities.

He began with a transcript of that racy journal entry, EXHI-BITIONISM, which made me feel fluttery and aroused and alarmed.

And he wrote about . . . I frowned and reread. Hm, something he felt when we drove past my parents' house? It was the night he proposed to me. Something between the lines.

I closed the Word document with the definite sense that I was missing something.

Or worse, choosing to ignore something.

The homes listed in Marion's e-mail ranged from suburban to country, two-bedroom to ten-, and affordable to impossibly expensive.

But impossibly expensive *was* affordable for us.

Still, I couldn't help but notice more seven-figure listings than not. In fact, Marion included only three houses that looked reasonable for a two-person family.

Matt's chapter loitered in my mind for the rest of the day. As I read queries and responded to e-mails, I thought about that word—"exhibitionism"—and how we might go about attempting such a thing.

Why am I considering this? I tried to ignore the thought, but it kept creeping back.

The logistics of it.

Who watches other people having sex? Voyeurs, that's who. But they watch in secret.

My mind drifted to the Dynamite Club, where a year ago, Matt had watched a stripper give me a lap dance. I shivered. That was hot.

A bulb winked on in my brain.

The club. The strippers! Surely one of those dancers, at least, was into exhibitionism. I knew some stripped because they'd hit rock bottom, but others seemed to revel in the work—the exposition of the body, the tease and play of it.

I was muddling over how my request might go—"So, heh, me and my fiancé"—when I snapped out of it. *The hell?* Was I planning this for real?

I stared at my lap and questioned my sanity. I could no longer tell where Matt's desires ended and mine began, or what I wanted and what I just wanted to give him.

I put in eight hours that day, making up for lost time in April.

Matt sent a volley of filthy texts: *I know you're alone at the agency. You* are *alone, right? Remember, it's the Fourth. My hands have plans related to your—*

Oh my God. Matt!

The building was eerily quiet as I left. My sneaker squeaked in the lobby and I jumped.

On my way home, I texted Matt.

Outside, wind tore along the sidewalk and ripped at the manuscripts wedged under my arm. A slate of blue-black cloud hung over the city. The smell of ozone filled the air.

I jogged the half block to my car, but a few yards from it, I stopped sharply.

What . . . the fuck?

White spray paint spelled the word SLUT clear across the windshield of my Civic.

Bethany.

I knew her handiwork immediately, but embarrassment blotted out my anger. I glanced around. Thank God for the holiday and the gathering storm. The street was empty.

I edged toward the car and slicked my thumb over the paint. It was dry, but recent, judging by the lingering chemical odor.

My heart squeezed. I touched the door and hesitated. What if she'd done something more? Cut the brake line, or worse?

A drop of rain hit my forehead.

I pulled out my phone and forced myself to relax. If I called Matt, we would spend the rest of our night at the police station, Matt on the phone with Shapiro, me filling out endless paperwork while strangers took pictures of my car.

The SLUT-mobile.

No . . . fucking . . . way.

I found Chrissy in my contacts and hit her number.

Seth's rental car, a silver Lincoln, slid up to the curb.

He leapt out.

I didn't see Chrissy in the passenger seat, which, strangely, was a relief.

"Just me," Seth said, his voice breathless. Fifteen minutes had passed since I'd called Chrissy and she'd promised to catch a cab over. She didn't mention last night. Her voice was papery and faint: *Don't worry, we'll figure something out.*

"Where's Chrissy?"

"We were at the house." Seth coughed into cupped hands. His black T-shirt and dark jeans emphasized the ashen tone of his skin. "She wanted to tell your parents. You know, about . . ."

"Did she?" I frowned. No wonder Chrissy sounded off.

"We did. That's why she stayed. She wants to have it. The baby."

"Are my parents okay?"

The rain began to pelt, frizzing my curls. The wind sucked our voices up the street.

"I think so," Seth shouted. "Don't worry about it now." He glanced at my car, then dashed to the Lincoln and lifted a plastic jug and a sponge off the seat. He sloshed soapy solution over my windshield and began to scrub.

Nothing happened.

He grimaced and ground the sponge in circles. The white curve of the *S* flaked away.

"Thank God," I said. "Can I help? Let me help."

"Just get in the car. You're getting soaked."

"So are you."

"Get in the fucking car, Hannah." He coughed into his shoulder.

Get help, Seth.

He looked strung-out and edgy, a shadow of the man I'd met five months earlier.

And I remembered that man. I remembered him sneering at me in Nate's house, charging across the graveyard to deck Aaron Snow, playing the piano onstage, singing with a rough, beautiful voice. I remembered the goodness and fierceness in him, which reminded me of Matt.

Good and fierce, both of them, like avenging angels.

The rain fell at a sharp angle, chilly drops stinging my face.

"I'm scared to get in," I stammered.

Seth had cleared the *S* and half of the *L* from my windshield. His expression softened. He set down the jug and sponge and guided me away from the car. We stood close for a moment, his fingers around my arm.

"You okay?" he said.

I nodded.

He jerked his head toward the car. "One of Matt's psycho fans?"

My chin fell to my chest. "Something like that."

"Well, that ain't you. That word. Not in a million fucking years."

He opened the door. Nothing exploded, and my silly fear dissolved. He lifted the hood and scanned the engine. He knelt and stared under the car.

"Get in already," he called. "Everything looks fine."

I hovered uselessly for another minute and then I climbed behind the wheel. Thunder bowled across the sky. The rain reached a frantic tempo. I huddled in the shell of my car while Seth Sky strained over the windshield, furiously scrubbing off the letters *UT.*

Once the glass was clean, he splashed the remaining solution around my wipers, sluicing away white paint. The rain stripped the soapy film from my car. Seth gestured, turning an invisible key, and I started the car. It revved on smoothly. I let out a breath.

He gave me a thumbs-up. I grinned and gave him two. God, he was soaked to the skin.

My phone chimed and I fumbled for it. Shit, a text from Matt.

Where are you? You okay?

I tapped out a reply.

Sorry, tried to wait out the rain. Just gonna brave it. See you soon. Love you.

I looked up in time to see the Lincoln's taillights glowing. Seth pulled away, no wave, no good-bye.

I drove slowly to the condo, my wheels spinning up water and rain streaming down the road. In the parking lot, I took a few personal minutes—to think about Bethany, to let myself forgive her, and to worry for Seth. Against my better judgment, I texted Nate.

> *I'm worried about Seth. He's here helping my sister. Doesn't look good. Thin, pale, etc. Do you know what's going on? Please don't mention to Matt.*

Nate's reply came within minutes.

> *Haven't seen Seth for a while, probably worn out from touring and always was lean. Great that he's stepping up re: your sister. You look to Matt. I'll check on Seth when possible. Together we'll keep these boys in order. Aunt Ella favorably mentioned you to me. Quote, she's quiet but has a great sense of style. See, she comes around.*

I smiled at my phone.

Okay, Aunt Ella was actually complimenting Matt's style, since he bought every piece of the outfit I wore in New Jersey, but no one needed to know that. And more important, Nate's confident tone, which transmitted even through text, set me at ease.

Look to Matt, he said.

Yes, Matt was my troubled boy.

Seth was . . . Chrissy's troubled boy, or Nate's, or Ella and Rick's. Definitely not mine.

The rain gave no sign of letting up, so I darted from the Civic to the condo, my work papers clutched to my chest. *Bethany,* I thought, *you are petty and cruel, but you are also hurt and cornered by pain. We wronged you. We require your forgiveness.*

I sent my little missive into the universe.

Matt met me in the lobby. He hugged me and took soggy items off my hands: the manuscripts, my purse.

"More potboilers?" He eyed the stacks of paper.

"Eyes off, you." I slapped his butt as I followed him up the stairs. Like a curious animal, he was forever getting into the manuscripts I brought home. He laughed at me for printing them, said I was following in the footsteps of Pam the Luddite, and disparaged every hopeful's novel.

"Aw, come on. This one actually looks cool. *The Midnight—*"

"You're a big bully." I laughed and bumped our door shut, prying the papers from him. "If I didn't know any better, I'd say these new young writers threaten you."

"Threaten me? Ha." He yanked me into his arms. I gave him a giddy smile. "And if they're new and young, what does that make me? Old and old?"

Young and *old,* I thought, wrapping my arms around his neck. Like a child in a man's body, sometimes. And I imagined he had sometimes seemed like a man when he was just a boy. Too sad and serious. I feathered kisses along his jaw.

"Mine," I said.

"I can work with that." He tugged at my wet hair so that I tipped back my head, and he kissed my mouth. "Poor thing, you really got stuck in that weather."

"God, you have no idea . . ."

We made out for a full quarter-hour before I noticed the tent in the living room.

"Matt!" I snickered. He'd moved the coffee table and couch to accommodate the tent. It was new, or new to me—a tall gray and orange dome.

"Aha, she finally sees it." He stalked over to the tent. Yes, it was definitely new. Matt wore his distinct "Do you like my new toy?" expression, and he circled the tent and folded his arms and studied it, signaling that I should also take a moment to admire it. I did.

"Wow . . . it's nice." I touched one of the poles. "So big. So . . ."
In our living room.

"Mm. I got it at REI. Had to throw it together, make sure nothing was missing." He frowned at the mesh-and-polyester palace. "I thought we might take it for a spin this evening, but not in this weather."

On cue, thunder crackled and boomed outside.

"Oh, babe." I rubbed his back. "Lemme get into dry clothes and we'll 'take it for a spin' right here, okay?" I kissed his cheek. "Happy Fourth."

His eyes lit up like a child's.

"Perfect," he said, already halfway into the tent.

I peeled off my wet clothes and changed into my Shell Belle Couture chemise, an expensive little gift from Matt. I never bought such nice things for myself. The champagne silk complemented my pale skin and felt luxurious. The lace cups, well . . . I resisted the urge to grab a robe as I felt my nipples hardening. Matt liked the lace cups best of all.

In the bathroom, I untangled my hair with Moroccan oil and washed my face. On my skin, I left the scent of rainwater.

I returned to a living room devoid of pillows.

The tent flap was shut.

"Knock knock?" I said.

With a swift zinging sound, Matt unzipped the door from inside.

"Why, come in." He was laughing. The tent was tall, but taller Matt stood stooped beneath the dome. All our pillows lay around his feet.

"Don't mind if I do." I took his hand and stepped inside.

He stared openly at my chest.

"Oh," he said.

His expression grew somber. I wanted to burst out laughing. *God, his cuteness . . .*

"Very swanky in here." I sat cross-legged on a pillow and looked around. The tent was cozy, the inner flaps a vibrant orange, and adorable Matt had stocked a wall pouch with snacks and drinks: two cans of Coke and a bag of goldfish. In another flap, two books and a flashlight.

"I was just testing those pouches," he mumbled, gesturing to the snacks. "Hi." He shucked off his shirt—*yum*—and crawled to me. "Hi . . ."

"Hi," I said, giggling. "Hello. Did I ruin storytime with lingerie?"

I slid my fingers up his arms. Whisper of skin on skin. My hands curled over his shoulders.

"No." He closed in on me, his body pressing mine back and down. He went for my neck with his teeth, like an animal. Bit the column of my throat. Licked away the hurt.

"Ah," I gasped, arching under him. I pawed at his abs and pulled at the band of his lounge pants.

An electrical pop sounded in the condo and the room went dark.

Matt and I froze.

We laughed in unison, sitting up and holding one another.

Pure darkness. I clung to his torso.

"Well, this is a first," I said. "Our first power outage."

"Always be prepared." Matt groped around until he found the flashlight. He turned it on and hung it from the top of the tent. A cone of light shone over us.

His erection tented the front of his pants. I reached for it, my hand drawn to it. I gripped his head through the fabric. God, I loved seeing him turned on.

"I'm glad that happened." He flexed into my hand. "Slowed me down."

"Baby, you don't have to slow down."

"I know. I want to." He caressed the undersides of my breasts and my nipples. The intricate lace of the cups scratched gently at my skin. I twitched and moaned.

He reached up and turned off the flashlight.

Darkness rushed back in.

It was better that way, never knowing what was coming. His hot, wet mouth on my nipple. His tongue between my legs. The weight of his dick along my chest.

Ah, he was something else, moving against me, and I thought of that "something else" I'd felt while reading his chapter. *I know that I'll die with these memories in me,* he wrote. I understood something, there with him in the dark, my toes curled against the tent wall. Not the sadness of death, but the silver clarity of these moments, casting a lifelong memory.

Afterward, we lay in a tangle on the pillows.

Satisfaction burned away my bashfulness. I stroked Matt's ass and he panted softly against my hair.

"So," he murmured, "you like my tent?"

I laughed breathlessly.

"Very much. Close quarters, but we made it work."

"Well"—he scooted down so that we lay face-to-face—"I know a girl who's into small living spaces. Won't take anything too grand."

I huffed. "Your realtor lady is obviously favoring the higher end of our price range."

"*Our* realtor lady, Marion. And I noticed that."

"Maybe I'll have a talk with her."

"You do that, little bird." He tapped my nose and I scrunched it. "You can always e-mail her. Still, let's at least see the larger places. Room to grow . . ."

I rolled onto my back. *Room to grow.*

"You want children," I said. Matt stayed quiet and I continued calmly, the awareness forming as I spoke. "What you sent me today, Chapter four. You said you pictured me as a child, playing on the lawn of my parents' house. You said it made you feel . . . sadness. You want to give me a home. And you want children, don't you? I mean, you really want them."

I glanced at him.

He sat up, avoiding my gaze.

"You don't have to tell me, then. I know. I just don't know how important it is to you."

"Don't say you haven't thought about it," he said. "I don't know exactly what I want. If you'd talked to me a few years ago, I would have said I never wanted to get married. You made me want marriage, though, and you make me want . . ." He shrugged.

"I *have* thought about it." I sat up and forced him to look at me. "Matt, I've gone so far as to picture it. A little boy with your beautiful eyes. A girl with sandy curls. But I'm confused, too. I'm scared. I never really wanted kids. There's so much to consider."

His eyes widened.

"We have to be careful."

"What?"

He shook his head. "We could be happy. Too happy."

"Too happy?" I frowned.

"Yes, God. Don't talk about them. A boy . . . a girl. Stop that."

Whoa, where was this coming from?

"I thought you—"

"You thought wrong," he snapped, and I flinched. They were figments of my imagination—those small children, the boy and the girl—but when Matt said, *Don't talk about them,* ferocity reared inside me. It was an instinct to protect . . . what didn't even exist.

I stared at my hands, dazed. I didn't want children. And now, mysteriously, part of me did. And I already loved the children that I wanted Matt to give me.

This new self-awareness stunned me into silence.

But suddenly Matt didn't want children? He'd just said—

The power returned with a rising whirr. The AC chugged to life.

"Thank God," Matt said. He grabbed his pants and kissed my shoulder. "I'll fix the clocks." He scrambled out of the tent.

Chapter 24

MATT

Hannah and I viewed homes with Marion twice a week, on Tuesdays and Thursdays.

After Hannah got off work, we dined quickly and Marion picked us up in her Prius, the car and the woman always looking freshly polished. She was middle-aged and pleasant—not the pushy woman I expected, but a knowledgeable and confident realtor.

She avoided talk of my books, which I appreciated, but she had obviously done her research. To me, she often said, "This room would make an ideal office or library," and to Hannah, "This area is great for newlyweds—private, but with so much to do nearby."

We traipsed through three to five homes per day.

Ranch-style homes, two-family homes, suburban monstrosities, luxury townhouses.

The more we saw, the less we knew what we wanted, and the longer Marion's listing e-mails grew. I pitied her—and us. That July was insufferably hot and we attacked house-shopping like a New Year's resolution: at first with great energy and excitement, by the second week with diminishing zeal, and toward the end of the month with forbidding faces, dragging steps.

Marion pulled into a neighborhood just outside Denver.

"No," I snarled. "Too suburban. Head to the next."

She took us to a country home with a stunning view of the mountains.

"I don't want to see it," Hannah grumbled. "I'm not living in the sticks."

We argued. We returned home late, disillusioned and depressed. We wanted out of the condo—once, our sweet little nest—and we picked on it and everything. *If we had one extra room—one!—I wouldn't have to put away my fucking weights every day. Well, how do you think I feel about my yoga stuff? All I can hear is the fucking street. Then go live in your tent!*

Back and forth. More homes, nothing suitable. My Monday-morning sessions with Mike became one-hour rants about the state of housing in Colorado. Hannah left for work early and stayed late. I imagined her savoring the solitude of her office—a room of her own, which I couldn't seem to give her.

Our story continued. *Untitled*, a novel by Hannah Catalano and Matt Sky. We threw ourselves into it, making progress with words where we couldn't with homes. Four, sometimes five chapters a week, fired back and forth in frustrated volleys.

One evening over dinner, Hannah announced that Chrissy was twelve weeks pregnant.

"Wait . . ." She counted on her fingers. "Thirteen."

"Mm." I plowed my rice into a pile.

"She really wants to keep the baby. She quit smoking and everything."

"Ah." I rolled an olive around the rice.

"I guess pretty soon they'll be able to find out the gender."

"Yeah." I speared the olive on my fork.

I'd also quit smoking, though no one seemed to notice, and I was acutely aware of Chrissy's thirteen weeks to the day. I found myself Googleing strange things throughout the month. *When does pregnancy start to show? How long does morning sickness last? When can ultrasound determine gender?*

"If you don't want to talk about this, you can say so."

"Have you seen her?" I continued playing with my dinner, prolonging the meal. Dinner and sex were our last bastions of togetherness. And sleep. Just the necessities. Otherwise I was writing out my frustrations or searching the Internet for our nonexistent dream home, and Hannah was doing the same.

"No. We've talked a few times. Um . . ." She cleared her throat. "They did that prenatal DNA test thing. So that was confirmed."

"Ah . . . good to know."

"Yup. Not that she wasn't sure, but, double sure now. And he's back—"

"You can say his name." I frowned.

"Sorry. Seth is back east. Now that everything's confirmed, and Mom and Dad know, he's moving her into a place of her own. One of the Beauvallon condos, apparently."

"Oh. Those are . . . incredibly nice." My shoulders fell. I felt a plummeting sense of inadequacy. Nate had a family and a home. Seth had a pregnant girlfriend and he was providing for her. I lived in a hovel and wanted a family and couldn't bring myself to talk about it.

I flattened my rice tower.

Cue the self-pity.

"I was thinking of helping her move in, since we'll be close."

"Yeah." My mind spun unhappily, churning up bitterness. Maybe it was time for a new car. That Mercedes I'd been wanting . . .

"That was sort of a question."

"What?" I glanced at Hannah.

"I mean, I want you to be okay with the ways I help Chrissy, like we discussed."

"Oh." I waved a hand and began to clear the table. Cooking was Hannah's department; cleanup was mine. "Sure, help her move. Whatever you want."

I stood at the sink, static.

She slipped up and hugged me from behind.

"Thank you." She kissed my shoulder blade. "Her mood's been getting more stable. Our talks have been nice."

"Mm."

Another invisible strike against me. I couldn't, or wouldn't, repair my relationship with Seth. Meanwhile, my fiancée was a model of mercy and love.

Her fingers grazed my abdomen. I moved a plate to the dishwasher.

"Baby, I made some plans for us this weekend."

"Oh?" I tried to sound upbeat. Hannah's last weekend plan had been a *Godfather* movie marathon. She knew I loved those movies. All I remembered, though, was Marlon Brando drawling that "a man who doesn't spend time with his family can never be a real man." And I wouldn't talk about starting a family because fear locked me up every time I tried to think about it. And if I couldn't think about it, much less talk about it, I wasn't a real man. Clearly.

"The house-hunting is wearing us down. I'm not myself. Neither are you. And I know we're both growing out of this place." She rubbed my back. "So, I booked us a room at Four Seasons for tomorrow and Sunday. I thought we could—"

"Four Seasons?" I tensed. "Why there?"

"Because." She kissed my cheek. "I want to make some good memories there. Memories with you. We'll pack overnight bags, eat out, see a movie, whatever you want. Say yes . . ."

"Well . . ." I turned over the idea and found nothing wrong with it. We *were* worn down. Maybe a night out would help. "Yeah, all right."

"Awesome. I'm gonna pack." She hugged me and scampered out of the kitchen.

On Saturday, Hannah insisted we take a cab to the hotel.

"I don't want you to have to do anything," she said. "Not even drive."

I shrugged and called a cab. I liked driving, but she sounded adamant, and something told me tonight was personally important to Hannah. She'd talked about making "good memories" at

Four Seasons. In other words, she wanted to replace the bad memories of Seth.

I was more than happy to oblige.

Hell, I would fuck her so thoroughly that she forgot my damn brother existed. It might be cathartic for both of us.

We checked in at four.

In the elevator, Hannah fiddled with her purse and fluffed her hair. She was quiet—wouldn't look at me. I smirked and brushed her cheek. Mm, so she wanted it like that? Shy little bird . . . I'd hold her down, make her watch.

She wore a short, tight dress with a galaxy print, the lovelock necklace I gave her last year, and combat boots. She looked young and playful. Tempting. I squeezed her ass in the hallway and she jumped.

"I'm looking forward to you," I said quietly.

She stared at the carpet and my heart rate rose. God, she did everything right.

Her hands shook as she slid in the key card. I pressed against her, heedless of anyone else in the hall. Let them see us. Let them know we were about to fuck like animals.

We stumbled into the room.

The door dropped shut.

I breezed past her, tabling my lust for a moment.

She'd booked us a one-bedroom suite with a sweeping view of the city. A cream-colored sofa, chairs, and glass tables filled the adjoining living room. I flicked on a light in the bathroom: full marble with a deep tub.

Hannah hovered.

"It's perfect." I tucked a curl behind her ear. "Hungry?"

"Not . . . really. You?"

"No. I'll get you a drink. Calm your nerves a little." I nuzzled her neck. "But not too much. I like you this way."

I ordered up a bottle of Moscato and poured her a glass. We sat in the living room and I watched her drink, and I wondered what she was wearing under that tight little dress.

Hannah drained her glass with a rapid gulp.

"Look"—she grabbed her handbag—"I did something. I . . ."

With trembling hands, she pulled several folded papers from her purse and thrust them at me. Frowning, I smoothed the pages on the table.

DATE . . . July 26, 2014 . . . PARTIES . . .

Of course I would recognize a document such as this.

I had many on file, though they were obsolete now.

"Nondisclosure agreement," I muttered. I noted Shapiro's letterhead. I flipped through the pages and then returned to the top sheet. "Who the hell is Rachel Mox?"

"A . . . a stripper. There are two NDAs there. Don't get angry." Hannah poured herself another glass of wine and guzzled from it.

"A stripper? Baby . . ." I half-smiled, my head tilted. "What did you have in mind?"

"Not what you think. Not, like, a threesome or anything. Um, more like"—she withdrew my black notebook from her bag and opened to the first entry—"this."

Chapter 25

HANNAH

Matt stared at his own handwriting with a mixture of shock and bewilderment.

EXHIBITIONISM

Even upside down, the heading was legible. As for the entry itself, I knew most of it by heart: *I want to fuck her with an audience. I want to see her embarrassment. I want to make our most private act a spectacle.*

I took another gulp from my wineglass. My arm shook.

"You called Shapiro?" Matt paled. "For these?"

"Y-yes. But look." I separated the NDAs, one signed by Rachel Mox, the other signed by Nicole Williams. "None of the initial language was specific to—"

"So you didn't tell him anything about this?" He pointed at the journal.

"No. Not even a hint, I swear. I called him and said that I was planning a surprise for you, and could he draw up two NDAs preventing the participating parties from spoiling the surprise. That's it. I kind of said it was like . . . a big wedding gift." I cringed.

Matt almost smiled—a twitch of his lips—and then his expression darkened.

"Okay. Ah, I need . . ." He stood and began to pace between the table and the flat-screen, gesturing. "I need more, Hannah. Give me more."

If not for my massive anxiety and Matt's almost about to be rage, I would have admired him. Serious Matt was a thing to behold. His every motion was measured and tense; his gaze sharpened fearfully, as if he could see into the soul of a problem . . . and tear it out.

"I've thought a lot about this," I stammered, "and I w-wanted to do it. For you. But also for me. I got thinking about how, and where and when, and . . ." I poured out the story of Mission Exhibition, which had grown from an idle curiosity into a full-fledged plan.

My voice wavered at first, but as I continued talking, it evened and strengthened. I explained how I had visited Dynamite after work—not once, but three times—and observed the girls. I singled out a woman who seemed to relish the work, asked to speak with her privately, and asked for her discretion.

"You trusted her to be discreet?" Matt butted in. "Even that conversation could have been damning. People recognize you, and they know we—"

I held up a finger. *Shush.*

"I had her sign an NDA before we spoke in detail."

He narrowed his eyes, but he looked impressed. "Go on . . ."

"Well, it was kind of a leap of faith. I asked if she or anyone she knew was into, uh, alternative lifestyles . . . or entertainments. I told her about our experience in the back room at Dynamite. She picked up on my meaning quickly."

He snatched the NDAs off the table and scrutinized them.

"Is this why we're here? Do I want to know how much money was involved?"

"It's only why we're here if you want it to be." I paused. "Four hundred each. I let her set the price. Shapiro sent the paperwork as PDFs and I added in some specific clauses."

"And Nicole is . . ." He sounded exasperated and incredulous. "Is who?"

"A friend of Rachel. She's a swinger, not a dancer. I don't know them well, but they took the paperwork seriously and they understand what we want."

"Which is?" The NDAs fluttered onto the table. Matt drew close to me, his legs touching my knees. Denim against skin. I shivered and gazed up at him.

"Nothing but a silent audience," I said.

"Finish your wine."

I blinked and drained the glass. He touched my cheek.

"Where are they now?"

"I got them a room for the night. They understand we might not call. I've paid them for their time regardless."

"You trust these people?"

I nodded.

"Nicole is a paralegal. She told me so and I double-checked online. She's into this lifestyle; she appreciates the need for privacy. Plus she has something to lose. Rachel . . . I trust her to understand that she can't afford the type of lawsuit we would bring if she breached our contract."

Matt smirked, one golden eyebrow arched.

"How cutthroat, little bird. And so cunning."

"I've learned some things from you and your family."

His eyes widened, his smirk fell—then he laughed.

"Fair enough. You thought of everything, did you?"

I lifted my chin, a little shock of pride racing through me.

"Yes," I said. "I did."

His hand fell, his fingertips leaving cool trails down my cheek. I must have been blushing from my hair to my toes, but I felt calm. The sort of calmness at the center of a storm.

He walked toward the door and stopped.

He shoved his hands in his pockets and stared at the carpet.

I was past wondering if I really wanted to try this, or what it meant about me that I was willing to try. Matt had shared his fantasies with me freely. After the night I gave him the whip, his journal lived on our bedside table. It was no longer a secret or an object of shame, but an open invitation to his mind.

I reread it when I was alone. I let it excite me. I let the strangeness and wildness of his desires sink into me; and his self-criticism, I treasured that, too.

What's wrong with me? I'm ashamed of myself. Confused by myself.

Oh, Matt . . . I ached to hold him when I read those words. He was the freest man I knew, but something—maybe regard for me—constrained him.

Tonight, I didn't need to rethink my decision.

I'd thought about it and planned it for weeks.

I studied his back, my head light with wine, until he turned and said, "Call them."

So much for my eye of the storm.

As soon as I heard a knock on the door, my Zen turned to panic.

Was I out of my mind?

"Stay put," Matt said.

I did, gladly. My limited store of courage had gone into sharing Mission Exhibition with Matt and risking his wrath. This was his rodeo now. I sank into the corner of the couch.

He greeted Rachel and Nicole at the door.

They smelled of floral perfume and looked . . . surprisingly classy, given the occasion. Nicole wore white linen shorts and a beaded sweater. She'd straightened her thick, black hair. Bronzing powder gleamed on her chocolate skin. Rachel, whom I'd seen previously in stilettoes, a thong, and gold-star pasties, wore a simple black dress and carried a clutch.

"Come," Matt said. He led them into the bedroom, where he'd arranged two chairs near the foot of the bed. From the living room, I heard his low, calm voice, and their voices. I couldn't make out what was said, but everyone sounded pleasant, as if we were getting together for tea.

God help me . . .
You can leave!

The thought obtruded sharply. Yes, I could leave. I could dart out the door while Matt and the women were in the bedroom. He would understand . . . wouldn't he?

He strolled into the living room and I sucked in a breath.

"Hi," he said.

"Hi."

"Sweet thing." He took my hand and I stood, fighting the urge to fall against him. If I showed my anxiety, he might call off everything, and I'd worked so hard to accomplish this . . . for both of us. He pulled me close and stroked my face and hair. "You all right?"

"Yes."

"Truly?" He chuckled. "Because I think you're nervous, which would be appropriate."

"Maybe . . . a little. Aren't you?"

He cocked his head and shrugged, as if normal criteria didn't apply to him. *Fuck,* he was cute. I laughed and leaned against his chest, drawing comfort from him.

"I want this," he said. "You know how much I want it. I can't believe you . . . arranged it, that you're even willing to try. Am I dreaming?"

"You're not dreaming." I kissed his throat.

"Be just like this. Like we're alone. Ignore them. I'll take care of you." He led me into the bedroom. Rachel and Nicole gazed placidly at us, their legs folded, wineglasses in their hands. I was instantly aware of them.

Ignore them.
How?

Matt knew how, apparently. He dimmed the bedside lamp—the only light—to a soft amber glow. I had interfaced so boldly with Rachel and Nicole in the past few weeks, but now I could barely lift my eyes. They became indistinct shapes on the edge of the room.

He tugged me into his arms and kissed me. As if we were alone, his hands went straight for my ass, squeezing and pulling.

My short, elastic dress rode up.

Cool air hit the skin of my bottom, which peeked out. Matt turned us so that my back faced our audience. *Oh God . . . they could see . . .*

The first small tongues of desire licked at me.

He broke the kiss and panted in my ear. His fingers gathered my dress higher, up over my ass. Nothing covered me but the strip of a thong.

"Fuck," he whispered.

I gasped. I knew they could see and were looking, and that Matt's growing hardness owed to that knowledge. He parted my cheeks, lifted my ass, slapped it. In front of them. I buried my face against his chest, burning with arousal and embarrassment.

Again, he turned us, leading our dance.

His back to them, my body hidden behind his tall frame.

"Go on." His husky voice hit my ear. "Do it to me. Show them."

I froze, my wine-soaked mind churning. *Huh?*

I peered up at Matt. He moved my hands to his fly and nodded. *Oh.* A wave of heat rolled over me as I understood.

I held his gaze as I undid his jeans and shimmied them off his hips.

"Boxers, too," he said calmly.

I licked my lips. *My God.* This moment. It had everything to do with us, and nothing to do with the onlookers. What Matt must have felt when he bared my bottom to them, I felt as I pushed down his boxers. My nails grazed his exposed ass. Pride, not jealousy, lanced through me. He was mine to touch. Mine to undress.

His breath came faster. I squeezed his ass and he groaned.

"You see?" he gasped. He pulled off his T-shirt and dropped it. I knelt, dragging his boxers and jeans down his thighs, my hands devouring him. He kicked away the garments.

Fuck. Matt said he would take care of me, and he was. He shielded my body with his. He let me reveal him completely.

When I stood, he turned to face our silent audience. I hugged him from behind, my cheek pressed against his back. He inclined his head toward me. Smiled.

"Show them all the little things you do . . . that drive me mad."

I envisioned us through Rachel and Nicole's eyes: Matt's nude, stunning body, and my hands devouring him. I stroked his stiff cock and massaged his balls. I caressed his abdomen. *Mine. All mine.* I laid a hand over his racing heart.

"Close your eyes," he said before we traded places. "I'm steady behind you."

I closed my eyes, and I kept them closed as he undressed me and touched me. He showed me off wordlessly—bending me over, sitting me down on the bed and spreading my legs, then spreading my sex and putting his fingers inside.

I could feel their eyes on me there, and Matt's trembling excitement.

He entered me. Covered my body. Nothing for Rachel and Nicole to see but his muscled back, his strong thighs and ass, and that most intimate motion that brought him against me, again and again, until we both unraveled.

But that unraveling wasn't the half of it.

I couldn't forget how it felt to own him. The fierce, simple trust in his eyes when he told me to do it to him. *I'm steady behind you.* Words I believed. Words I believed for my life.

"Open your eyes," he said.

I did, and we were alone.

Chapter 26

MATT

"When did you send them out?" Mike said.

I smiled and shrugged. "Does it matter?"

"To my curiosity, yes." He shook his head, but he looked pleased, and I felt one of my rare surges of gratitude for my psychiatrist.

I had spent the better part of my appointment describing Saturday night at Four Seasons. I told Mike how I shared my journal with Hannah, and how I whipped her, and how she organized my wildest fantasy into a reality.

"It's jarred us out of our frustration," I said. "I mean with the house-hunting. I feel . . . refreshed." I leafed through my journal, which contained no new entries. I studied a bare page. "Some fantasies one expects to remain in the realm of fantasy. I'd thought exhibitionism was one of those. This has been . . ."

I closed the journal, which had been more than a useful tool.

"Well, thank you," I finally managed.

"You don't need to thank me. Without Hannah's open-mindedness, the journal would have been nothing but a sounding board for your thoughts. Thank *her*."

"I have."

"Good. I don't mind saying I wasn't sure about her role in your well-being—whether she was good or bad for you. But that's clear to me now. She seems very extraordinary."

"She is," I said.

"If you would consider a group session or two . . ." Having triumphed with my aberrant desires, Mike started in on the efficacy of group therapy and marriage counseling. I could only laugh. I felt sure he was right—a few appointments with Hannah, Mike, and me might smooth out our engagement—but I wasn't ready to talk about children, and I knew we would end up talking about children.

First, I needed to settle that score with myself. Did I want children, or didn't I? I thought I did. I considered the idea, I imagined the child, my mind lurched through a reel of happy images, and then horror seized me and I recoiled.

Too much happiness . . . is a dangerous thing.

I'd tried to explain that to Hannah in our story, just as I'd tried to explain it to her when we drove through my hometown in June.

We were happy, I wrote, *with this happiness so cosmically unfair . . . I knew it couldn't last . . . that somehow I would have to pay for it.*

I e-mailed Chapter 10 to Hannah on Tuesday. We wouldn't have time to discuss it—I didn't want to discuss it—because we had a full evening of showings with Marion.

Hannah got home early and changed into jeans and a T-shirt. We ate a quick dinner of takeout Chinese.

I pulled on my Brooks, my favorite running shoes, and we grinned at one another.

We'd been doing that—grinning dopily at one another—ever since the weekend and Mission Exhibition's completion. We spoke about it remarkably little. To me it was surreal, a moment in time that too much talk might jeopardize, and it must have been the same for Hannah.

Later, we could process it into writing.

For now, it had revitalized us, just as I'd told Mike, and we were excited to hunt for our future house. Our future home.

I let Hannah sit up front with Marion. First we drove to Pradera, a community of luxury homes in Parker. Hannah frowned at the colossal house, but she listened and held my hand as Marion extolled the four-car garage, the hickory hardwood, granite counters, oversize laundry room, and finished basement.

I loved it.

Hannah endured it.

Next, as we toured a two-story shanty in Longmont, I tried to show her the same courtesy. I sort of smiled at the bland siding, the postage stamp of a yard, and the window through which we could literally pass notes to our neighbors. *Awesome.*

"Cute place," Hannah said as we climbed back into the Prius.

I grimaced.

"I want to show you a new listing out in Clear Creek County, different from this and very exciting." Poor Marion sounded defeated. "Is a thirty-minute commute feasible?"

"That's up to Hannah," I said. "There's not much I need in Denver."

Hannah shrugged. "I'm willing to look."

We traveled west, toward Mount Evans. The city receded; flat land gave way to foothills. Sometimes Marion talked up a listing as she drove, but she said nothing about the Corral Creek place. Maybe she hadn't familiarized herself with it.

We turned onto a dirt road and Hannah glanced back at me.

I frowned and shrugged. *No idea.*

"Here we are," Marion said. We pulled through an open gate. The road extended into a meadow toward pine-covered hills. Lodgepole fencing followed the curve of the land as far as I could see. Where was the house?

Spruce and aspen were interspersed through the meadow. The sun was going down, showing the land to great effect. Long shadows and golden light. Fringes of prairie grass shining like torch heads.

I have always had a weakness for meadow landscapes, and I felt my soul expanding to let in that place.

"As you can see," Marion said, "the property is extremely private and secluded, but just a thirty-minute drive to the amenities of Denver. The ranch covers two hundred and ninety acres and one-fourth mile of Corral Creek, which—"

"Ranch?" I blurted. "Two . . . what?"

"Yes, this tract was originally a gentleman's ranch and summer home for the—"

"Ah, could we"—I touched Hannah's shoulder—"step out briefly?"

"Sure, of course." Marion parked and remained in the car while Hannah and I stumbled around to one another. Cool, pine-scented air and stillness surrounded us.

I snagged her hand and pulled her into the meadow.

Several yards from the Prius, we stopped.

"Is she out of her mind?" I laughed. "Have we finally driven her crazy?"

"Maybe she took us out here to shoot us." Hannah giggled.

"Right? I mean, Jesus." I stared at the vista. "Did you hear that shit? A creek? Almost three hundred acres? Hannah, that's more land than . . . I even know what to do with. I'm sorry, I"—I wrung my hands—"we'll have to be clearer with her."

"Yeah, for sure." She glanced at me and then at the meadow and mountains. "I mean, it's definitely beautiful."

"Oh, very. Too bad it's so, ah . . ."

"Crazy?" she offered.

"Yeah, ridiculous."

I cleared my throat and we stood there in silence, surveying the land.

In retrospect, I realize we were feeling one another out. The house itself didn't matter. Nothing could be said against that land and its absolute beauty. Thick groves of trees stood in the distance, filled with mystery, and forest carpeted the mountainside. I wanted to be there when night fell. How powerful that night would be, and the wind and the stars.

196 | M. Pierce

I wanted to own it. I had never conceived of owning so much land, and maybe part of the allure was the insanity of it.

And now, I thought, *you have to say good-bye to it. Hannah would never*—

"Let's see the house," she said.

"What?"

"Just for fun." She toed the earth. "We came all this way."

I led her back to the car, the phrase "just for fun" digging at me. See the property of your dreams, *just for fun!* Rub salt in your wounds, *just for fun!*

"Honestly, I'm not sure I want to see it," I said.

"Well, I do."

I frowned as we got back in the car.

"Stunning, right?" Marion smiled uncertainly at us. I glared out the window. *Fuck all this house-shopping, and so much for my rejuvenated mood.*

"It really is," Hannah said. "Can we see the house?"

"Just for fun," I muttered. No one heard me.

"Of course!" Marion stepped on the gas and we rolled deeper into that gorgeous world. It closed around us and filled me with longing. I must have looked like a little boy staring out the window. *Can I have it, please?*

Marion pointed out "improvements" as she drove: a paddock, a horse barn, another, smaller barn and a cabin.

I refused to look at Hannah, who was probably snickering.

The house stood on the northwestern side of the property, at the base of a large rock outcropping. It was, quite simply, the killing blow to my hope—a chateau-style refurbished lodge with a white stone exterior and a giant, solid joke of a front door.

A joke, yes. This house and land were a practical joke at my expense.

Nine bedrooms. Six bathrooms. Five fireplaces.

I sneered at the rustic, elegant interior. Light wood and pale stone gathered the day's last sun. Hannah squealed in the kitchen, skirting around the granite island like a child.

"So beautiful," she said.

"And completely modernized with new appliances," Marion put in.

On the second floor, they tried to lure me into one of the two libraries.

"You'll like this," said Marion, and Hannah yanked my sleeve. "Matt, look how many shelves this place has."

"I don't want to see it," I snarled. "I'm tired." I threw myself into a nook at the end of the hall. Hannah's phone buzzed.

"I'll give you two a moment." Marion drifted down the hallway.

As Hannah thumbed her cell, I stared out the window at the blue evening.

I pretended it was all mine.

Soon, I could go for a run across the meadow, or an ambling walk with Hannah. Two hundred and ninety acres. We could get lost . . .

"Shit," she said.

I snapped out of my daydream.

"What's going on?"

"It's . . . Seth. Well, Nate." She wiggled her phone. "He texted me. Seth was in the hospital last weekend. They just released him. God, why didn't we hear about this sooner?" She stabbed at the screen.

My dark mood shifted.

"Why was he in the hospital? Who are you texting?"

"He collapsed after a show on Friday. And I'm texting *Nate*." She glared at me. "He didn't say what happened, exactly, but I'm pretty sure we can guess . . ."

With Marion in hearing range, Hannah just gestured.

I snatched her phone and read her half-written text.

Out with Matt. Will call ASAP. Pls give more

"More *what*?" I said. "*Out with Matt*? What the fuck? How long have you been—"

"More details, obviously. Give me that." She pried her phone from my hand. "What is wrong with you?"

"I almost put him in the fucking hospital myself. Do you realize that? I don't care how much he fucks up his life right now. When are you going to get that? I despise him."

"Well, I don't. And Nate doesn't. When are *you* going to get *that*?"

"We are getting married, for God's sake." I slammed my palm into the wood-paneled wall. Hannah flinched. It was the first anger I gave that house, but not the last.

"That doesn't mean you get to tell me how to feel about people. Your brother is sick. He's suffering. You should empathize."

Seth's invisible intrusion into my night, which was already going so poorly, infuriated me. Why did Hannah continually throw herself between Seth and my rage? Couldn't she see that she was at the heart of that rage? Seth touching her . . . Seth trying to take her from me . . .

"I am done . . . talking about him." I made my voice low. It shivered with emotion. "Done for good. Stop bringing him up. I am not going to fucking forgive him."

Tears shimmered in Hannah's eyes—whether from frustration or sadness, I couldn't tell.

"You are always so upset," she said. "Always. You don't know how to be happy."

"That's not fucking true."

"It is." The first tear rolled down her cheek, and then the next. And I hated Seth, and the possibility that she might be crying for him. "I found this listing. I actually thought you would like it. I sent it to Marion"—she snuffled loudly—"for a surprise for you. Y-you said to meet you in the middle, but there is no middle with you! You don't like anything!"

She started to cry in earnest.

I grabbed her wrist, my eyes wide.

"What?"

"M-maybe you don't want to live w—"

"You said you didn't . . ." I stood swiftly and cradled Hannah. In spite of her anger, she clung to me. ". . . didn't want to live in the sticks. I don't understand."

"Thirty minutes from Denver *isn't* the sticks."

"Hannah. Bird." I kissed her damp cheeks. I wiped away her tears until only her lashes were dewy. "Would you seriously live here?"

"Yes." She laughed—a little hysterically—and her eyes filled again. "I would. I'm tired of the city, tired of the condo. And I know it's . . . ridiculous and huge, but . . . we could get people to take care of the—"

Seth faded from my mind like a ghost, paler and thinner . . . gone. My anger faded with him. I lifted Hannah off her feet and I turned and turned, laughing.

Chapter 27

HANNAH

"You can touch it," Chrissy said, frowning at the subtle swell of her stomach. "If you want to, I mean. I just hope random women don't try to touch me. Ew."

I eyed my sister's belly. At seventeen weeks, she definitely had a baby bump. The band of her yoga pants hung beneath it and her tank top stretched over it. I wondered if that was good for the baby. *Poor little guy . . . or girl.*

I looked away.

"I'm good, thanks. Maybe when it's . . . kicking and stuff." I laughed nervously. The idea of feeling something moving in my sister's stomach appealed to me less than touching the bump. Was I lacking normal maternal instincts?

Whatever the case, I planned to support my sister all the way. She didn't need to know that pregnancy, well, freaked me out.

"Hey, I can't get over how nice this place is. Seriously, you live in a palace." I gave Chrissy's new digs a sweeping look. For the past three and a half weeks, I'd spent all my spare time in moving mode: angsting over the Corral Creek home inspection, boxing up stuff at the condo with Matt, and driving Chrissy and her piles of junk to and from our parents' house and her swanky new down-town condominium.

"Right? I kind of hit the jackpot." Chrissy traipsed through the living room, which was filled with stylish furniture, to the wrap-around balcony. Denver sprawled below.

"I mean, it's really . . . nice that Seth set you up like this."

"Nice? I guess so. It's the least he could do, if you think about it."

I pursed my lips. I didn't want to get into a fight with Chrissy. Still, I didn't like her tone: the jackpot, the idea that Seth owed her anything. *It takes two, Sis.*

"Have you heard from him much?" I said.

"Sure, we talk all the time."

"How does he seem?"

"Fine. Busy." She folded her arms over her stomach and beamed at me. "Can you believe we're dating brothers?"

"It's . . . pretty crazy." Again, I wanted to snap at her. I wasn't *dating* Matt. We were engaged to be married. Our love was real and trial-tested, whereas Chrissy's only hold on Seth, as far as I could tell, was the baby.

But maybe she sensed that, and maybe her attitude grew out of insecurity.

"I'm sure he'll move in here when he's not touring so much." She hummed and fluttered the drapes. "He wants me to get an ultrasound to see about the gender, but I'm waiting for him."

"Waiting—what do you mean?"

"I think it's something we should do together. Hey, are you gonna give me that, or what?" She looked at the flat cardboard box in my hand, one of Matt's old shirt boxes. I had tied a purple ribbon around it.

"Oh, yeah." I handed it to her. "I just came over to give you that, really. Kind of a housewarming thing, now that you're settled."

While she opened the box, I tucked my fingers into my pock-ets and surveyed the condo again. Matt still wanted nothing to do with helping Chrissy, but at least he "let me" help her. My arms

ached from carrying boxes and moving furniture—heavy lifting
that my pregnant sister couldn't do. In a matter of weeks, she'd
transformed from carelessly smoking mother-to-be to neuroti-
cally terrified of anything that might harm her baby.

More proof, I thought, that she viewed the baby as a means to
an end.

That end being Seth Sky.

She'd quit her job at the Dynamite Club, taken up prenatal
yoga, and, with a stipend from Seth, started eating organic. But I
wasn't buying it. The baby was a nuisance to Chrissy before Seth
stepped into the picture.

"A . . . lantern?" She lifted the collapsed lantern from the box.
The thin paper, turquoise-colored with circling koi, opened into
an orb. Tears pricked at my eyes. This was the lantern I'd hung in
my basement bedroom last year when I moved back home. It was
a spot of color in my haze of depression. The first time Matt had
visited my bedroom, he'd noticed the lantern.

He wrote about it in *Night Owl.*

Damn, the room was small, made smaller by Hannah's queen-
size bed and piles of boxes. The only window was high and narrow.

She'd hung a paper lantern from the ceiling. The sight of it
tugged at my heart.

Now, the sight of the lantern tugged at *my* heart. What a long
way Matt and I had come . . . full circle, it seemed. Writing together, living together. I blinked back emotion.

"For good luck," I said. "I better get going."

"I hope I don't need luck." Chrissy laughed and tossed the box
onto a couch. "Thanks, Han. It's adorable. Are you going to call
your mystery man?"

I froze.

"What?"

"Ha! You look guilty. I've seen you from the balcony, always
out there on your cell."

"I'm . . . planning wedding stuff," I said. "And house stuff. Yeesh. And soon I'll be calling you for dinner dates with Mom and Dad, so don't be dodging me."

I scuttled out.

Whoa, Chrissy had noticed me making calls? Good thing she and Matt weren't on speaking terms. That day, I waited until I was safe in my Civic to take out my cell and make a call.

"Hannah," Nate answered. "Hi."

"Hey. How is everything?"

"Fine, thank you. Congratulations on the house closing. Shouldn't you be knee deep in boxes, or maybe learning to drive a tractor?"

"Pfft." I laughed. "We'll hire people to help with the land. And thank. We're so excited. We've been moving stuff slowly. It's a process. I don't know why Matt won't get a company for the move; something about the *experience* . . ."

I rambled awhile, giving Nate details on the Corral Creek house and closing. It had happened quickly, inside of a month. The owners had moved to California and were eager to sell. We offered, they countered, and because Matt was impatient, we paid just shy of the asking price, five and a quarter million. Whew.

"And he's been elated. It's worth it just to see him this way, he's . . ."

"Like a boy, I know." Nate chuckled. "His happiness is something else. He's been sending pictures. That is quite the piece of property. I eagerly await my invitation."

"Don't be silly. Come any time." My big smile started to fade. "Anyway, I'm calling—"

"To ask about Seth. I know." A pause. "Should I be worried?"

"Huh? I don't know. You tell me."

"Not about Seth." He sighed. "About the degree of your concern, Hannah."

The degree of my . . . ? I almost dropped my iPhone.

"Uh, no. Er . . . it's nothing . . . nothing like that, I—"

"I don't mean to put you on the spot, but you can see why I worry. Your concern is very touching. Of course, Seth is involved, and I know there's some history." Nate sounded effortlessly blasé, while I wanted to disappear beneath my car. "The fact is, I feel a little guilty, and I wonder if Matt shouldn't know how often you—"

"No! Nate, you can't tell him. I'll call less. Or not at all." I pressed my forehead against the steering wheel. *Stupid!* Of course all this Seth-worry sounded suspicious, but . . . "Who else can I talk to? Chrissy doesn't think anything is wrong, Matt doesn't care, and I can't be calling Seth and asking *him* how he is. That leaves you."

"As far as I can tell, he's fine. Touring on the West Coast. His discharge papers from last month cite exhaustion as the cause of the collapse."

"Okay . . ."

"I worry, too." Nate sighed in my ear. "But there's only so much I can do."

Untrue, I thought. Nate had done much more when Matt was in trouble. And sure, Seth wasn't drinking himself to death, but couldn't it get there?

We said good-bye and I ended the call.

My face slowly resumed a normal temperature as I drove home.

Maybe I couldn't see straight about this Seth issue. Maybe there *was* no problem, just a tired, hardworking lead singer, and maybe I felt extra guilty for fooling around with him and for the faked death fiasco . . . which must have hurt him so terribly.

If only I could talk to him. I could call him. I should.

"God, just let it go," I said aloud to myself.

Matt was moving boxes in our barren living room. Laurence shuffled and stamped. The chaos frightened him.

Matt smiled when he saw me.

Oh, that sight dispelled my cares—shirtless Matt, every muscle in his torso defined as he lowered a box. BIRD'S BOOKS, he'd written on the cardboard. I smiled softly back at him.

"Hi," I said.

He came to me and kissed me full on the mouth. "Hi . . ."

We did our dopey-grinning routine, which had only gotten

worse since we'd acquired a house, and packed quickly for our first weekend at the new place.

Our first weekend at the new place.

We hadn't even moved our bed.

We slept on an air mattress on Friday night and in the tent, in the meadow, on Saturday. As I watched Matt, I remembered what Nate had said: *His happiness is something else.* It was.

He stormed around the house, dragging me with him.

"Look at this room." Ducking in and out of bedrooms. "Look at this window! This view!" And then he had to go out, onto our land.

"Hannah, we *own* this," he kept telling me. "Look at it. Look!"

I would look with him and see the field, the trees and layers of hillside . . . beautiful, magnificent, no doubt about it . . . but I never saw quite what he saw. Whatever he saw drove him a little crazy. "It provokes me," he tried to explain, charging toward this or that glen. "It's the same thing I feel when I look at you. I want to have an experience of you, possess you . . . in a way that I don't understand."

I didn't ask for clarification. He was deliriously excited, and his excitement passed into me like a current. All day he was a boy—all night, some kind of animal, making love to me as if his life depended on it.

On Sunday evening, we built a fire in the great room—a fire, in August!—and sat on the cool stone floor. A wall of windows gave view to Mount Evans. Night came down cinematically, and I realized I hadn't been online, watched a TV show, or even listened to music all weekend. I hadn't wanted to. Matt and this place absorbed me.

I smiled and nestled against him.

The phone rang—the single phone we'd plugged in—and I jumped. Matt smoothed a hand across my brow. "Nate," he said. "Or Ella or Rick. I wanted to test the landline." He kissed my temple and jogged out of the room.

I grinned and admired the view.

"It's Nate," he called a moment later, his voice echoing down the hall. He sounded so pleased with himself. I laughed and flopped onto a pile of pillows.

Several minutes passed.

The fire started to die and I let it.

Shadows and light flickered on the wall.

Gosh, this place would be a little creepy if I were alone. I sat up and hugged myself. Well, Matt didn't really go places without me . . . plus, we'd get a dog or two.

I stood and stretched.

I thought I heard the front door, which made me laugh.

Crazy boy. He kept going outside! He could barely stand to look out the window without vibrating like an excited dog—and then, *whoosh*, he'd go stalking out the door.

I padded down the hall.

"Matt?"

A faint, angry digital pulse grew louder as I walked. I turned into the kitchen. The cordless phone lay on the counter, the off-hook tone blaring.

"Damn it," I muttered, slamming it into the cradle.

I hate that sound.

The phone began to ring and I yelped. I checked the caller, my heart hiccuping.

TRENTON, NJ.

I picked up quickly.

"Nate, I am so spooked! I just—"

"Hannah, where's Matt?"

"Um, I think he's"—I drifted toward the front of the house—"out in the yard?" I laughed. "But there's a lot of yard—"

"Listen. Can you find him? Can you see him?"

The first rising note of panic sounded in my brain. *Something is not right. Nate's voice is wrong . . . different.*

"It's dark . . . it's getting dark." I cupped a hand against a window and peered out at blackness and my reflection. "I can't—"

"Go out and call for him. Keep the phone. Stay on the line."

"Nate, what's—"

"Hannah, go."

I'd never heard Nate speak like that—with that kind of anger and urgency. I ran to the front door, which hung open. Looking at it, and the panel of night beyond, I wanted to cry.

"I'm scared," I said, stepping outside. "What's happening?"

"It's okay. Just call for him."

I lowered the phone and called Matt's name. Somehow, I knew he wasn't there, but I strained to see. Maybe if he heard me . . .

"Matt!" I screamed. "Matt!"

The evening swallowed my voice and sent back no echo.

Chapter 28

MATT

"I tried your cell," Nate said, "and Hannah's."

"Oh, I don't even know where they are." I laughed and leaned against the island, smiling indulgently at my new kitchen. *Our* new kitchen. "We're living like hippies. This place—"

"Could you sit down? Is Hannah around?"

"She's nearby." My smile fell. "What's up?"

"I'd like it if she were—"

"Tell me what the hell is going on." My heart began to pulse palpably, audibly in my chest. My mind went to the baby. Yes, the baby—Chrissy and Seth's child—which Hannah seemed to think I didn't care about, but which was never far from my thoughts.

"Okay. All right, I'm sorry." Nate's voice broke. "It's Seth. Please, go get Hannah." He started to cry—guttural, shivery sounds. Horrible sounds. He apologized and begged me to call Hannah. He said that he would come to see me.

I began shaking like a frightened animal.

"God, please," I said. "What's happening?"

This is the big breath before you go under.

* * *

I ran barefoot down the dirt road.

Stones and burrs tore at my soles.

Get on the grass, I thought, and I did, but the grass was dry, full of points and toothy vines. Nothing is kind.

I searched for the creek. I don't know why. Everywhere, I thought I heard its whisper.

I fell and lay in the road.

Headlights came bouncing toward me. I crawled into the grass.

The car crunched to a stop and I pressed my face against the earth.

"Hey, are you all right?" called a baritone voice.

Go away. I breathed in dust and coughed, my spittle tangy with adrenaline. A car door closed and hushed voices bickered quickly. *I'm exhausted*, I realized. My eyes wanted to stay shut. I felt the energy going out of me and the deep, sweeping pull of sleep.

I won't be able to find the creek.

I could barely make a fist.

"Hello, sir?" said the voice, closer now. A shadow blocked the high beams.

I flopped over and gazed at the man.

"I fell," I said.

"Okay, son. You look pretty torn up. You alone out here?"

I wasn't alone. I probably wasn't far from the house. I didn't know, though, and the man asked too many questions. I closed my eyes as he propped me up in the grass.

"I'm calling the cops," said a higher voice.

Oh, she sounded angry.

"We're going to help you find your people," said the man.

When I opened my eyes, I saw a little boy peering at me from the backseat of the car. The way he looked at me, I knew I was becoming a memory—slightly menacing, surely strange. *Remember that man we found by the side of the road, all dazed and scratched up?*

I felt sorry for him, because he was just a kid.

You don't know what you're getting into, being born.

Chapter 29

HANNAH

Nate Sky talked me through the worst night of my life—a night I have convinced myself I deserved. Didn't Matt and I play with death once? We did. I lied and pretended; he wore it like a cheap Halloween mask.

Now it had come to collect.

"Sit down somewhere," Nate said. "You stay on the phone. Matt might be in trouble. Listen and do what I say—it's important."

Then he explained that Seth's heart had stopped.

"He was found in his hotel room. He was partying all weekend."

"Where is he now?"

"Hannah. He's gone."

"Okay," I said. But it wasn't okay. But it had to be okay. Now I understood. My mind began to spin at the speed of panic. "You told Matt?"

"Yes. Are you sure he isn't in the house?"

"Pretty positive. I'll check right now." I was already on my feet, running. I flicked on lights as I went. *Flash, flash, flash.* That huge house lit up room by room. Would I find Matt curled in a corner? Sprawled on the floor?

Gruesome images intruded.

"Get your cell and his. Keep them with you. Call nine-one-one."

I started to shake—*call 911?*—and forced myself to be still.

"What do I say? Are you sure?"

"Yes. This is an emergency. I'm not sure if you . . ." He trailed off, then started over. "Tell them your fiancé just received news of his brother's death and has gone missing. Give them the timeline. Tell them there's a history of suicide attempt."

Again, the shaking.

Again, I made myself relax.

"Okay. Calling now. I'll call from my cell. Be right back."

I dialed 911, which I had never done before, and after a series of quick questions, the dispatcher told me police and EMS were on the way. She instructed me to remain calm and double-checked my address. "Do not leave the residence," she said. When she told me I could hang up, I ended the call robotically.

"Thank you, Hannah," said Nate. "Are you okay?"

"Uh . . . no, yes . . ." I touched my chest and forehead. I couldn't actually tell if I was okay. My mind kept spinning, spinning—*this is an emergency, Seth's heart stopped, Matt might be in trouble, I need you to stay calm.*

This was not a dream.

Despite the dispatcher's instructions, I walked around outside the house while I waited for the police. I called for Matt every few minutes. Chilly wind billowed through the meadow.

"The suicide attempt," I said to Nate. "Tell me about it."

"You didn't know?"

"I read about it online—last year, when Bethany outed him. *Fit to Print* published a bunch of stuff." Fear suppressed any embarrassment I might have felt. I spoke in a too-calm, measured voice, covering the receiver and lowering the phone when I hollered Matt's name. "The article wasn't detailed. It mentioned a psych ward . . ."

"Right. If—when we find him, we might want to move him for a while."

Move him. Code for "have him committed."
Over my dead body.

"Tell me what happened. We never talked about it." *But we should have,* I realized. I should have pushed Matt to tell me about his past instead of ignoring it or waiting for him to mention it. As if he ever would.

"There isn't much to tell. He . . ." Nate's confident tone wavered. "Our parents' passing . . . he never dealt with that. Emotionally. Psychologically. The drinking didn't help. He was in grad school, and . . . tried to overdose. He left a note."

"I'm sorry," I whispered. "Nate, I'm so sorry about—"

"Please. I'm not ready to discuss that."

My heart constricted. How could Nate compartmentalize so well? Seth Sky was dead. *No, God*—I couldn't believe that. Thumbs-up . . . we gave each other a thumbs-up after he cleaned the word "slut" off my car. I saw his sad smile. He was so alive.

"When he got sober," Nate continued, "he wanted to leave everything behind. Ella and Rick, the East Coast. He bought a place in Montana and stayed there awhile, then moved to Denver . . . maybe to be close to his agent, I don't know. She was his only friend for a while."

I leaned against the house and shuddered.

Matt knew almost everything about me—he'd teased out my life story during our first few phone calls—and I knew almost nothing about him.

One dry, hoarse sob escaped me.

What if I never got the chance?

I slid to the ground, folding under the weight of guilt. Seth was gone. He'd needed someone, anyone, and no one helped him.

It would serve me right if Matt was gone, too, because I didn't deserve him. He'd come alongside me for a while, never belonging to me, and now he was gone.

"Hannah, you've got to hold it together."

"I can't. How? How are you doing it?"

"Faith," he said.

"I don't have any faith."

I heard sirens—a faint tremolo growing louder—and soon I saw blue and red lights flashing in the dark.

When the police and paramedics arrived, I had to get off the phone with Nate, which made me cry.

"You're all right," he said. "I'm here; I'm not going anywhere. I'll be buying a ticket to fly out tomorrow. Call me back as soon as you can."

Then I sat in the kitchen with a female officer and told her everything.

Her partner searched the house.

Another group of officers combed the property, their flashlight beams glancing eerily off the windows and their calls making me flinch. *Matthew Sky! Matt Sky! Matt!*

Lost boy, I thought, just like Seth. And I had played a cruel game with Seth's heart. Matt had played a cruel game with Seth's mind. *I should disappear, too . . . join them . . .*

"Miss Catalano?"

"Huh? Sorry. What was the question?"

"We need some assurance from you that this isn't another hoax. We're exhausting lifesaving resources here and—"

"It's not a hoax." I rubbed my eyes. When the officers had arrived, they'd strolled up to the house—hands on belts, no hurry—exchanging weary looks. I couldn't blame them. Matt and I had cried "wolf" last year and the whole nation heard our cry. Search-and-rescue teams had risked their lives in the mountains, looking for the missing author. More than once, I'd sat down just like this, feeding lies to the police. People had grieved for him. Seth had grieved . . .

Tears of fear and frustration seeped into my fingers.

"Please," I said. "I'm sorry. Please find him."

Hannah, you've got to hold it together.

I sent up a prayer for strength.

I said to God: *Don't make me pay for my sins with his life.*

The officer's partner returned to the kitchen.

"All clear," he said. "I'm going to help outside."

An hour later, only one police car and the ambulance remained. The female officer began talking me through filing a missing-persons report. "You can do that tomorrow at the station," she said. Her radio buzzed. "Take notes on what you remember tonight—"

"You can't"—I clutched my cell—"you can't go. He has to be . . ."

What was Matt wearing? Why couldn't I remember?

"Ma'am, we have to—" Her radio buzzed again and a garbled voice said something. She walked away and responded. I clung to the counter.

Was this how my happiness ended?

"Miss Catalano," said the officer. "They've found him."

It turned out to be a family of three that had found Matt on a road beyond our property. Unable to get much information from him, they'd called the cops. Somewhere, wires got crossed. One car was taking Matt to the hospital while other officers responded to my call. Matt heard the word "hospital," panicked, and demanded to be taken home. He must have seemed cogent, because the officers turned and brought him back to the house.

They escorted him out of the car. He was barefoot and limping slightly. Bits of dirt and grass clung to his shirt, which was torn.

I ran and threw my arms around him. He didn't move. He wore a dazed expression, eyes unfocused, and let the officers handle him.

"We'd like to get him stabilized in the ambulance," said the female officer.

"He's fine." I stepped in the way.

"We can't be sure about that, given your call. Excuse me—"

The paramedics popped open the back of the ambulance and Matt's eyes widened. He pulled against the officer's grip.

"Mr. Sky, it's all right, we just want to make sure you're—"

His nostrils flared. He tried to yank his arm free and the two paramedics grabbed him. *Oh shit,* this was not going to end well.

"Stop it!" I shrieked. "Please." I forced my way to Matt and cupped his face. His wild eyes panned over mine. They didn't catch with recognition. "Matt, listen. We have to get in the ambulance, and then we'll get out. No big deal. Come on . . ."

I stepped backward and he followed.

We climbed into the ambulance together.

He sat on the stretcher while the paramedics checked his eyes and cleaned his feet, which were cut in several places. They kept asking for a verbal okay. I squeezed his hand.

"He's had a shock," I said.

"We need to make sure he's not *in* shock. We're trying to prevent—"

"I'm okay." Matt's voice silenced everyone. I stared at him and kissed his hand. The paramedics frowned at one another.

"There," I said, "he's okay. And his brother's a doctor and he's coming tomorrow, and he has a psychiatrist, and I'll watch him around the clock, so . . ."

The paramedics and I argued for twenty minutes—it felt like forever—while Matt sat on the stretcher and stared at his feet.

Finally, with a lot of "at your own risk" warnings, they left.

Matt was docile, completely tractable as I led him into the house.

I held his hand and took out my cell. I wanted to handcuff him to me. A firm grip was the next-best thing.

"I'm calling Nate, okay?" I said.

He gazed at the floor. *Fuck*, had I made a mistake in sending away EMS? The silence of the house closed around us. I tightened my hold on his hand.

I knew, I just knew, that if I'd let the paramedics take him to the hospital, and the physicians there got hold of his medical records, they would "move him" to a psych ward . . . medicate him, observe him, put those pitiful socks with paw-shaped grips on his feet. His room would have Plexiglas windows. His meals would come with only a plastic spoon.

I rubbed brimming tears across my sleeve. *You've got to hold it together.*

Nate answered the call instantly.

"Hannah, what's happening?"

"He's here. It's okay. Everything's okay."

I stumbled through a narrative of the night. Matt appeared oblivious. Now, it was Nate's turn to panic. "Can I talk to him?" he said. "I don't like this. He needs a hospital."

"Um, lemme see." I muffled the cell against my shirt. "Matt? You wanna talk to Nate?"

Matt's foggy stare stuck to the floor. He shook his head and I stroked his knuckles.

"That's okay, baby." I lifted the phone. "He can't talk right now."

"Hannah, goddamn it. Is he there?"

"Yes, and he's fine. He . . . said he doesn't want to talk. Maybe tomorrow."

Nate chastised me for dismissing the ambulance and demanded a picture of Matt, which I took and texted as we talked. I sort of angled the shot to avoid the muddled look on Matt's face. That would go away soon . . . *right?*

"If something happens," Nate said, "if he disappears again—"

"I've *got this*," I snapped, but cringed immediately. "Sorry. I'm sorry. It's been—"

"I know. Look, go on. Please call tomorrow. Call or text with any updates."

I gave Nate promises and assurances and said good-bye.

"He's doing fine," I told Matt as I led him up the stairs. Silence. I smiled and chattered away as if nothing had happened. A thought flashed through my mind—*am I the one in shock?*—but I dismissed it. I couldn't afford to worry about me right now.

In the bathroom, I cleaned his face with a damp washcloth and he pulled off his shirt.

"I'm . . . so sorry," I said. "About—"

He looked at me sharply. The motion startled me.

He shook his head once—a gesture I would learn meant *we aren't talking about that*—and climbed onto the air mattress in the bedroom.

Chapter 30

MATT

I eased my finger off the trigger of my pistol, relaxed my hands on the grip, and lowered the gun. The sound of its shot still sang in my ears. Four of the five cans that I had balanced on the fence now lay in the grass.

There is a clean, controlled violence in shooting. And now that I owned almost three hundred acres, I hardly needed to visit a range.

I left one can standing.

I walked back to the house, but circuitously, roaming through the woods and splashing cold creek water on my face.

Lately, I spent more time outdoors than in. Nate was visiting. Hannah worked from home. Mike made house calls three times a week. I had nothing to say to them, though. They suffocated me with their concern.

I slipped into the house by the back door, kicked off my boots in the mudroom, and hurried upstairs. I knew Hannah would be waiting for me in the family room. Sure enough—no sooner had I reached my study than I heard her bounding up the stairs.

I dropped into my armchair and glowered at the window.

The door opened; Hannah's head popped into the room, forced cheer on her face.

"You're back," she said.

That was self-evident.

I closed my eyes and listened as she walked across the room. I heard the heavy metal scrape of my pistol on the desk.

"Did you . . . put the safety on this thing?"

"No." I sighed.

"Do you want to shower? With me?"

I heard her drawing closer. I smelled her perfume, piquant and almost masculine. I usually loved that scent on her body, but right now it was cloying.

"No," I said. "I'm tired."

"Where have you been?"

I rested my head against the high back of the armchair. Some nights I drove to Denver and slept in our unsold, desolate condo. Other nights I camped on the Corral Creek property. Other nights I didn't sleep at all. I explored our land or walked around Denver. Why should I sleep if I wasn't tired? I preferred to sleep in the day, avoiding my battery of well-wishers with their painful, tedious questions.

How are you feeling?

Have you eaten?

Do you want to talk about Seth?

No. No. *Never.*

"Matt?"

"Mm."

"It's September," Hannah said. Her fingers sifted through my hair, which was getting too long, and over the scruff along my jaws. "Look." She turned the page on a wall calendar. I studied it from the armchair. Ah, yeah, I recognized that calendar: a gift with an appeal from The Nature Conservancy. September's page showed a beach at sundown, golden sand and rocks green with lichen.

I would not like to go there. I looked away.

"*Night Owl* comes out in paperback tomorrow. Can you believe that?" She kissed my mouth. I knew that I loved her and I wanted to hold her, but I lacked the energy. "I'm actually excited," she said. She sat on my lap and nuzzled my neck. "Have you been outside? You smell like pine. Matt . . ."

She cried for a while and told me she missed me.

"Hannah." Nate strode into the room. He held a cup of coffee, black, which he set on my desk. He guided Hannah off my lap. "Morning, Matt."

"Three's a fucking crowd," I said. I stood and brushed past them, heading for the bedroom. "Don't touch my gun," I said at the door.

I have a recurring dream.

In the dream, I drown my brother.

We played together when we were young.

I hold him under until he stops moving.

I killed my brother. I loved him. I killed him.

Chapter 31

HANNAH

"He's getting better every day." I cradled the cord-less phone between my shoulder and ear, both hands occupied with bracing a bowl and stirring batter. Muffins for Matt. I smiled. I loved to watch him eat. He never really ate with me now—he tore through the kitchen like a hungry animal, wolfing down the nearest thing—but he ate, and that's what mattered. "Oh yeah, more communicative about it all, more . . . just everything."

"That's great. God, such a relief." Pam sighed.

"It shouldn't be long before—"

"Hannah, please. Work from home for the rest of the year if you need. I understand. You have to let me know when I can visit, that's all I ask."

My smile dropped.

"I'm sure it'll be soon. Um, whenever he's ready. Is Laura in New York?"

We chatted about book stuff for a while and she let me go. As soon as I hung up the phone, I felt Nate's presence. I turned.

He was leaning in the kitchen doorway, head cocked. It gave me a rush of relief to see someone—anyone—besides my haggard reflection and wild Matt. Even under duress, Nate looked sophisticated and carefully put together. His black hair was clean and combed. He wore slacks and a thin charcoal sweater.

"Getting better every day?" he said. *"More communicative?"*

I resumed stirring the batter.

"In my opinion, he is."

"You're lying to Pam. You're lying to yourself. I can't stay out here forever, as much as I want to, and Ella and Rick will break down the door soon. When they do—"

"Stop."

"When they do, and when they find Matt stalking around with a loaded gun—"

"He has *never* talked about suicide." My hand trembled.

"They will have him committed. You can't stop them. And at this point, I'm not even sure it would be the wrong thing to do."

I bit my lip until it hurt. Then I breathed out.

"I realize you can't stay forever. I'm not letting anyone take him away."

"Do you think I don't love him and want him to get better?" Nate came around to look at me. "But what we're doing here? It's not working. He hasn't breathed a word about Seth. I'm not even sure if he knows Seth is gone. That person upstairs isn't my brother, and he isn't your fiancé. Where is he even spending the night?"

"He needs more time. It's only been a few weeks. Mike is coming tomorrow—"

"Perfect." Nate threw up a hand. "You invited that psychobabbling idiot back here?"

Nate and Mike did not see eye-to-eye. Mike wanted to shoot Matt full of benzos. He talked about "depression and features of catatonic excitement." Nate quoted from medical journals, raised his voice.

"Look, I think he can help. He's helped Matt through . . ." I looked down. "A lot."

"I think you're grasping at straws, but suit yourself. All I'm saying is that time is running out. Ella as good as told me they're coming out next month if they don't hear from him."

My heart fluttered strangely. *Stay in there*, I thought, because sometimes it seemed to want to burst out of my chest. I was holding myself together by sheer willpower.

I began to line the muffin tin with papers.

Nate loomed, wanting something that I would never give: Matt. If Matt went into the psych ward, I went into the psych ward.

I glanced up, expecting angry eyes. Instead, they were soft and sympathetic.

"I'm going to drag him out for a walk," Nate said. He patted my shoulder and left.

I spooned batter into the muffin tin and listened to Nate striding around the house. It was an old house and no one could move through it undetected. A creak here, a pop there, signaled even the lightest footfalls.

And I loved the house, in spite of everything. Twice, Matt and Nate and I had gone shopping for home décor. Those trips consisted of Matt glaring out the car window, sitting in back with Nate, and me driving and dashing in and out of stores.

I would return to the car with a basket or lamp and show it to the boys.

Nate and I would enthuse.

This will be great for one of the libraries. Maybe we could put this at the end of the hall. What do you say, Matt?

We thought the work of fixing up our home might bring Matt out of himself.

We were wrong.

He showed no interest in anything but getting away from us. He went out with the tent or his gun. He left his cell phone in the study. He drove sometimes to God-knows-where and returned with scratches and sleepless eyes.

He was changing . . . moving away from me. And how could I blame him? I knew what he saw when he looked at me or Nate or anyone.

He saw Seth.

The front door opened and closed. I slid the muffins into the oven, put on my glasses, and climbed the stairs to watch Nate and

Matt from a bedroom window. I loved to watch their walks, just like I loved to watch Matt eat. Seeing him in any semblance of normalcy gave me hope.

Matt, clearly irate, stormed across the meadow. Nate hurried to keep up. I could tell that Nate was talking, gesturing and laughing in his amiable way.

I cupped my hands to my mouth.

For eighteen days Nate had been here helping me. When he returned to his family and his medical practice, I would be alone. What then?

I rubbed my eyes and readjusted my glasses.

Nate and Matt grew smaller, two figures near a stand of aspen. The dark-haired brother and the light-. All the aspen on our property had changed, green to gold overnight. Those yellow leaves looked beautiful against the sky, but their beauty meant something terrible to me. *Goldengrove unleaving.*

Matt clung to Nate abruptly. Nate held his brother and stroked his hair. Then Matt crumpled to the ground at Nate's feet.

Nate stood there for a moment, speaking down at Matt and gesturing. *What the hell?*

The silence, the smallness of the spectacle, framed by a panel of window, entranced me.

Matt cowered; Nate shook his head and gestured sharply. Then he crouched, wrapping his arms around Matt. My trance broke. I dashed down the stairs and out of the house, sprinting across the meadow. "What are you doing?" I shouted.

Nate glared at me with red-rimmed eyes.

Matt was balled up, shaking.

"Telling him the truth," Nate said.

"And what exactly is that?" I slid to my knees and pulled at Matt. "It's okay, love . . ."

"That Seth's funeral is today. That our brother is dead. That we should be there."

"Stop it!" I gathered Matt into my arms. He wasn't crying, but his breath came hard and fast and he covered his face. Crying without tears, maybe. I held him until the shaking stopped.

* * *

That evening, Nate and I built a fire in the library across from Matt's study. Though Matt showed no interest in the house, I had filled the study with his favorite things—his desk and books, Laurence, his computer, notebooks, framed prints, and many little things meant to cheer him up (cut flowers, pictures of us, and some of the plush animals he'd given me).

For once, Matt was in the study, not out in the cold night.

I sat in an armchair from which I could see his door.

"I'll check on him, if you want," Nate said.

"No, that's okay. I will soon. Anyway"—I sighed and lowered my face into my hands—"he's fine, I'm sure. He's the same."

Despair opened up inside me.

Nate had done his worst today . . . and nothing happened. After collapsing in the meadow and shaking for a while, Matt had returned to his seething silence. He'd walked back to the house and locked himself in the study.

"I'm not sorry," Nate said, staring into the flames. "I would try anything."

"I wouldn't forgive you even if you were sorry."

He chuckled and I smiled bleakly.

"We can't be impatient with him," I said. "We can't inflict our desperation on him."

"What if he's sinking deeper? What if this is a small window of opportunity, a chance to pull him back, and we're wasting it?"

"Hey. Was it really . . . today?" I softened my voice and leaned forward. I couldn't answer Nate's questions; I shared his fears.

He walked to the mantel, braced an arm against it, and lowered his head like a man in prayer. *So, it was today.* A late-summer funeral in Oak Grove Presbyterian Cemetery. A small group of mourners, I imagined. Both living brothers . . . absent.

I pictured the cemetery and I remembered Seth saying he had a plot there. I remembered him alive. Could it be that he was in the ground?

I went to Nate and we seized one another.

"Oh, God," he said, clutching my back so hard it hurt. "I couldn't go. You saw it coming. I didn't. God help me. Now it's done. Hannah . . ." Nate cried in a terrible, suppressive way, with breathless, gasping gulps. I told him no one saw it coming. I told him no one could have done anything. Gradually, he let himself weep unrestrained. His tears dampened my hair.

We swayed together and his sadness and my hollow reassurances faded to silence.

Motion caught my eye.

I jolted away from Nate.

Matt stood in the library doorway, staring at us.

"M-Matt," I said. His eyes were calm and clear. I flapped my hands. "Hi. We—we were just being sad together."

"Matt." Nate wiped his face hurriedly.

"Let me get this," I whispered. I scurried over to Matt and kissed him. "You want to sit with us? We made a fire." He shook his head, and after a moment he turned toward his room. "Okay, we can go back. I'll go with you."

I trailed Matt back to his room and he sank into the armchair.

His MacBook stood open on the table.

"Were you online?" I sat on his lap and pulled the notebook onto my thighs. He gazed off at nothing while I studied the screen. I hoped to find he'd been writing, but no such luck. A Wikipedia page on Virginia Woolf was open. He'd scrolled down to . . .

"Matt, baby . . . why are you looking at this?"

I tried to make him look at me. He wouldn't, or couldn't.

He'd highlighted section four of the Woolf entry, DEATH. It summarized her suicide by drowning and contained a transcript of her last note to her husband.

Dearest, I feel certain that I am going mad again . . . I am doing what seems the best thing to do. You have given me the greatest possible happiness. You have been in every way all that anyone could be. I don't think two people could have been happier . . .

"No, listen to me . . ." I closed the tab and cleared the browsing history. I shut off his laptop and glanced toward the library. Nate was deliberately not paying attention, his back to us but his head inclined. "Darling," I whispered. "You can't look at things like that. They'll take you away from me. Please, don't you understand? I need you here with me." I stroked his face and pressed soft kisses all over it. "Come to bed with me."

When I led him toward the bedroom, Nate stepped into the hall and eyed us warily.

"Everything all right?"

"Fine," I said.

Chapter 32

MATT

On Friday morning, Mike, Hannah, and Nate filed into my study.

They brought chairs and sat.

I grimaced and tossed my book onto the desk.

"I was reading," I said.

"Well, good morning to you, too," said Mike. He grinned at me, then at Hannah and Nate. "Surprised you're home at this hour. Is that new?"

"Quite," said Nate.

"Sort of . . ." Hannah flushed and I wanted to laugh. I'd been *home* last night, when, for whatever reason, she'd become determined to have sex. I hadn't wanted sex in weeks—but Hannah applied her hands and mouth vigorously, and then she rode me like her life depended on it. We came. I fell asleep. Experiment over, I suppose.

But I did grasp her wrists in the heat of pleasure. I did sit upright and meet her gaze and scrape my teeth along her throat. Yes, I enjoyed that feeling, a touch of death, and I missed it.

"I wanted you to see these." Hannah offered a stack of printed pages to Mike. What were they? I tried to get a look. "It's a story he and I have been writing. This chapter—"

My hands tightened, nostrils flared.

Everyone looked at me.

Mike said, "You don't mind if I read this, do you?"

In response, I snatched the pages—Chapter 10 of our untitled novel—crumpled and tossed them on the floor. Hannah laughed. Nate smiled broadly and Mike chuckled.

"The fuck?" I spat. "You look like a bunch of clowns."

"I'll give you the gist," Hannah said. "He has this idea, this belief, 'deeply held,' he wrote, that the price of happiness is pain. From what I can gather, he blames the happiness of his early childhood for the loss of his parents."

I disliked the direction of the conversation.

"Very disordered thinking," Mike said. "Black-and-white. Typical for him."

Typical for me?

I felt like a specimen.

I wanted to leave, but for the first time in a while, I also wanted to stay.

"And once, when we were talking about whether or not we wanted children, he said, 'We have to be careful. We could be too happy.' Something like that."

Nate chimed in with some unhelpful bullshit about my childhood.

All three of them began to discuss me openly, encouraging and questioning one another.

"I'm fine," I snarled into their dumb conversation.

Mike barely glanced at me.

Hannah mentioned Seth, and Nate said, "I'm sure Matt blames himself."

"He must," she said. "He probably thinks our engagement and this gorgeous house, all this happiness, somehow relates to Seth's overdose."

"That's a great point." Mike scribbled notes.

I felt myself rising into the moment, where I had not been for many days. It stung. I wouldn't be there—couldn't—in that reality where Seth had died. I couldn't. *That's it.* I couldn't. I told Mike and Hannah and Nate that I couldn't, and I nearly took the door off its hinges on my way out.

There was excitement in the house.

No one came to tell me what was happening.

Fucking typical. No one cared about me anymore.

Nate didn't drag me out for walks; Hannah didn't leave muffins and other treats around the kitchen. How long had my brother been staying here anyway? One night, I returned to the house and found them at the dinner table, Hannah and Nate, the happy fucking couple. Hannah quickly set me a place at the head of the table, but Nate said grace.

After that, I had resumed sleeping at the house. In bed, I pulled Hannah against me possessively. I woke tangled around her.

Shrieks of laughter sounded from outside.

I pulled on my standby layer—a rugged navy blue sweater—and went to the window. The afternoon was gray. I wanted Hannah to come read with me, the way we sometimes did. Instead, she was outside with . . . a white horse? It wore a saddle and bridle and Hannah held the reins from as great a distance as possible. I snorted. What the hell was she doing?

Nate appeared, jogging across the field to the paddock. He climbed over the fence and tossed an apple to Hannah. She fumbled it, let go of the reins, and squealed when the horse lunged at the apple.

Amateurs . . .

I tugged on socks and sneakers and checked myself in the mirror—not that I cared what I looked like, just to be sure I looked better than Nate. I did, of course. I'd lost a little weight and needed to gain back some muscle, but I was clean-shaven and clear-eyed.

I bounded down the stairs and out toward the paddock.

Hannah and Nate didn't see me. He sat astride the horse and she stood on a fence rail, holding Nate's hand and teetering.

"I can't!" she said.

"Just throw your leg over. Come on."

Hannah looked delightful. Her long curls were tied back and she wore a wooly red sweater. A burst of color shone on her cheeks. I wanted to bundle her up.

I stalked into the paddock.

They ignored me until I snagged the horse's bridle and looked it in the face. It was a mare with a subtle crimp of the mane and tail, completely white and too thin.

"Hey Matt," said Nate, casual as you please. "Tell Hannah to get on this saddle."

I glanced at Hannah. She smiled shyly at me.

"I bought her," she said. "Can you believe it?"

I gave her a flat look. "No, I can't believe it."

The tack, at least, was very fine—used, but of good quality. The horse had been groomed recently. I smoothed a hand down her leg and she lifted it, making me smile. Clean hooves.

Then I folded my arms and cleared my throat.

I looked at Hannah.

"You don't know shit about horses," I said.

She and Nate stared at me. Was I speaking in tongues? They glanced at each other, then Nate started to laugh and Hannah grinned.

"Well, you don't have to be an asshole about it," she said.

A smile twisted my lips. *Oh, you're funny, little bird.* I studied her, assessing, smiling. The red sweater . . . the lippy attitude. I liked this girl. *Fuck,* I loved her.

I jerked my head at Nate in a gesture that said *get off.* He slid down from the saddle and handed me the reins.

"She's a . . . a Saddlebred," Hannah said. "She's seven."

I stroked the horse's neck.

"Her name is Written in Verse," Nate said.

"They always are weird," I said. "Horse names."

"True," he said. "You remember Overtime Magic?"

I laughed spontaneously. Overtime Magic had belonged to Aunt Ella. She was an ornery old quarter horse, nothing magic about her and no overtime in her.

"And Razzle-my-Tazzle," I said.

"Yeah. Seth got a kick out of that one."

A hot, uncomfortable feeling simmered up my throat, so I gripped the horse's mane at her withers and swung onto the saddle. My sneakers felt clumsy in the stirrups. She danced sideways and I shortened the reins. Nate gave her cinch a little tug.

"That's right, he did," I said, focusing on the horse below me. I was always a good rider, but I was out of practice. Slowly, I found my equilibrium, weight in my heels, my body relaxed.

Written in Verse hugged the fence.

I leaned down and kissed her neck.

"You're a pretty lady," I murmured, "but a little too skinny for my liking. We'll feed you well, don't worry."

Hannah shimmied along the fence and laid a hand on my thigh.

"You look good on that horse," she whispered.

I glanced at her and felt the pull of her. *Her hand on my leg . . . God, if Nate wasn't standing there.*

"You look fine on that"—my mouth twitched—"on that fence."

The corners of her eyes crinkled. She seemed about to laugh, then about to cry. *My God, if everyone would quit crying at me.*

I tightened my legs against Written in Verse and she walked on, and I took her around the paddock at a trot. That young horse wanted to run. I knew the feeling.

"I'm going to take her out," I said, nodding toward the meadow.

Nate frowned. "I'm not sure that's a good—"

"Go ahead," Hannah said. She beamed at me and I smiled at her. I remembered these compulsive smiles we used to share, like starstruck idiots.

I urged the white mare out of the paddock and took her up to a gallop. That speed always comes with a thrill of fear. Written in Verse ran smooth and fast. I couldn't hear anything above her hooves and the rushing wind, which was just the way I wanted it.

When I returned to the paddock, the sun was halfway behind the mountains. Nate sat waiting on the fence. I dismounted and he caught the reins.

"Just because I'm talking," I said, "doesn't mean I want to talk about everything."

"I don't need you to." He slid off the fence and I looked sidelong at him.

"Do you need to talk?"

He shook his head.

"I'm going home soon. Tonight I think I'll go out and buy supplies for this girl." He patted the horse's cheek. "I'll walk her to the barn."

"I don't want you to go yet."

"No?" Nate chuckled. "You've seemed ready to see me go for a while."

"I wasn't myself. I haven't been . . ."

"That's all right." Now he patted *my* cheek. "I'll come back. I need to see my family."

"I *am* your family."

"Matt . . ." He kept one hand around the reins and pulled me in with the other. He brought my face against his shoulder.

I know something about grief. I learned it the hard way, which is the only way. The thing I know is that grief is no feeling—no feeling at all. When it comes, we expect a terrible pain or drawn-out, stinging sorrow. Then we learn that grief is a vacuum. Even tears would be preferable. It is no feeling that comes and comes; it is loss itself.

After a while, Nate told me to go up to the house. He said that Hannah was my family, too, and not to be angry with her about the horse.

I thought about the horse as I walked back. An impulse buy, it seemed. With Nate leaving and Hannah ignorant of horses, I would need to care for the animal, which was no simple task. I wouldn't sell it, though. I already loved it. Hannah must have known that the moment I saw the horse, I would love it.

And if I didn't care for it, it would die.

Animals are that simple. They need our care and we love them for needing us. Children are the same.

I stopped midstride, and then I ran.

Chapter 33

HANNAH

That evening, Matt returned to the house alone.

I met him in the doorway.

His hair was wind-mussed and he was panting.

"Where's Nate?" I said, looking him over.

"Taking the horse to the barn. He said he's going to buy some things for her. He said he's leaving soon. Did you know that?"

I gazed dumbly at Matt's mouth as it moved. I don't know what I expected, but it wasn't this—an abrupt return to clarity and full sentences.

"Are you . . . okay?"

"I'm not angry about the horse. I like the horse. Hannah, what—Chrissy, the baby . . ."

"Come in, come on." I closed the door and led him to the great room. He refused to settle on the couch. I sat while he paced. "What do you want to know?"

"Is Chrissy . . . all right?"

I nodded quickly. Matt's energy was contagious. I wondered if this was phase two of a protracted breakdown—some kind of mania.

"She's fine. I mean"—I searched my memory—"we spoke . . . a couple times on the phone. After, uh . . . she moved back home. She's back with our parents."

I watched the color drain from Matt's face.

"Out of the condo? That nice condo?"

"Well, S—" I bit my tongue. *Seth didn't leave Chrissy anything.* But that wasn't Seth's fault. He didn't know death was right around the corner. "She can't afford that place."

"We can. She can stay, for God's sake."

"No, love . . ." I smiled softly. Matt was concerned for my sister? Strange, but touching. "It's more than the money. She needs people right now, family. The condo isn't good for her. Isolation isn't good. It's been . . . hard for her."

"Okay." He dragged his hands through his hair. "The baby?"

I shrugged. I did *not* want to be having this heavy conversation. Any one of these topics—Seth, Chrissy, children—could send Matt back into a tailspin. And God, it was heaven to have him here and communicative and engaged with the real world.

I stopped his pacing with a hug.

"Baby, are you hungry? Do you want dinner?"

"Not at all." He squeezed me, his voice thin. "Please. Is she still pregnant?"

I stared up into his wide eyes. Was *that* the problem here?

"Yeah, she is. For now."

"For now?"

"She doesn't know what she wants anymore." I stroked his cheek. "She's twenty-two weeks this week, so she could still—"

"Don't." He pulled away from me. "Don't say it. I get it." His gaze panned rapidly around the room. "Right. She only wanted the kid to get to him."

I'd had the very same thought about my sister, but when I heard it from Matt, spoken with such contempt, protectiveness reared inside me.

"Hey, you don't know that. She's going through her own issues, okay?"

"No. It's not okay. You don't understand." He hurried to the window and looked out in the direction of the paddock. "If she does that, I will never be okay. I'll do anything she wants. It's not just some child. It's my brother's child, and my brother is dead." His eyes snapped to mine. "Get her on the phone."

Matt locked himself in the study with my cell.

He spoke in a low, continuous murmur. Not once did he raise his voice. And that sucked, because I couldn't hear a damn thing he was saying.

I hovered outside the door until I heard Nate returning.

With a sigh, I descended the stairs.

"Everything okay?" Nate said. A long receipt dangled from his hand.

"Uh, sort of. What's all that?"

"Supplies for Written in Verse. It's all in the barn. A couple more pieces of tack, hay, oats, a concentrate mix." He set the receipt on the mantel. "In case you need to return anything."

"Thank you." I looked at my feet. I should have bought food and supplies *before* having the sellers drop off the horse. Desperation made me rash. "That all went well, huh?"

"Amazingly well." Nate approached me. For the first time in weeks, he looked happy and confident, like his old self. "You know what you are?"

"What?" I peered up at him.

"Saving Matt with a white horse. You're his knight in shining armor."

I laughed. "I hadn't thought of it that way."

"Well, you are. You're a regular heroine, in my book. Make sure he teaches you to ride that horse, because I want to see you on it—jumping fences, fending off doctors, throwing yourself like Pocahontas onto ungrateful men." He hugged me and kissed my cheek. "Where is that ungrateful man, anyway?"

"In the library." I cringed. "On the phone with Chrissy."

"Oh, Lord. Really?"

"Really. He gave me this fire-and-brimstone speech about how

she *must not* get an abortion and—" I covered my mouth. *Oops.*
I'd momentarily forgotten Nate's Christian status.

"It's fine, Hannah. I'm also a doctor." He took a swift stride toward the steps, then stopped. "No . . . I suppose I won't interfere."

"Probably a good idea. He's . . ."

"Being a bit of an asshole?" Nate raised a brow. He swore so rarely that when he did, I had to laugh.

"Exactly."

"Then he really is feeling better. Listen, I'm packed already and I got myself a hotel for the night. I'll fly out tomorrow or Thursday. You two have put me up long enough."

"Oh . . ."

"Yes. You both need this place to yourselves."

A twinge of fear pinched my heart. For weeks now, we'd been a team, trying to help Matt—and though we argued more than we agreed, I would have been lost without Nate.

"What if he's not actually better?" I fought the urge to grasp his sleeve.

"He's coming out of it. I can see it. I'm a phone call away, and don't forget Mike."

"But you can't just sneak off. He'll want to say good-bye."

"Oh, no." Nate smiled. "He won't."

I watched him walk away and climb the stairs two at a time. The thick wedding band on his finger skated up the rail. My future brother-in-law. He truly felt like a brother now, after all that we had been through. I would be proud to call him my brother.

And there were things I wanted to ask Nate, with his unwavering faith—did we bring this pain on ourselves, did we deserve to lose Seth because we played a game with death?—but I think the time for those questions had passed.

He returned with his bags. I walked outside with him, we hugged again, and I watched his rental car roll into the dark, crunching and kicking up dust.

When I got back inside, I found the study door open.

I heard a loud *thump*, then a grating noise.

"Matt?"

"In here," he called.

I peered into his room. He'd moved Laurence's hutch to the door. All his weights were rolled into a clump on his exercise mat.

"Whatcha doing?"

"Mm, moving things. This room is ridiculous. Here." He returned my cell and frowned. "Rather, not ridiculous. It was nice, having all my things in easy reach. Thank you . . ."

"You're welcome. Any time." I swallowed and touched his cheek. The words "in sickness and in health" passed through my mind. *For better, for worse.* "Any time . . . ever, Matt."

My eyes watered. I'd begun to hate my emotionality, and also to expect it. These, at least, were tears of happiness and relief.

He kissed me. I laid my hands on his chest and leaned against him.

"I want us to have an exercise room. You need an office. I'll put my books in the library and Laurence, I think, somewhere downstairs. You know he likes to be centrally located, privy to all our comings and goings."

"I think he's been privy to too many of our comings." I grinned.

Matt laughed and I soaked up the sound.

"I'll make this into my office," he said, "and we can go from there. Whatever you want. And a . . ." His arms tightened around me. "A room for the baby."

Matt had tightened his arms with good reason. I jumped and tried to pull back.

"The . . . baby?"

"Your sister doesn't want the baby."

"I'm not following."

"I've convinced her to have it . . . and I'm going to adopt it." Matt's tone cooled and hardened. He released me and walked back into the room. "She was very reasonable. She simply doesn't want it. The whole situation is too painful for her, and she doesn't want to be a young, single mother. Completely understandable."

He moved books from the shelves into stacks on the floor. I had never, not once, heard Matt speak so sympathetically about Chrissy. My mouth hung open.

"And she doesn't want to have an abortion. You see, she already . . ." He paused, lifting one of the small plush owls I'd put in his room. "Well, she felt it move. She's giving it up for adoption. I'll call Shapiro tomorrow and get the ball rolling, and schedule an appointment for an ultrasound. Sort out the . . . gender question."

I braced my hands against the door frame. Oh, Matt was back, all right.

"Excuse me," I said. "Do I have any say in this?"

"I thought you would be happy. I can see that you're not."

"Matt, this is . . . huge. This decision."

"I'm well aware." He brushed past me, carried a pile of books to the library, and returned. "I know we never properly discussed . . . all that. And I'm not asking you to carry a child. This isn't about that."

"So, it's about what?"

"Making things right." He answered without hesitation. As he passed with the next load of books, he paused and looked me in the eye. *Yikes*, I'd wanted this Matt back—commanding and stubborn—but I'd forgotten how intimidating he could be. "Don't you understand?"

"I might, if you'd asked me or talked to me."

"There's nothing to talk about, and this isn't a question. I'm going to take care of that child. I'm going to love it the way I didn't love him."

"Married couples make decisions together."

"No one's forcing you to marry me."

His words slammed into me with physical force. I inhaled.

Ungrateful man. Nate got that right.

I twisted the engagement ring off my finger. My knuckle burned, the skin around it bunching. Matt watched with a passive expression, which made me want to scream.

"You're fucking right about that." I slammed the ring atop his stack of books.

He balanced the books with one hand and pocketed the ring.

"I'll hold on to that for you," he said, and he breezed into the library.

Chapter 34

MATT

"What did she say?"

"Buckle your seat belt." I glared at Chrissy until she banded the belt across her body. Her unmistakably pregnant body. My eyes lingered on her belly.

"Relax," she said. "Everything's fine in there."

"We'll know that soon enough." I pulled away from her parents' house.

"How'd you get this appointment so fast, anyway?"

"Easy. You're overdue. You were *supposed* to have a twenty-week check."

"Okay, chill out, Frosty. Better late than never."

Chrissy's abbreviated nickname actually made me smile. She'd donned me Mr. Frostypants over a year ago, in happier times.

"So, what did she say after you took the ring? 'Cause I really don't want this baby, like, messing things up with you and Han."

"She said . . ." I cleared my throat. I remembered the argument well. It happened three nights ago, and Hannah hadn't slept with me since. She took the air mattress if I got in our bed; if I joined her on the mattress, she darted to our bedroom. "She said something like, 'You're a selfish fucking jackass.' I'm paraphrasing."

"Great," Chrissy muttered. "And you're still 'holding on to' the ring?"

"Mm. She'll come around. Either way, I'm adopt—"

"You're adopting this child and it means everything to you," she droned.

I glared and kept quiet the rest of the way to the clinic.

Excepting Hannah's surly attitude, everything was falling into place. Shapiro had another lawyer working with an agency on the relinquishment form and kinship adoption lawsuits, and my home study and background checks started next month. I wasn't worried. Thanks to Shapiro's tireless work over the years, my record looked pearly.

Now, if only Hannah would conform to the idea, get the ring back on her finger . . .

Chrissy clutched my hand while the ultrasound technician slid the wand over her belly.

Would I be required to fill this hand-holding role during the actual birth?

I felt light-headed.

The technician seemed too quiet. The thing on the screen moved constantly. Chrissy and I watched, rapt. *Seth, why did you do this? You should be here. I'm not ready.*

But there it was, ready or not: a grainy child-shape, my atonement embodied.

"Everything's looking good," the technician said.

Chrissy and I exhaled simultaneously.

"You can see the spine"—she pointed—"and the head right here. And . . ."

And it was a boy, though it didn't even look human to me. *Ready or not, here I come.* I slipped into autopilot, nodding and listening, asking questions of the technician and then the doctor, and all the while thinking about hide-and-seek. A children's game. *Here I come.*

Children need games, diversions, and food.

Constant care.

I couldn't do this alone.

"You okay over there?" Chrissy said. It was midafternoon. I had taken her for ice cream after the appointment—she ate two chocolate cones—and drove her home. My car idled outside the Catalano residence.

"Fine. Thinking. Lots to think about." I unlocked her door.

"I'm glad it's a boy, you know?"

I glanced at her, my jaw tight.

"Don't look at me that way," I said. "I'm not about to fucking cry in front of you and lose all my man points, got it?" I smirked and she laughed, her eyes shining.

"Got it. Me neither. I have badass-girl points to protect."

She scrubbed her face and climbed out of the car.

I watched her until she stepped into the house, and then I drove through Denver and wondered where the hell people buy baby stuff. *Online,* I decided. *Boyish things. Solid, dark, modern furniture. A mobile of some kind. An extravagant playhouse.*

Buying things, I could handle. And when the kid was old enough to read and fish and ride, I might even enjoy his company. But what to do with an infant?

Panic.

I swung by the agency and visited Pam. She hugged me like I might break and I joked that it was the gentlest she'd ever been with me.

Afterward, I wandered Denver again.

I got coffee and lurked in a used bookstore. I bought a second copy of *Swann's Way.*

At last, I went home.

Home-sweet-fucking home.

I avoided the house for a while, going directly to the barn and checking on Written in Verse. She was a sweet creature. I brushed her coat and picked her hooves.

"Pretty soon I'll be sleeping out here with you," I said.

She rolled her eyes toward me. She'd seen a lot of me in the past two days. Hannah's anger drove me out of the house. The stalemate between us refused to break, and I found myself seeking her out, only to confront clipped answers and quick departures. *How are you? Fine. Feel like furniture shopping today? Not really. Do you want to see my garden? No.*

My fucking garden: a barren rectangular patch into which I'd churned my frustration, because planting in September is pointless. I said good night to the horse and went to the garden. I stabbed at the earth with a spade. Laughable, the idea that I could nourish anything. I was a writer, not a gardener. Not a father.

"Go easy on that dirt," Hannah said.

I stood quickly, brandishing the spade. "Hi. Hey. Didn't hear you coming."

She frowned and closed the gap between us. "You got some in your hair." She brushed a clod of dirt from my hair.

Mm, she smelled good, like clover honey. She hadn't stood this close to me since our argument, and her nearness affected me. I wanted to touch her. I wanted to look her over the way a man can look at his fiancée's body.

"What did you get?" She pointed.

My book lay in the grass.

"Oh." I dropped the spade. "*Swann's Way.* Different translation than I've got."

"I haven't read it." She didn't move away from me.

"It's a . . . cycle. Series-type thing." Oh, how the tables had turned. Me, elated to get a word out of Hannah. "It's got the perfect first line: 'For a long time, I went to bed early.'"

She smiled and tilted her head. "Yeah."

"It does something to you, right? The writing is dreamlike. The narrative. It moves under you. I'd kill to write like that."

"How was Chrissy?"

"Okay. Good. I guess it's—" God, was I about to utter the words "It's a boy"?—"A guy."

"A . . . guy?"

"Yup." I used my superior height to its best practical use: to look way over Hannah's head and pretend I was cooler than this baby conversation. "Everything looks fine, healthy. I took her for ice cream. She had two cones. One for the guy, evidently."

"Ice cream." Hannah chuckled. "That's a thing with you Skys, huh? I wrote about it."

"You did?"

"Yup. Chapter eleven. It's in your in-box. My fiancé charges off to New York City"—she didn't hesitate, though we both knew what had happened that day—"and his saintly brother Nate takes me out for ice cream, saving me from the clutches of Aunt Ella."

Tentatively, I ran my fingers over her curls. They hung loose and fell past her shoulders, pooling in the hood of a pale blue sweatshirt.

"Well, I can't wait to read that. And maybe my fucking brother should stop furtively taking you on dates."

She giggled and I smiled.

"Come here." She took my hand and led me to the side of the house, where a long bale of hay lay in the grass. A bright quilt hung over the bale. "Sit."

"Okay . . ." I sat on the block of hay.

"How does it feel?"

"You want the truth?"

She nodded.

I patted the quilt. "Lumpy? And a . . . piece of hay is . . . poking me in the ass."

Laughter burst out of Hannah. "Okay, get up, you dork. I guess they need more padding. But it looks cool, right?"

"For a quilted hay bale, sure." I laughed helplessly. "What the hell, babe?"

"Don't judge me." She grinned and perched on the bale. "This is the seating for our wedding. I got the idea online. 'Instead of chairs, throw brightly colored blankets and quilts over bales of hay.' It's gonna be quaint and . . . country cool."

"Our . . . our wedding?"

"Yeah. Our wedding. Which we're not waiting forever to have, because we're getting married next month. See? I can be Matt Sky, too. I can make unilateral decisions like a dick."

I stood there in the fading light, blinking at Hannah.

She clambered up to her feet on the hay bale, looming over me.

"That day Nate took me out for ice cream, I asked him for advice. Like, marriage advice. And he said to be honest about everything, what you feel and what happens. He said little secrets are like water, but if water gets into a rock and freezes, it can break the rock."

I tilted my head. Thank God, Hannah had a speech, because I was speechless.

"And honesty starts with communication," she said. "I need you to get that I am okay with us adopting the . . . guy. The baby." She pounded her fist into her palm. She was beginning to unravel, blinking rapidly and sniffling. "That was never the problem, once I sat down and thought about it. The problem—" Her voice quavered pitifully.

God, what had I done to this girl?

I hugged her legs, pressing my face into her jeans.

"The problem is that you made me feel like you didn't care what I wanted. And I have been waiting"—another weak fist-palm slap—"waiting for you to show me that you care. And you're stubborn and you won't ask what I want. And all I can think is that . . ." She hiccuped. "That you can't choose between the two loves, and you know that I would never walk away from you because I love you, you arrogant asshole. The way I love you . . ."

Hannah was right, of course. She always was. And she was the better person in our romance, always, in all ways. She was stronger, truer, and steadier. She was the making of me.

I dragged her off the hay bale and hauled her over my shoulder. I carried her into the house like that.

In the great room, in the dark, I pressed her against the wall.

"Here," I said, "now, always like it's the last time."

We moved from the wall to the couch and from the couch to the floor.

"Breathe," she said as I moved against her. She lay under me, on the rug in front of the fireplace, and I was inside her. "Breathe . . ."

Excitement practically closed my throat. I shuddered and slowed, gulping air.

It was good to be like that—so exposed to her, excited and desperate—and good to see her undressed and blushing, so exposed to me.

When I became frantic again, pushing us both to the edge, she grasped my thigh and back and let me feel the bite of her nails.

This happiness, I thought. *Here, now, always.*

This happiness, no matter the cost.

Chapter 35

HANNAH

"He wanted me to give you this." Chrissy tapped a cream-colored envelope against my arm. I took it and she slipped out of the room.

The envelope contained two folded pages. I shook them open.

October 18, 2014

Dear Little Bird,

You may be south of the border right now, having finally decided that I'm insane. In that case, I can't blame you, and I salute your sister for delivering my note.

However, I hope you are up in our room, wearing a gown I am about to see. I already know you look beautiful. That is a certainty and not praise. I have been the beneficiary of your goodness and beauty for quite a while now.

Tonight, when you walk down the aisle and our eyes meet, only you and I will know <u>all</u> that has passed between us. That is the way it should be. This love is thickly plaited. And you know I am a little sad (are you laughing?)—of course, I have to be sad. I have written two full novels about you, and now I understand that no novel will hold you.

My heart can barely hold you. All that I feel for you.

Here's to you, Hannah, and our life together—my greatest happiness. Let me carry you to bed. Let me bathe you and make love to you. Let me fuck you (you know how I like it) and let me know you. Let's fight and make up. Let's be together in triumph and failure, here and abroad, as a family of two and a family of three. I want to do the good days with you and also the bad. Let me show you with my whole life how I love you.

I'm steady behind you.

Love, now and always,

Matt

I read the letter twice, though it threatened to ruin the makeup my sister had carefully applied. *My greatest happiness . . . now and always.*

I blushed and hid the envelope in our bedside table.

Let me fuck you (you know how I like it).

Oh, yes, I do, Mr. Sky.

Thank God, Matt had issued that toast on paper, in private, and not at the reception. One never knew, what with his exhibitionistic flair . . .

I giggled and spun, my gown whispering over the floorboards.

"All good in there?" Chrissy called through the door.

"Yeah. Come in. I need some touch-up."

"Did that asshole make you cry?" She bustled in, one hand hoisting her long maroon dress. The color suited her, and the empire waist and flowing skirt sort of hid her bump, not that I cared. The baby belonged at this wedding as much as Matt and I, and Chrissy was my maid of honor. "God, I feel frumpy." She steered me to the vanity and dabbed at my eye makeup.

"You look beautiful," I said.

"No way. You're the beauty tonight, Han."

My fingers twisted on my lap. I'd chosen a simple gown—airy tulle covered with petal shapes, a glass bead on each, which faded from white to a subtle blush at the train. Jamie, our neighbor from the Denver condo and my only bridesmaid, had styled my hair in a loose braid. A Sakura halo and Dalloway Earrings from BHLDN completed the look.

Fresh. Light. Simple.

I smiled at my reflection. *A simple girl. Just what you wanted, Matt.*

"Are you sure you won't be cold?" Chrissy rubbed my bare upper arms. My gown was, admittedly, springlike.

"Positive. I'm kind of burning up, honestly."

Jamie peeked into the room. She squealed and almost dropped my bouquet, white orchids and calla lilies, the first flowers Matt gave me.

"Hannah, you look amazing! Your father is out here . . . whenever you're ready."

"She's ready," Chrissy said. I stood and she hip-checked me. "Ready as you'll ever be, right? See you at 'the altar.'" She made ridiculous air quotes around "the altar."

Because we had no altar.

We had a loose arrangement of hay bale seats, an aisle of grass lined with tiny white bulbs and flowers, and synthetic rose string lights and hanging lamps in the trees. A broad tent covered the reception tables, and camping lights glowed beneath the tablecloths. Our drink coolers were old flower boxes, the gift table just a picnic table.

Everything was the way I wanted it, makeshift and rustic. Magical.

I met Dad in the hallway.

He didn't cry, God bless him, but he also barely spoke.

"Beautiful," he managed. "You. All this." He gestured to my home. Matt and I had made great strides in the past few weeks, filling our rooms with tasteful country-style furniture, art, and lighting. We rushed nothing, but we brainstormed excitedly and shopped together.

Some rooms looked classically Matt: spartan and elegant.

Other rooms were all me: cluttered and colorful.

Somehow, our disparate visions melded harmoniously throughout the house.

We agonized over one particular room.

Though I knew Matt and our guests were waiting, I led Dad into the nursery. I had to show him. When we'd told Mom and Dad about our plan to adopt Chrissy's baby, they clung to one another and cried. Then they clung to us and cried. Everyone knew Chrissy wasn't ready for a child, Chrissy included. In that single moment, Dad's low estimation of Matt skyrocketed and Mom's sky-high estimation of Matt reached space.

"He won't call it the nursery," I said, squeezing Dad's arm. "He calls it 'the little room' or 'Seth's room.' I swear, he's more put off by domesticity than I am."

"Seth? Is that . . . ?" Dad cleared his throat.

"Maybe. We don't know. Too morbid?"

"No, no. So long as it doesn't upset anyone."

"It seems to make Matt happy. I've been thinking . . ." I watched Dad drift through the nursery, which wasn't little at all. We'd left the walls light beige and hired a designer to paint Deco birches along one surface. Light, distressed furniture and linen curtains gave the room a bohemian feel. Matt lined a shelf with books he intended to read to the child. I placed a round crib with a pretty skirt near the window. "Um, thinking about . . . Seth James Sky Junior."

Dad laughed from deep in his belly.

"You're bringing out the big guns, huh? I'm not going to be that father, blubbering my way down the aisle."

"Daddy." I hugged him tight.

Matt once said to me that losing his parents was like having the authors of his story destroyed, so that no meaningful narrative could follow. I understood.

"Come on," Dad said, offering his arm. "We've got a ways to go."

The night was cool and bug-free, thanks to an early autumn

frost. I could see our lights glowing in the meadow among the trees. Dad held me steady on the uneven ground. My heart thumped and fluttered, unsure whether this was the best night ever or entirely terrifying.

As we drew closer, I began to recognize guests: Aunt Ella and Uncle Rick, Mom, Jay, Nate's wife Valerie, Pam, Laura, Kevin, Stephen. Someone gave Owen and Madison their cue; I saw their small figures moving up the aisle, Owen with a little pillow and Madison scattering petals. I smiled as I watched Nate's children, my soon-to-be nephew and niece.

There was Mike, who'd loaded me up with intel during two intensive "marriage counseling" sessions. *Matt has abandonment issues, anger-management issues, fear of static states, manic-depressive tendencies, paranoid tendencies, masochistic tendencies . . .*

I remembered leaving his office dizzy, wondering what *wasn't* wrong with Matt.

I also remembered seeing Matt at his worst, and staying.

Other aunts, uncles, cousins, and colleagues filled out our modest seating.

Nate, the best man—of course, the best man—stood by Matt. And Matt . . .

I took my time in letting my gaze go to him, because I knew that once it did, I wouldn't look away. He wore a gray slim-fitting tux with just a limning of satin on the notched lapel. A white satin tie with a Windsor knot disappeared behind his vest.

My heart can barely hold you.

The almost silver-gray of the tux, and his golden skin and fair hair, drew in the light of our lamps and candles.

Those hands of his, those long legs, that elegant frame—my eyes roamed. That chest, those shoulders, the neck and throat, his smooth jaw . . .

His face.

Our eyes met and I forgot the audience staring at me. His lips parted slightly, eyes widened fractionally. I wanted to run to him.

Was it the surrounding darkness or the chill in the air, or maybe the presence of others? *Something . . .*

Something clicked, and I understood that no one wanted me the way he wanted me. To have and to hold, for better or worse, in sickness and in health, until death.

So I went to him.

That is the story: I went to him.

"Were we idiots to let people crash here?" I whispered.

Matt chuckled and held a finger to his lips. *Right,* Nate and Val were just across the hall.

For the last four hours, we'd wined and dined our wedding guests and toasted and danced. Tomorrow we left for New York—the first of many cities I needed to see, according to Matt—and then Greece. No one had dared to deface his cars with cans, which made me grin. They also spared my brand-new Mercedes, a gift from my husband.

My husband . . .

He ruffled his hair and stretched gloriously, opened the bedroom window but left off the light. Outside in the dark, our little wind chimes tolled.

I watched him pry off his shoes and drape his coat across the bed.

God, he still made me shy.

I went to him only when he beckoned.

"There you are," he said softly in my ear. "Are you real? Little bird, I think we can be quiet tonight." He kissed my mouth and spread his hand across the V of skin on my back. He found my gown's tiny zipper and tugged it down.

The garment dropped around my feet.

"Come sit on my lap," he said.

He settled in the armchair in the corner of our room and I—calmly as I could manage in a garter belt, heels, and sheer bra—tottered over to the vanity and removed my accessories.

Be calm, be sexy, I chanted inwardly. *This is your wedding night.*

I turned to Matt. My jaw dropped, and my calm and sexy soared out the window.

He had his dick in his hand, eyes on me.

"I will never get tired of that reaction," he murmured. "Come here."

Sit on my lap . . . oh, boy, that made a different kind of sense now.

I shuffled over, unclipping my garters as I went. He smiled at me, not with his usual wicked amusement, but with simple, youthful desire.

I kept on my heels and thigh-highs; I kicked off my panties.

"God"—he touched my hip—"let me make sure you're wet enough . . ." He stroked himself while he swirled a finger around my folds. The whole display mesmerized me. He still wore his shirt and slacks, only the thick rod of his arousal protruding from his fly.

Because I knew it would drive him crazy, and because his teasing touch was driving me mad, I lowered my body onto his fingers . . . lifted and sank again.

"Ah, *fuck*, Hannah. Are you fucking my finger?"

I nodded and rolled my hips, biting my lip to suppress a moan.

"Turn around," he whispered. "Sit."

I obeyed, gripping the arms of the chair and lowering myself onto his lap. He positioned his tip at my entrance. I took it slow, loving the way his thighs trembled and tensed.

At last, with a gasp I couldn't subdue, I sat.

He unhooked my bra and tossed it aside. He hugged my back to his chest.

The way his heart beat against my shoulder blade told me he could barely keep still and quiet, which made two of us.

We sat like that, husband and wife, locked together intimately.

"Even if they can't hear us," he said, "everyone knows what we're doing." He cupped my breasts and lifted them. I felt his cock shift deep inside me.

"You like that they know, don't you?"

"Oh, yes. All the men present today wanted you secretly, guilt-ily. Probably some of the women, too. You were a vision . . ."

He pinched my nipples and I squirmed, my body clamping around his. *Delicious.*

"I think . . ." I panted. "I think the women were focused on you. Matt, you looked—"

He covered my mouth. *So handsome, so graceful . . . so beautiful, brave, and strong.*

"Shhh," he whispered. "Don't. Don't make it about me tonight. It's you, Hannah. It's always you. I was proud to be on your arm tonight. I was proud . . ."

I wanted to look at him, but I couldn't, the way we sat.

And that's how we did it that evening, sitting together in our home. His hands played me and I moved on his lap. He told me how it felt. He told me many things. No book can hold them.

Epilogue

HANNAH

April 2016
Matt and Seth Junior are in the meadow.

Seth is one and walking, which has thrown Matt into a panic. Last week, I caught him crawling around the main floor of the house (my husband, not our son). I laughed for ten minutes straight. Matt didn't crack a smile. "I read that you need to get on the child's level," he'd explained, "to spot potential hazards."

Then he crawled away, glaring at walls and furniture.

I doubled over with laughter—again.

As it turned out, anything within Seth's reach constituted a hazard. Matt stripped our house of knickknacks from the floor to a yard up. He'd already put plug covers in every outlet and gated not just the staircase, but most of the doorways. "So we can control his movements."

My husband is a worrier, you see.

So am I.

I watch my boys from the nursery window, a smirk on my lips. *I know what you're up to, Matt.* Ever since I caught him reading *Dracula* to Seth (and confiscated the book, which is way too dark for a one-year-old mind), Matt has taken their reading sessions outdoors.

I pull on a light jacket and stride out into the meadow.

The April sun is warm; the wind is cool. Seth's white-blond curls, which we leave a little long, toss in the breeze. He caught the rare fair-haired gene in the Sky family pool and has his father's deep brown eyes. From Chrissy's side, he got the same thick curls I inherited.

I know he will look like Seth when he grows up: devastatingly handsome, tall, and kind.

"What's going on here?" I say.

Matt, who is lying on a blanket with Seth's pudgy hand on his knee, snaps upright.

"Bird! Hey . . . hi."

I squint at the thin volume he holds: *Beowulf & Other Poems.*

"*Beowulf*? No. Okay? No."

"Oh, come on. He likes it. He likes—"

"He likes the sound of your voice. I don't want weird, dark ideas infiltrating his mind. Stop trying to turn him into Heathcliff." I go to swipe the book and Seth's bubbly laughter distracts me. I am as powerless against Seth's charms as I am against Matt's.

"Ma-ma-ma-ma-ma," he trills, pushing away from Matt and walking toward me. His little foot catches on the blanket. Down he goes, peals of delight turning to wails of unhappiness.

"See?" Matt demands.

I scoop up Seth. "Yes, I see that it's nap time."

"Here, I'll take him." He pulls Seth out of my arms and cradles him as if he were a much smaller child. "He still likes me to hold him."

Seth is inconsolable. I twist away so that Matt can't see me smiling. He is too painfully cute, and this routine reminds me of Seth's infancy. "He likes me to hold him," Matt would say to anyone who tried to take the baby. I had more than one picture of my husband standing in a corner, facing the wall, rocking Seth.

My two babies . . .

We walk to the house together, my hand in Matt's back pocket.

Inside, he passes off Seth. He refuses to put him down for naps or bed. Too much like good-bye, I guess.

"Say night-night to Daddy." I wave Seth's hand and then carry him to Laurence's hutch. The rabbit turns an ear. "Say night-night to Lor Lor."

"Lor Lor," Seth sobs.

"Do you have to make it so sad?" Matt snaps. He bolts upstairs before I can roll my eyes. Nap time: a Sky family tragedy.

Two hours later, Seth is sleeping soundly and I have just finished reading a client's manuscript. It's good, which makes me proud. My stomach grumbles and I glance at the clock on the mantel. It's past lunchtime. I should prepare something for myself and Matt, whose eating habits are still woeful.

Still. I smile.

Not much has changed, if I think about it, and I wouldn't have it any other way.

I find my husband upstairs in his office, which is spacious and light. He looks like a prince in there, surrounded by his books and artwork, and I am quietly grateful for our home. At last, I understand why a small house would never work: because a soul like his needs room for its roaming and passion.

I knock gently on the door frame and walk to his desk.

He is writing in a notebook. His hand stills and he smiles at me.

"Chapter thirty-two," he says.

My throat tightens. It took half a year for Matt to pick up the pen and resume our story, and now we are in the thick of it, describing his depression after Seth died. My chapters are lucid and filled with concern. His chapters are fragmented, lost.

"We're getting close to the end," I say.

"Are we?" He frowns.

"It has to end somewhere. Why not here?" I touch the frame on his desk, which holds a picture of Matt and me on our wedding night.

"Ah. You want a happy ending."

"I do." I smile. "You want a sad one?"

"I don't want any ending." His hand tightens around the pen.

"Come downstairs. Let's make some lunch."

He remains seated, immobile.

"Life is out here," I whisper.

"My life is in here." He spreads his hand on the page.

Oh, Matt. I slip around the desk and extract the pen from his fingers. He watches me with a bemused expression.

"I know you don't know how to say good-bye. I'll do it for you, sweet man." I flip to the final page. There, under his steady gaze, I write:

I met a man online; he called himself a night owl. We played a wicked game in the last light of day. We were married in October, after dark.

I place a gentle kiss on his lips. He pushes away from the desk. "It's a good story, Matt. It's an even better life."

Acknowledgments

Warmest thanks to my agent, Betsy Lerner, for *The Forest for the Trees* and for believing in me, and to my editor, Jennifer Weis, for incisive suggestions and incredible patience.

Thanks likewise to Sylvan Creekmore and my team at SMP for bearing with me and for pushing the Night Owl Trilogy to be the best version of itself.

Thanks to the following book blogs for invaluable support: *Maryse's Book Blog, Aestas Book Blog, Totally Booked, The Rock Stars of Romance, True Story Book Blog, Smut Book Club, Talk Supe, Shh Mom's Reading, Love Between the Sheets, It's Andrea's Book Blog, SMI Book Club, The Book Bellas, Dirty Laundry Review, MRBOD, Literary Gossip,* and so many others.

Thanks to Aimee, the original bird, and to Anna, with great affection. Thanks to Naomi for writing opposite Cal; you know what makes a good story.

Thanks to Jennifer Tice for tireless support, friendship, and administrative work in the Night Owl Facebook Group. Thanks to Lisa Jones Maurer for much-needed advice and friendship. Many thanks to Michele for encouragement and friendship, and to Angie,

Chrissy, Cristiane, Deb, Jaime, Jen, Kayti, Kris, Kyleigh, Laurelin, Lex, Mel, Paula, Sheri, and Tarah.

For counsel and friendship, thanks to Alan and Michael.

And thanks to you, my reader, for doing the very best thing: reading.

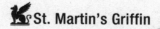